from your heart.
bleed.

3rd Edition

Copyright © 2014 by *Eckhard Gerdes*

Dirt Heart Pharmacy Press edition made possible in collaboration with author and press.

Design & Cover by *Norman Conquest*

ISBN – 978-0-9944167-6-6

You've begun a journey. Don't stop now.

Hugh Moore

by

Eckhard Gerdes

Acknowledgements

The author would like to acknowledge several people for their dedication to this project and their invaluable contributions: my brilliant late wife Persis for her original version of "Mary's Meditation," which she generously contributed to the novel albeit in a somewhat different form; Jean Starr, editor par excellence, whose assistance was a true godsend; Brad Johnson and Ann Meyer of the sadly now-defunct *No* magazine, in which a small part of *Hugh Moore* originally appeared; and the late great Kenneth and Miriam Patchen, whose guidance and influence has meant so much to me over the years—Kenneth's through his brilliant oeuvre and Miriam's through our delightful conversations and correspondence regarding Kenneth, writing, the academic life (which Miriam fervently warned me against pursuing), and the world in general. Also, thanks to the wonderful folks at Dirt Heart for breathing new life into this undertaking. Without their help, the book might have needed a different sort of undertaker.

Foreword

It's a strange, hard action to try to talk of someone else's core as if speaking of a person's very private life. Of that we really know nothing. So it is in speaking of Gerdes's *Hugh Moore.* As you read you think you know Moore. One should. But he remains one you think you know. Would he like you? Would you get along well with him?

Hugh Moore is like all of us. He has problems as we do—perhaps not the same as ours but he experiences each—as we do. Finally—find out for yourself. Gerdes has worked out a true study with no escape. The reader is stuck with a pattern of his own growth.

—Miriam Patchen
Palo Alto, California

Prologue

A carny barker on the dais attracts a few people with his cries. "Here! Come here, sir. Step right up and try this amazing formula, this fantastic elixir! It's guaranteed to cure what ails you. You can brush your teeth with it, shine your shoes with it, wax your car with it. It'll remove the tarnish from your silverware. It'll lead the old to the fountain of youth, it'll give wisdom to the young. It'll cure quarrels between lovers and introduce new lovers to each other.

"You, sir! You, madam! Look at each other. Get to know one another. See? This elixir has already made you friends. And you haven't even tasted it yet."

Use it only in well-ventilated areas and avoid prolonged usage. Administer carefully. If no change in condition after ten days, consult your physician.

Part One

Hugh Moore

Chapter One

In Which We Meet Our Protagonist

Hugh Moore finally wakes up only to go back to sleep.

Brrr... Nnn... Who... Ttt... Hum... Crackle...

Hence free. Ya bu boy shing. Ah... who... so... yeah... this is it... ah... sitting down... ah... I've got a beer here with a boilermaker—tequila and beer... shot glass is inside the beer glass... gug... god that tastes shitty... ooosh... blecch... uh... sittin' down...

Wasn't it a stupid... uh... yeah, well, it's last but, well, you know, it's not much, and it'll be gone real soon anyway, doesn't matter anyhow, so it's okay 'cause there's something's that's gonna, and before you know it, time to go on through and, uh, find yourselves, like, around to, urn, like, back into the place where, like, there's breathing and, uh, uh, it's not so difficult, uh, to keep on with what you're trying to do because it's, like, mostly what's important is a sense of trying to, uh, ah, realize that motion in a person's life has to be forward and, uh, if there were a point where it would need to move sidewards for a reason, urn, a lot of the forward momentum would be lost and it might mean, at the end, like, you wouldn't be able to get as far because you lost a lot of the speed.

Hugh rolls over on his right side onto his cat, St. Charles. St. Charles skreeks and pulls out from underneath and jumps off the bed where he had settled, looking for shared space.

Hugh opens his eyes for an instant, then drifts away again.

Dharma wah-doop had. Chew on a ruin? Turnip grounds and locket watch your dune.

A cuckoo breeze hovering Indy nights. Ain't it right, ain't it rice?

Radio seaway. Baby opiate.

Commentary marlin promontory shore line. We're all fishers of meat jelly.

We're all fathers of mint jelly. Julips, not ruins. Tulips congruent.

Beer for me, not money. Dope.

Mr. Fox says, "Truth is something to be felt, an aura in the room."

Quadrapennate
pnemonoultramicroscopicsilicovolcanoconiosis. Fucking right.

Not to be confusing, it all makes sense to me.

Even an interregent feels the need to be the court fool.

Goobydoobyfluffy.

In accordance with the stigmata in the eyes of seers, our world was to end this year.

Or I was.

Reveal. Gumata.

I was hers, you were his, he was hers, she was his, and we are all together. Dmess jujube. Sudow von Bulow fly-paper picture, this sky with a gaberdine suit in his eye—how gone. How gone. Carmelita Pope with a cardboard candy stand. See how she fries without dicing the guys arm wrestling.

Whisker against whisker, St. Charles wakes up Hugh again.

"Get the fuck outta here, cat. Leave me alone. Or else. No food for a year."

Sinking onto a rubber raft, bouncing along the river. Whisker-like reeds stick up along both shores. Visions of Rain Pain cloud his mind, but he steers the raft successfully—until she appears next to him. They continue downstream together.

A knock on the door. They open it. It's a man who leaves them a candygram. For Hugh, who's afraid to open it—it might be a bomb.

Rain says go ahead.

He does.

It clicks upon opening but no explosion. Inside is a black hole which sucks them both through. They slip onto a gigantic water-slide which spirals, circles, and loops them into the vortex of a whirlpool carrying them through and down into a stalagmite-filled cave through which they must pass bare-footed. Hugh gives Rain two suction-cups to put on the bottoms of her feet so she can traverse the stalagmites, which could be explosive. Hugh puts on his own cups and shows Rain how to negotiate the stalagmites. Hugh and Rain lift off into darkness.

At the end of the darkness is a scepter turning 'round. Beams emanate from it as it withdraws into the tower of a lighthouse. Bears walk down the long, winding staircase. Chinks missing in the wall reveal marbles glued there in their place.

Punctures at the bottom of two tires reveal that Hugh's car won't move for a while, at least not horizontally.

He panics and awakens.

"Rain!" he moans, shaking his head awake. "Where are you today?"

He smiles his eyes open.

Well, no more of that shit for me, says he, and he flushes it away. I'm in love with my world and this is going to be a good one. Forego the bullshit—ain't no better bullshit to be forgot. It be there to infest you, dude—cut it loose. What can you lose by being honest that you really don't want anyway?

Beers are in the fridge—better get one. Mellow into this one soft. No more of that hard shit—goddamn I feel bad—all fuckin' down the toilet—I guess I could have sold it—oh fuck it—grab a beer, okay? There's nothing new to be learned there—man, I mean, I know the lines before they're spoken, dig? So what's next? I'll try to find out, that's for sure. So hang tight, relax, and put this down for breaks as often as desired, okay?

Life's kind of fuzzy. I think I need me a shower, babe. Hugh strips off his clothes, in mockery of cheap thrills, and steps into the bathroom, kitty krunchie kat litter underneath—what a sensation! He walks out, scrapes his feet against the carpet, and finds a pair of blue socks in a drawer for when he gets out of the shower.

Phone rings. Four by the time he gets it. His best friend's wife looking for his best friend. Don't know, he says, ain't been here. Not at all.

In the shower his pores absorb water as if mouths. He pisses into the plughole. He begins to think about coffee. Basic maintenance. Vitamin C. Aspirin. Yada.

His poems absorb water. Forgotten by the time he dries off. I wonder if a waterproof pad of paper and pen exist left, blue sock right, underwear, robe.

He calls the national weather service to decide how to dress. First time through he can't focus and misses the message. Second time he hears everything except today's temperature, which is what he wanted. Third time he makes it. Upper seventies. Good deal.

Tired. Too tired. Lie down for a minute. Flop. Going away again, drifting. Sleeping wide awake. The guy upstairs is listening to loud blurry music.

Hugh groans and gets it up. What an asshole. It's only noon in the morning. I swear god I'll never do it again. Just let me live. Tears stream. Vitamins. Aspirin. A shot of schnapps—the hundred proof. I'll be human yet.

Better than mouthwash. Where's my John Entwistle album? That'll blow the jag-off away—my wattage outstrips his. *Peg Leg Peggy, she really knows how to hump.*

Kinda like Neal Cassidy, *one wooden eye, one wooden leg, Mumbly Peg.* What a party, man. Shoulda left it alone after I got left alone. Something back there about Rain—strong strange bitch—I think I'm falling in—fuck it—who's the bozo here? Me, prob. Still, want to get between those legs, that's for sure. Dig it—nose ring and all (especially—what a fun broad). Brrr... Do I got time to whack off over this babe? Nah—gotta get under way. Sooner or later. Wrider.

Slider. Gump. Gotta be somethin' better for breakfast than that (the thought of 'em made Rain blow her lunch last night). Maybe have time for a real breakfast at Fat Bill's Restaurant.

Culminator your type hell. She'd told him about a guy who'd written her an eighteen-page love letter, so I thought, drunk and stoned last night, I'd write one too. Ended up with a poem.

Then he remembers the weird goddamn dreams:

A silo-like building in Indianapolis with the words "Geiler" or "Keiler Geyser Co." on it. I think Geiler.

I'm in a hotel up north in Wisconsin and Rain calls, disguises her voice and says I'm someone from chemistry class who tried to pick her up in the hall. I finally recognize her voice. She tells me she has fetalitis—a dead baby inside. I ask whose it is, Guerin's? She says "no—why can't it be yours?" That's impossible says I. Meanwhile my mom's muttering at me, "Don't believe her! She's probably just trying to get you to marry her." I tell my mom to shut up. I even go to the trouble of explaining that Rain's the single sweetest woman (or is that the sweetest single woman) I ever met and that I'll defend her to the death. I talk to Rain again who says it's just polyps.

Then the cat throws up.

"St. Charles! You asshole! Fuck it—this day ain't ever gonna start." We're talking about a cat who digs in the litter before it shits and leaves it untouched and uncovered afterwards. A cat so smart that squirrels play practical jokes on him by running up trees, him in hot pursuit (St. Francis he ain't), and jumping off onto others, which Charles cain't do. He be treed, the maroon. Meow meow! A one-way tree, him needing a pet vacation for overstressed animules.

"What are you? Stupid on purpose?"

Dumbo expression back, as if to say "god any drugs, man?" Brrr.

Sit down. Stand up. Remember the vomit. Get a paper towel. Clean it up. Wash.your hands. Sit down. Stand up. Fill the coffee pot with water. Find a mug. Find the coffee funnel. Find a filter and put coffee in it. Put the pot on a lit burner. Sit down.

Ah. Emit a yawn. Stare at the lily-of-the-valley wallpaper design on the kitchen wall. There's a tiny roach moving along the stem of one. So what? It'd take too much energy to kill it. Damn booze tires me down.

Steam whistles through the spout of the coffee pot.

Sitting down again drinking the cup of coffee he made, staring at the wall.

Hugh's eyes begin to open. He begins to focus himself into his person.

Another day. Hey. It'll be okay.

Caffeine shudder.

Salmon Song (for Rain)

Swimming around
     your brain I examine its cracks,
     marvel at the depth,
          attractiveness
of your grooves,
     Life your god,
     energy his breath,
          youth,
          attention
to friends,
     particularly the disabled,
     hurt,
     hungry.
          Selflessly

              aground
you should be the one
      to fish
      my person
      up
      as

            I
            swim
            into your
            net.

Beautiful day. Should get outside. Walk around. Maybe walk to the funeral. Least I don't have to work today. The day job takes up too much energy. But without a source of income I go nuts. Depressed and shit. It's like I'm *worth* nothing. What a drag, to tie your emotions to money like that. Fat Bill's it is.

Shoes.

Sidewalk strut, bounce-walk in a good mood.

Several misspelled signs in store windows. A store during remodeling has a sign that says "pardon the inconvience." The singular of potatoes or tomatoes is made by dropping the "s." "Weird" is spelled as "wierd." A sign in a bike shop says "we have used bikes."

Sears has an ad claiming to have "the world's largest waiting room."

In one window a legal or business form has the words "SAMPLE VOID" printed on it diagonally in red outline letters.

A sign in a rib joint reads "IT'S THE SAUCE—DONT GO HOME WITHOUT IT. No apostrophe in "don't."

Under a train overpass a white plastic owl hangs from a girder to scare away the pigeons.

See that Japanese guy walking a Malamute? An old man throws a disposable razor into a mailbox.

A picture framing place with a clock that's stopped after at least a year of accuracy in the window has placed a sign proclaiming "Sun Dials" next to the clock.

Pigeons and sparrows pick at the bodies of processed food cousins—fast fried chicken bones discarded to the street.

Whoops. Slow Down. Too much too fast. I deserve a slow

day. Sit on a bench for a while, watch traffic pass by. Light the first cigarette of the day, let it lighten your head and loosen your sphincter. Better find a john. Ah—a portojohn in the park. Walk there.

Walk in. Strong shit. Look at this, man. They got toilet paper here with a dark brown floral pattern on it. Does that make any sense?

Out. Fresh air. Bench again. Another smoke. Watch the women's breasts. Ah. There's one with R. Crumb legs.

I don't think this thing with Rain will work. "What's this with these redheads—always with redheads."

"Better red than dead."

"Yeah?"

Rain's complacency certainly has its parallels in the past. She doesn't make reliability her strong suit. No shows and forgotten phone calls. See what happens when she gets the poem. Silence maybe? The smarter they are the dumber they fall.

Nervous sliding break, my absorbent brain needs to be fed some beauty. Not games of love. Isn't there any honest affection in this world? Shit, babe, I'll do just about anything for you. Don't fuck it up. Treat me right and you've got yourself one loyal lover.

Switch it off. Wrong track right now. Not after last night's forgotten communication. I'm just low in her priorities. At least I'm not as bad as that ragpicker over on that other bench. Yet.

Hey. Where's my cheerful day gone? Maybe some more coffee. Hope a friend's over at Fat Bill's.

She was probably out fucking some dude, probably Guerin.

Goddamnit, Hugh, shut up. It's none of your business what the hell she does. She doesn't owe you jack shit.

There's a lot she learned from him. There's a lot you learned from him. There's a lot you learned from her. There's a lot she learned from you. There's a lot he learned from you. And we are all together. Dmess jujube.

Stop by a pay phone and call Guerin to invite him to Louisa's show at Orphan's. He says hello and immediately mentions Rain's having been over. "The kids were asking for her." Don't know about the show though, says he.

Rain next. She may have received the poem.

Oh yeah. I received your letter today.

It wasn't a letter.

Poem. Thanks. It was very nice.

Want to do something tonight?

No.

Who me? Paranoid?

Breakfast for Hitler and Germany. Fat Bill's is another three blocks zig zag.

Let it lie. There are other women who've expressed some interest in you.

No games, pal. Try to come straight from the heart.

Let it burn.

Ah! Fat Bill's should be good for that. Those nuts and that mediocre food—what a combo!

Stroll on down there. Start to smile thinking 'bout their shiny breakfast burgers. And a breakfast beer, eh? And some coffee, 'course. Gotta balance shit out to keep it even as possible. Better throw some hot peppers on that burger. Swiss cheese. Kraut, yeh everything but that radioactive relish. Really? No. I'm sorry—it's just that it's a very funky color, don't you think? Kelly Green? Like the Chicago River on St. Pat's. St. Charles better not be fucking up the place.

"Hey, buddy. Gimme a quarter."

"Sure, here ya go."

"Gimme another."

"Aw,man. Now don't be greedy."

Leaves just enough for a number one and a bus to the money machine.

Rain calls you at Fat Bill's. "It was a beautiful poem. Thank you very much." Zoom. The day goes off.

Thank you, babe. Energy my way from you juices me up like you wouldn't believe. I do love you.

There's the face of a fat man with a beard embroidered into the cushion of the chair. That's Bill.

His place is a legend. Yeah, but they say that 'bout lots of dumps.

"Grubs in gruel, please."

"Fuck Hugh."

"Ha."

"Thumb chowder."

"So long's there's no crabs."

"Nah. Washed today."

"You're sick. A Diet Perrier too."

"We don't carry it, sir."

"Nevermind. Coffee and a greasebomb with cheese and extra fuel, hold the radioactive materials."

"Yeah, wiseass."

"Careful—you won't get your tip."

"You never tip."

"Bull."

"Okay, okay. Man, it's good to see you. How's life with what's her Pain?"

"Cool."

"Bummer."

"Oh, nah. It's all right. I got a funeral to go to today, Bill."

"Who croaked?"

"Someone croaked?" asks a horn-rimmed heavyset fifty-year-old Irish woman.

"Oh yeah, Molly," says Bill. "Hugh was just gonna explain."

"I know that," she retorts. "Well?"

"Old Rose."

"Rose Moore?"

"How'd she die?"

"It was natural. She came home, put away the groceries, and collapsed in her kitchen. Dead almost instantly. Kinda like Gramps, but he died in the tub. Peaceful deaths. The best kind."

"What's John going to do?"

"Fuck John."

"What?"

"Look—get me a drink. I don't want to talk about it, 'kay?"

"Yeah, sure. Warm Old Style?"

"Fuck you."

"Cold Pilsner Urquell?"

"Now you're talking. Yeah, thanks, Bill."

A beer later everything's starting to focus better. Rain is a good woman, but you don't want to crowd her. She did say you were a terrific guy and seemed to genuinely like you. Let it gel. No hurry. Be yourself. Jeez, reads like a primer in cliché. Hard to avoid sometimes when they're entirely accurate.

"Hugh?"

"Huh?"

"Zillion miles away, man. Whatcha, out there checking out the space-worms?"

"Ah, no, man. I don't do that anymore."

"Hugh?" asks Molly, drunk and slurry.

"What?"

"Do you still love me?"

"Yeah, sure, Molly."

"Yeah. I love you, too."

Hugh leans over and plants in Bill's ear the words "Man, is she drunk, Bill. How long she been here?"

"Since near opening. Seven fifteen, maybe."

"Should try it in the purple."

"What? You're fucking weird, dude."

Bill, weighing in at a fat, greasy, dark-haired two-fifty calls me weird. Yeah, sure. I'll take that. Bill's trip's still 'Nam. Thing turned him conservative.

"No, I mean, Molly can't get a decent man, should get a woman instead."

"Fuck off. You know I hate that shit."

"Just kidding, Bill. Lots of people into that, though, these days."

"Yeah, tell me. My buddy's wife turned lesbo, man. What a trip. "

"Whatever blows up her skirt."

Both laugh. Molly comes closer to find out what's funny.

"Hugh just told me the size of his thing."

"He wasn't laughing, he was crying. Check out those tears."

"Been peeling onions."

"Been pulling your onion, you mean."

"'Least I got one to pull."

"You guys are disgusting" and Molly leaves for the ladies'.

"Hey, Bill. You got a paper around here?"

"Yeah. The Daily Poop. Here." He reaches into the counter under the register and removes the morning edition. He tosses it onto the counter in front of Hugh.

"Hey, easy. You almost spilled my coffee."

"You ain't got no coffee."

"That's my point."

"Oh, yeah. Sorry. Forgot."

"'Oh, yeah. Sorry. Forgot.' What a guy."

"Ease up, Hugh."

"All right. Coming to the picnic next month?"

"Don't know."

"Hey, do. It'll be a blast. Bring Portia."

"Rain going?"

"I think so. I won't know until five minutes before it's time to go."

"Oh."

"Hey, I'm going to read this paper a while, okay?"

"Oh, yeah. Sure."

Fold it open and accidently hit Molly, who's just sitting down next to you, upside the head with the back of your right hand.

"Sorry, Moll."

"Bastard."

"Yup, I am."

25% IN SCHOOL GET DRUNK WEEKLY

Should that be "weakly"?

NEW YORK—One in four high school students admits to getting drunk during school and one in three has smoked marijuana between classes, according to a poll conducted by Conservative Nonmotion magazine. The study also states that drug and alcohol abuse is spreading into elementary schools. The survey involved more than 250,000 10- to 18-year-olds in 37 states, most of them in the Midwest, according to the magazine.

Coffee! 'Bout time. Slrrrp... Ow! Fuck!

APALACHIA, WV—In these parts they come pretty horny. Take Clem Fletcher. Please. Call him a cab. *This writer's a rip-off.*

Fletcher is a 90-year-old retired shrimp, wimp, transmitter of communicable diseases, dip shit, gong farmer, hand-job giver. Get the drift?

He's been harried five times and has fucked five divorcees. Yet he's still got a gamey leg and is in the shopping mall for no sex.

"I fear women," he says, "but I need them." That's why he

welcomes Hurricane Stupid Bitch into his life. He lives on his three-acre spread waiting for her fist to pound into him. The rest of the county had evacuated, leaving them alone together.

"Unh-unh. Ain't leaving," he says, farting loudly. "Oh I did go and buy some tape worms. They're for my mule. Boy's she dumb."

A clear complexion attracts a man's juices. Sometimes from his bowels.

This is really sick. man. I can't believe it's in the paper.

Outside his home 60 m.p.h. winds come crashing like the accusations of bitter women. The rains turn trees to mud.

"I grew up here. I wait for her to come to me," says Fletcher, a tall, scrangly, thick-browed Abe Lincoln of a guy without the bullet hole.

"Worried? No way. My bride's coming for me. I ain't going till she gets here.

"Once a man falls for a great lady, he falls for the rest of his life," remarks Fletcher, who goes under the nickname "Feltch."

His next-door neighbor, just before leaving town, threw a rock at him and yelled across a field "You ol' fool!"

"I ain't never going back there," said the neighbor. "I don't know what's worse, the storm or that ol' coot."

TEEN'S "ART" LEADS TO DEATH

Bull Monitor lived by the sword of art and died by it. Fear of being caught caused the youth, engaged in his artform on a subway walk, to fall onto the electrified third rail. He was pronounced D.O.A. at Rolling Hills Hospital.

A double-edged sword.

CHILD PORNOGRAPHY INVESTIGATION CONTINUES

A letter containing full-color snapshots of naked Asian boys and girls not yet in their teens engaged in sexual activity with men were confiscated by city police yesterday as the city-wide crackdown on child pornographers continues.

Straight news is heavy shit. Check out the personals.

"Stubborn Tom, let me know when I can have it my way—Suz."

Odd stuff, eh? She probably watches a lot of fast-food

restaurant commercials.

"If anyone saw an accident involving an 18-wheeler flat-bed truck and a green moped Tuesday, 8/27, approx. 12:30 a.m. on Lake Shore Drive between 47th St. & 53rd St. please contact Hank Sims 555-5555 or 555-5555."

SOCCER
Canada and Costa Rica tied with no score in a match played in San Jose, Costa Rica. Both nations still have hopes for a place in the 1986 World Cup Competition.

ASTROLOGY
Don't be impatient with the new. Clarify your position. Be diplomatic, willing to make adjustments. Harmony will be restored.

Rain's—

You seem caught between your responsibilities and your desires. Act cautiously. Emphasis on intensified love relationship. Take leadership position.

Here's one about three brothers named Moore. Not relatives, I don't think. Let's see.

ROBBERY ATTEMPT THWARTED BY STOOL PIGEON
He gets distracted when he hears a car horn playing "What Do You Get When You Fall in Love?" Answer: a car horn that plays "What Do You Get When You Fall in Love?"

Sees another article instead.

PEOPLE AT JAZZ FEST GET HIGH
For the last seven years Chicago's Jazz Festival has become the expression of the police loving the public so much that twenty at a time would carry a stoned Mexican away for god knows what.

But it was good for making out on the lawn with Rain.

Back home his doorbell rings, but he's not there. Relax a bit here. Contemplate the situation.

These are her words: energy, life, generosity, afraid of something I don't know, but brave in the face of it.

Worms in the tequila and roaches in the coffee.

Tequila! Ah! A real breakfast. Mexican coffee. But keep that creme de cocoa out of there. Banish that shit.

Should look for another nose ring for her—something elegant, simple. To remember you by.

A silver Reliant K's car alarm is out of control in the parking lot. An angry reaction ensues throughout the café, especially as the duration of the alarm increases.

After an interminably long time an irate neighbor treads heavily into Fat Bill's.

"Anyone here own that Reliant K?" threatens the newcomer.

Silence.

"Well, I'm ripping the fucking alarm out. I live right above that fucking thing."

He went in back, popped the hood and tore out the alarm wire, thereby negating the primary function of the alarm, that of deterring break-ins.

No more paper. Pay the bill and slide out back on the street. Head home and maybe call Rain. Maybe not. She wants to play distance call someone else. You even have someone in mind who really digs you. So if Rain can't love you someone might. Of course I really wish Rain would love me.

Aww...

Fuckin' third grade allover again. What a wimp.

Open the door, forget about the step and stumble in the sidewalk onto a guy with a riding crop walking his doberman.

"Uh, bonehead," you mutter. As soon as the words escape you hope they weren't heard. You're lucky. They weren't.

She doesn't want a boyfriend. Rose's funeral.

Outside sweatin' out the beers you just had.

Maybe do another shower at home. Change into my funeral gear.

One of my father's friends once told me if he could have picked his son it would have been me.

What? Cool.

NO, not cool.

Maybe a nap. Not enough time.

Glide down the alley, shimmy up the stairs, stick your hand through the hole in the screen and pop the lock of the screen door. Both locks of the inside door are opened. Shoulder and right leg hard into the door simultaneously and it opens in to your kitchen.

Home again.

Chapter Two

The Bungled Attempt

"These roads used to be horse paths, and all this was swampland. Then they drained the swamps and paved the paths. That's why none of them run straight," says Nick Moore, the brains behind the operation.

"What about the horses?" asks his youngest brother, Jimi.

"Glue and dog food," interjects their middle brother, Rob.

Nick is worrying whether anyone will be suspicious of their carpet-cleaning truck arriving at the house so late in the day. Most workers are home staring with beers at their TV sets. Westalian Brothers 24-hour carpet cleaning.

Drive over the wooden bridge past the tennis courts and park between the six-car garage and the swimming pool.

Nick knows none of the neighbors can see through the trees which surround the estate. A tourist trap laminated cross-section of maple with "The Cavanaughs" burned into it hangs over the rear patio.

"We're going in here—the patio door," Nick tells his brothers. "Jimi, do your stuff." All three put on their gloves.

Jimi kneels before the door and removes his unique tool. It doesn't take him long to open up the house. They glide in. The Cavanaughs are on vacation.

"Take your time. Look for the rare shit." Nick walks over to the bookcase. He pulls strands of book from the wall like spiderwebs, like pulling away an entire layer of artichoke leaves in the middle where they're soft when cooked. Each strand is a chapter. All chapters end at the same point, are given similar structures but vary contents and definition.

A book on phlebitis.

"What's that, Nick?" asks Jimi.

"That's what someone with flea bites has."

"Oh."

A book about someone named Howard Johnson. An amazing guy—restaurateur; jazz baritone sax, tuba, and euphonium player; and infielder for the New York Mets.

It is weird to sit down watching a piece of paper in order to scratch strange characters onto it.

A book by Jackson Berlin called *Hoy Tomb Mutilate the English Lingo.* Nick reads the forward:

Stake. a word, amy word, and fill it fulla stuffing, add it to a Liszt and play it on pianer. Inna da circuolumvercularnacular all dat's goa round coma roun and weebee sittstill lissening to the glistening. Glissandoing across the flow witchoo pardoner in yo grclaspowing ten sense a dance.

Prbudispose daytoona is wonderfully 500 Grayest Waschmaltzes den filling hootcha but yootcha and duhopes you dulude minnusota wit. Duntcha blinka' me. I dunno. Da freemoon ahdah road. Anna we wander away to gather. Picka da sun and keepud closet yhan, holda ta holda and gibba ta me.

Sitcha bossyda an itzgnats tomby toobey tallying da strees stress hoohoohoo. Shh. Glissen.

Icedabeedaboy withnut nope grether. Buttcher meet made me make mahpoyn. Hoy. Meatcha. Woods crewa fromma floor off my deepwoods moat. Seatzin sighed glookinoot trclprapp neweyatta he.

Sighland callous crocodile river highland palace alligator shiver ain't nothin' gettin' in no mo'. We're isolated in safety where we can destroy the English language without threat of retribution, thereby effectively changing the thought patterns of English-speaking peoples everywhere, possibly averting the coming apocalypse. The basic link between people is communication, but mankind must have been doing it wrong because we're here teetering on the edge. If we break down language and rebuild, perhaps we might stave off disaster.

Our community is hidden but our impact is being felt. The subversion of the language has already begun. We are responsible for the bastardization of English more than anyone suspects. A personal favorite of mine is the term "parenting." We have also disseminated the spelling of "weird" as "wierd," the use of "like" for "as," "irregardless," "same difference," the formation of the singular of "potatoes" and "tomatoes" by merely dropping the "s," the use of "paradigm" for "foremost," and the dreaded double negative.

I am expressing our aims clearly, I realize, which no doubt causes some confusion. Why do I use correct English in order to call others to help corrupt it? The answer is simple. Our community has elected me to approach the incarcerated and attempt to liberate them from their linguistic prisons (primarily because my companions are very busy with their own projects and I am holed up with a broken foot and nothing else to do). There are others like me working in other languages, but the responsibility for English has fallen to me and those who are willing to help.

We believe that if we can change the way in which we as humans communicate we will be able to leave the strict narrow path that has brought humanity close to its own destruction. We need your help. At every given opportunity, use the language wrong. Say to yourselves like Churchill did, "this is the sort of pedantry up with which I shall not put."

Weebeekneedfreed! Uffoo fyndus wee bee hefty programnin on dieland he. Come to joindus andy weebee t-shirt youwatchoo wahn.

Doot yer ow nway. Bu doot!

Abba won listery abba man cunity. Heebee: found 1953 by Wooly Arm Aspirin Toe, freeman lance teach at What Sopwith U. (namen da chain to Lautrec linaseed). Xcelpelled fa sudeducing a coat heedee tire toodee slylan in Lame buSuprior. Whawe ahlive (das seve tea seve) an we subbasuffishin' an we I ibbatooteashin' dway to DESTROIENGLECH (an Frunch an Churm an oil Indoiurpeein' an ideotgram an all da rest).

Lik Bab lawn wemee tasyuman anchoo mu too doo newey ta stroi holy warld.

Sport these burns of tension:

1.   What can replace the language that's blown off asunder?
2.   Won't chaos result?
3.   Won't this just hasten the destruction of our planet?
4.   How could anything get done?

First, as any traveler can tell you, there is a beauty in meeting someone with whom communication is reduced to essential humanity, stripped free of the debris of societal conventions and prejudices. Rather than meeting preconception to preconception, two can meet identity to identity, pure and human.

Rather than chaos, a greater striving toward cooperation must follow. Only by paying closer attention to those we encounter can we survive—an essential if we are to save this planet. All are equal, all must be met with compassion in order to be understood and to understand. Russian, American, White, Black, Conservative, Liberal, all become meaningless terms.

The planet can be saved because we will be involved with the tangible, that which is immediately in our environment, and the "evil enemy over there" will cease to exist.

Lastly, rather than spending our energy and money combating that thing over there, we'll need it all to get along right here—rather than bombs we'll be concerned with digging wells and growing food.

Sobadusee, itcha wanna hay pltoo stove awf denda whirl, lemon up da whey cyunicake. Visit our community or, if you can't find it, stake a word, amy word, and doot yer ow nway.

Bu doot!

Another book. This one by a dude named Hugh Moore.

"Hey, Rob? We got a relative named Hugh?"

"Dunno. Not that I know of." Rob coughs.

"Book here by him."

"Hey, take it along. We'll check it out later. Dig these collector's plates. Any way to transport these safely?"

"Shit, sure. Wrap 'em in newspaper and box 'em."

"Hey, why not?"

"Make sure you wrap 'em well, Rob."

"Shut the fuck up, Nick."

"Yeah, right here."

Check out the drawers. Trinkets. A watch with four other dials on its face. Two jumbo paperclips. A pack of condoms, ribbed and lubricated. A Malfeasance Proclamation. A cheap chapbook copy of Joyce's *Pomes Penyeach*. A metal Matchbox Mercedes Benz. Four calling cards (a Docker, a Liar, a Sign Tist, and an Injun Ear). Three French Fries. Two Turtles albums. An' a Partridge Family 45.

Behind the paintings. Who's there? An 'ole. Oy see an 'ole. Go fru dat 'ole and you'd be standing in the wall with the carpenter ants and the mice and the roaches and all their droppings and babies and silverfish and earwigs and centipedes and spiders. Fuck that hole.

Got a flashlight?

A shelf with a metal box sitting on it in the hole.

Pull that box out.

Hey Moe, Hey Larry.

Open it, you knucklehead.

No way. You open it.

Okay.

Emeralds, rubies, diamonds. Unmounted cut rocks.

Holy shit.

"Hey, Rob. Fuck those plates. We don't need 'em."

"Doesn't look like we do, do we?"

In the bathroom a woman's hosiery collection. Jimi thinks yes. Then he thinks no. Never hold a hose if you don't know where it's been.

It's hard for me to know where anything's been when I don't know where I've been or where I'm going.

But I keep on floating through, sinking to know I'll rise, rising to know I'll sink. Knowing somehow it's all worthwhile. It's a wheel, a switch, day and night, breathing.

I've got a feeling. I keep on going. Caught between wanting to change and wanting to stay the same.

Time to get a haircut. When I feel that straight-edged razor on my neck, I smile. Shave those neckhairs. Let a little blood.

The TV work okay? "And featuring Marlene Dietrich," pronounced "Marleen."

TV? We don't need no stinking TV.

"Hey! This dude's got files on his clients. Check it out. He's got one for his general clientele—"

"Isn't that stuff private?"

"—and one for his major clients."

"Those must be the kernel of his business."

"Their bank accounts, sexual habits, prescriptions, dealings outside the law, etcetera."

"Etcetera? You some kinda Latin scholar or somethin', Rob? Speak English. Fuckin' fag pussy wimp."

"Come here so I can throw up on you."

"Please."

"Come on, guys. Get serious."

"I'm Roebuck."

"You're dead in a minute if you don't shut up. You're driving me batty."

"Relax, Max."

"Holy shit—real snakeskin boots. I'm snarfin' these. Rattler skin or somethin'. This is cool."

"You're an idiot."

"Why?"

"Go away. Get out of here."

"Yeah, okay—I'll go check out the bedroom."

"You sicko."

Leaving Jimi and Nick in the living room.

"Guess I'll check the bathroom again, Nick."

"Not only are you sicker than he is, you're an even bigger idiot. What the fuck of any value could possibly be kept in the bathroom?"

"Under the sink, like in the movies. Taped up."

"I doubt this dude—oh well, go ahead take a look. Why not?"

What bozos I have for brothers. 'Least the real fuck-up ain't here.

Shiver through the spine.

You don't remember me.

I'm a believer in personal freedom and I know how to use it. No one'd say no. Claws for cause.

Be tweenya wanta.

Crowds of joy.

Yeah, it's hard enough to be an individual.

Life is Pan. American, theistic, ama, der, da, creas, ts, g, e, cake, ther.

Sometimes life goes to pot. Wonder if Jimi'll find anything. Probably not. Thinking he's Hendrix, changing the spelling of his name, and he can't even play *Smoke on the Water* half-decent. What a narr. Even the guitarist in Ada and the Evil Hearts is better. Ada Romp—what a great-lookin' broad. Love to nestle in that bushel. Hmmmm ooooh. Yeah.

In the bathroom Jimi reads a handwritten note on the toilet tank that says "keep the handle depressed until toilet is through flushing." Should I insult it where it lives? I ain't no gong farmer. Never mind. No one gonna send me back to the Same Asylum. They try to make everyone enjoy their fit.

Might as well use the facility for what it was designed. What? Brown floral t.p.? That's ignorant. Ignorance will get you in the end.

Rob's in the bedroom admiring his snakeskin boots and hoping he can wear them for a while. Then he remembers how little time he probably has. Going to Vailima. He coughs again. Good thing his doctor has small hands. Makes it easier to beat him in poker. Makes it easier to beat him with a poker. God I feel bad. Hope Jimi's found the dope I told him to look for. Anything to get me through.

I've led a hard life. Most of it working eight hours a day, transport there and back three, writing another four (remember when I pretended to be a writer—an artist?), sleeping five, which leaves four for chores and drinking and getting high. Don't give me your suburban preppy petty tiny imbecilic juvenile no-good ignorant asshole rectal mucus bull diarrhea. Lawn chairs? Colored TV? Swimming pools? Wine futures? Servants? Take this fuckin' shotgun up your mouth, rich motherfucker. I'll outlast all your kind.

Hello, John Giorno. "I don't need it, I don't want it and you cheated me out of it." If you don't know it you might as well buy a gallon of Sherwin-Williams and some bags for your LawnBoy because you're way too removed from real life. Put your faith in products—go ahead. Humanity's basic impulses, thoughts and drives are meaningless because they don't put money in your pocket.

I'll be fuckin' dead within the year so what do I care what I say? Give me a cigarette, a joint and a beer. Some tequila and no love at all. Thanks, planet. I've tried to do everything for you and

I've never gotten anything back. Goin' elsewhere, babe. This ain't the place for me. I've got too much love for this desert.

It's too late to even look for someone to love me. I'm gone.

I've been cheated and unappreciated.

Thanks again. Planet of death. World of horror.

Won't you let me go?

"The end of my life is an open door," quoting Mr. Entwistle.

Getting through softly is important.

Go alone, go quietly, don't fight it anymore. Dream it into freedom. Seed it. Watch it grow. What's ambition mean an inch away? What does anything mean except being held in by a loved one? But, perhaps, that's too much to expect a lover to go through.

Fuck it, might as well rip off this dude. Got nothin' to lose, right? Zam—Zap Jam. Free is the key. Donkey meat alcohol and a doggie treat. Cryogenic sleep. Corridor of dreams. Corridor of scars. Spent most my life sittin' in bars. Drink my liquor from mason jars. For profit. Two doin' the dangle.

High grade necking. Collecting bucks on past due bills. Nothin' to get me through but pain pills.

Friend of mine.

My friends are still alive. It's 1985. And the world we once lived in has gone away. Awry. Flowers springing up from the body of a dead pup make me glad to know that I am still alive. No jive.

Clowning in my room, no audience too soon, hoping it'll get somewhere someday. Then I see something like Jackson's new piece and I wish I could do that. Strong and self-assured. Young.

When I was young I thought I'd be famous by now.

Dead too. Can't always slide into your fantasies. But some do. May yet still get there. I ain't giving up or going away just quite yet. It's impossible to quit.

What about that dream last night? Some woman named Andy looking like a boy with ultra-short butchy hair—gotta scare men away. Set in Pittsburgh. Goin' to a show where she knew everyone and I didn't and she spent her time flitting about, not having any time for me.

'Least it wasn't my ex, social climbing, fucking one dude till something better came along, then him till something even better. She's not good enough to be pulling that off for long.

Fuck it all—there's nothing in here.

"Nick?" Bob calls out of the bedroom. "There's nothing in here."

"Oh shit!" Jimmy shouts in the bathroom. He comes out looking pissed off. "Found a quarter taped to the inside of the lid of the toilet tank, but I dropped it in and the fuckin' paper opened. Fuck."

"Oh man," Rob's disappointed.

"We didn't come here for that anyway, bozo. Here—let's load up all this shit I found."

They decide to start hauling everything out to their Westalian Brothers 24-hour carpet cleaning van. License plate FCW 226. FCW for "fuck Chicago winters. "

Nick picks up the Jackson Berlin and Hugh Moore books first to take them out and place them in the glove box if they'll fit.

On the way to the door he decides to pause to read a bit more Berlin.

"In the Land of the Estimos" by Jackson Berlin

Wantcha getoncha road you node. Trabble the pad you canfortable whip. Seeb whateye neeb?

Lerrming axe ya distance—whybe dat suppertime ice kraken govinda coffee and suppertime knot. White?

White knot.

A world of distance between north and south poles.

"Where'd you learn to kiss like that?"

"Penguins taught me."

"Yeah?"

"Yeah. They learned it from the Eskimos."

The estimos. "I'll be there in half an hour." "Just a couple of bucks." "I'll have it back to you right away."

Butcher block. Imagine an island.

We're pro's.

Some say there's only rum for one. I say bring your own. Find your horseless carriage. Keepud closet yhan. Drinka dribe. Fugga da systim and get up.

People be feedin' you shit to keep you in line. Resist it, man. When People talk to you about Jesus, Reagan or the Grateful Dead tell 'em no thanks man—you can think for yourself. Throw away your left crutches, liberals. Throw away your right crutches, conservatives. Abandon Jesus and God and all the antiquated myths and begin to think for yourselves. It's not hard to see that there are no liberals or conservatives but that many of us have accepted these limitations onto ourselves and should discard them *as* limitations. I doubt you would sink—the sea of life would keep you afloat. Be free. Tell your bosses to eat shit. Tell your schools they're off the mark. Or pander to 'em if you need. Do whatever you want. Don't take advice, not even mine, unless you really agree with what tile advice means—if you can feel in your bones it has something you can learn from for a little while—until you have to move in order to keep on growing.

A bee with energy coming from its belly. Wearing a mask and dancing in the sky. It'll sting you with ideas when the time is right.

Spelp ten.

It flies away once its message is imparted. Up your nose.

Stingstingstingstingstingsting.

A string of stings.

You've got W. C. Fields' nose. Just like a hermit, your peter's for no one. Will it ever be thus? Are you too old to quit the booze? Do you care? Isn't it a nice way to be put to sleep?

A monk hiding away. Where's safer to hide than in a group of friends? Some of them take a lot of drugs because deficiencies in their body chemistries require them to.

Others pack little boys in their crawlspaces. There's a problem with that. A basic instinct screams not to take another.

Are we not men?

So we're out here now, post-hippie, post-punk, post-modern. Do we push it higher or does it collapse? If we're gonna go, let's go for it. Push it. What do you think?

Frogmen on the terrace?

Palace guards at the lake?

These are weird times, man. These times were made

for walkin'. Hey, know what? When I was in high school I fucked the principal's daughter. Yeah, so what? I was just a P.K. anyway. Looking for a good lay.

Just discovered a nice drink: stout and diet cherry cola half and half. Try it. First thing every morning do aspirin and caffeine and fluoride. But leave that flower alone. It's illegal and bad for you—it causes tits on men, brain something and something else I forgot, too. Come on, do you really believe such bullshit? My only complaint is that it makes me pleasant and relaxed and then people take advantage of my good mood to suck my marrow. Another law of nature—if you feel good, you get drained; if you feel bad, you drain others. Inadvertently or not.

Fact is there's nothing I have to say unless I pursue a process through which I approach serious thought.

But I do know this—

Thab we detter geb ob whim tuh reconstootin' I of a butter whey. Fretget it owl.

Clour dowt.

Mungehead.

Wet.

Dot.

Drip.

Slip.

Mop.

Frim.

X·stttfen

kRmmy

gqdbsz-¼?

ah.

ah.

ah.

ah.

ah.

Bambambarnbamba!

Oh fuck.

"Open up! This is the police! We have the place surrounded!"

Oh shit. That's why the ass didn't show. Fes turned in his own brothers.

"Nick, what do we do?"

"I don't know, Jimi. Put this shit away in a closet. Sit back, relax, pretend we're waiting for our friends to get home. If questioned we could maybe be mistakened—had the wrong address. I don't know. Rob—crack open the scotch on the bar—let's sit back and relax with a few—I'll get the door."

Rob fills three highballs very quickly with Old Brown Shoe.

Nick walks over casually to the door and opens it.

"Hello, officer. How are you? What seems to be the matter?"

The policeman looked confused. "Uh, what's your name?"

"Nick. What's yours?"

"What are you doing here?"

"Waiting for our friends to get home."

"Friends?"

"Yeah, Lorrayne and Joyce."

"Who?"

"The Clancey sisters."

"This is not their residence. Come on, hands up. We've gotta take you in for questioning."

The three brothers get hauled in. They turn in their matching statements and are released uncharged when it is discovered nothing's been stolen and there's no sign of forced entry. Jimi's been good.

Chapter Three

The Vomitous Bar

The first thing anyone ever noticed was that everyone else was wrong. The second thing was that they didn't do it right.

Chuck takes a shower with his dishes to save time so that he can meet his second cousin Ralph at the bar before Rose's funeral.

Standing there, letting water spray forever on his face, Chuck runs the vision of death which had haunted him during the night past his closed eyes once again.

At two-thirty in the morning the doorbell had rung. Chuck buzzed whomever up and went out to the hall, expecting to see a drunk buddy coming up the stairs. A voice called up "help me, help me" and Chuck called down his buddy's name. "No—I—live—down—the—street. Help." The man's face and body appeared as he fell flat on his back on the landing halfway between the second floor and the third floor on which Chuck's was the only apartment. Chuck couldn't see him clearly—Chuck wasn't wearing his glasses. The guy was white, about 23, maybe a college student, a preppie (or someone disguised as a preppie).

Chuck said "just a sec," went back in his apartment to find his glasses so he could better assess this scene. The guy came up the stairs and knocked on the door, "help—me." Then he left and Chuck heard footstumbles going down the stairs as he hunted for his prey glasses. There. He fired them onto his face. Opened the door. Nothing there but blood on his door.

He closed the door, got dressed, got some moist t.p., wiped off the blood, threw the paper down the toilet, flushed, and went down the stairs, half-expecting to see this guy sprawled out dead at the foot. Blood on his neighbors' doors too.

The apartment building interior door, which contained eight large square windows in two vertical columns of four, was missing the two central ones on the door knob side except for the jagged broken edges where panes had been. Glass littered the foyer and hall.

Chuck finishes his shower, dresses and walks on out the door.

I am at the bar when he walks in.

"Hey, Chuck."

"Hiya, Harry."

"Goin' to Rose's funeral?"

"Yeah—I'm meeting Ralph here and we're going over after a few. You?"

"Nah—I'm just gonna hang out here—catch the game on TV maybe."

"Think they'll do it?"

"Better—I got a twenty on it."

"Whatcha drinkin'?"

"Shots."

"Tequila?"

"Yeah."

"Here—I'll buy us a round."

"A true shot-putter."

"Yeah, s'pose so."

"How'd the last meet go?"

"I was too hungover. I placed third."

"That's not bad."

"Yeah, I s'pose."

"Really."

I start thinking about my haircut yesterday and how much better I liked it after I washed it this morning.

When I felt that straight-edged razor on my neck, shaving off those long neck-hairs, I smiled.

Here's Ralph. These two are going to be obnoxious again.

Ralph sits down, joins us in a shot and begins watching the television. He talks to it.

An ad for designer jeans. "Eat it, bitch." Hard to believe Hugh's his brother.

Who am I to speak, though? I'm here dressed yuppie to fool people. Chuck and Ralph begin recalling their greatest automobile accidents.

"Yeah, I was drinking this stuff once and got the idea my Datsun was a dune buggy and rode it up on the beach and got it buried in a foot of sand. This guy drinking a Heineken came up and told me the same thing'd happened to him and the cops came by and he told them he'd overshot the parking lot and they let him off. So I tried it. The cops came by, I told them I'd overshot the parking lot and they offered to call me a tow-truck, which I accepted. Hell, they were probably getting kickbacks from the towing company they called, so I figured if I let 'em, they'd let me off. They did. The guy even took my personal check—I didn't have hardly any cash on me."

"Wild, man. Did I ever tell you 'bout the time my buddy and I were going up to Lake Superior to spend some time up at Jackson Berlin's colony?"

"No, not at all. Doesn't your brother live in the same building as him?"

"Yeah, but I don't think they know each other well or get along or anything. Hugh's always bitching about him.

"No shit."

"Anyway, we were headin' north. Takin' little highways that ran through towns all the way up through Wisconsin. Stoppin' in each town first at a bar where we'd walk in, order a couple of screwdrivers, hit the can, come out and drink 'em, buy a six to go, or if they didn't have packaged go to a beer store and get a six and drink 'em on the road till we hit the next town where we'd repeat the whole procedure.

"Needless to say, we never got there. I was playin' navigator and my buddy was drivin' my car and we got lost, or the map was wrong. But we were headin' up this hill, looking for a connection to another highway and I told him we'd have to drive two blocks farther and take a left. He gunned it up to eighty, blew the stop sign at the top of the hill and next thing I knew we were flying over a ten-foot ditch into a wheatfield that was four feet below road level. The road had ended in a t-intersection. Twin spiderweb shatters on the windshield, my buddy broke his nose on the steering wheel. I'm laughing up a storm, tellin' him to put it in reverse and get us the hell out of here 'fore the cops come. And he tries it. Nothing. The car's totally fucked. My buddy's bleeding like a pig so we climb out and, totally smashed, get out and walk up to the nearest farmhouse. The farmer's wife there is super nice to us and gives us washcloths and helps my buddy with his nose. She tells us they got towers pulling cars out of there every week, ever since the road was put in three years back. She lets me call my dad who tells me he knows the minister in the nearest town and that he'll contact him and have him meet us. He calls back in a couple of minutes and tells us the name of a restaurant where the minister'll meet us. He'll pick us up there and drive us to the Holiday Inn where my dad's made reservations for us using his Visa. When we get there we're supposed to call my dad again.

"A cop comes by to look at the wreck—county sheriff's police. We thank the farm lady and go to the car to meet the cop. He asks me what happened. I concocted a story about a yellow Camaro that cut us off. He said it couldn't have because of the skid marks. He took out a camera and began taking photos of the marks. I said 'Just a minute, officer. Let me talk to my friend to refresh my memory.' After a couple of minutes of talking with my buddy I came back and said, 'no, my friend assures me there wasn't another car. We didn't see a warning for the T-intersection though and the road was wet and it was overcast and we didn't see the stop sign,' and so on, and the cop interrupted and asked why I wasn't straight with him to begin with and threatened to run us in. Here my buddy was a genius. He asked the cop, 'so what's goin' to happen to us? Are we gonna spend the rest of our lives rotting in some stinkin' jail in Wisconsin?' And the cop cracked up. We all laughed and were glad to be over the tension. The cop said 'No, there's another option.'

"'Whatever it is I like it,' said my buddy.

"'I don't have to give you a ticket. I could let you go.'

"'I like that a lot.'

"'But next time don't stop at so many gin mills on the way, okay?'

"'Yes, officer. Thank you very much. You're a nice man.'

"'I'll call you a towtruck which'll take your car into town. The town's out of my county, but I'll drive you boys in so you can take care of your car, okay?'

"'Sure. Thanks. Could you drop us at the Caravelle Restaurant?'

"'Yeah.'

"'Thanks.'

"So we get there and eat some food. Real lousy food. Made us both sick. My buddy waited till after we got back to the hotel. I threw up all over the minister's car. Fuck was I embarrassed, but fuck it, I figured I had a mild concussion at least, but probably it was just the booze.

"So we called my dad from the hotel and he had arranged air flights back for us the next morning. I called the desk and left a request for a wake-up call and went to sleep. My buddy spent the night pacing the room, repeating to himself as he cupped his nose in a handkerchief, 'I'm bleedin' like a fuckin' pig.'"

"Wow, man."

"Really. It was weird, pal. And the farmer tried to get money out of us for damage to his crops. We blew him off."

"Good."

"Yeah. Fuck him. Why didn't he have a guardrail up or something?"

"For sure."

Another round of shots and beer chasers and they continue.

"I had a head-on collision once."

"Ow. What happened?"

"Ran into some Punjabi at the intersection of Michigan and Ohio. Christmas Eve 1979. Coming from a party at the Mark Plaza where I'd been drinking lots and smoking and tootin' up a storm. I had two accidents that night. First I couldn't even get out of the parking lot. I tried exiting through the entrance and popped up the bar that blocked the way and hotel employees stopped me, took my license and made me wait till they copied everything down back in the office, where I had to get my license back from. In case of any damage to the arm mechanism. Then when I finally got out of there I got lost. Ended up on Martin Luther King Drive with no idea of where I was other than I was headin' in the wrong direction. So I turned around and got back goin' north. Got on Michigan Avenue. Trying to get my bearings, you know? Cruised through the intersection of Ohio with the green light and barn! holy fuck! Some dude'd been facing the wrong way in my lane, too far out past the turning island there, with his lights off and his flashers not on either. His lip was bleeding. I went and called the cops who came and ticketed us both. We both called tow-trucks. The cops took the Indian guy to the hospital. I went into a diner to get food while I waited for the tow-truck. Bleedin' a lot, reeking of booze, they served me and didn't say a word. Pretended I was normal. Cool, eh? On Michigan Avenue?"

"Very."

"Yup."

"I had an accident because of Satan once."

"What?" They both started laughing loudly. Getting on my nerves already. Didn't they have a funeral to go to? And talking about Satan? That didn't seem like a good idea. Playing with things you don't know about. Like the Stones at Altamont.

"Really. I rented a truck to move back to Chicago from Iowa City. Got it late in the day 'cause we had to work. My gal and I stayed at friends' in Coralville overnight and came back along Iowa Avenue, on which I lived, forgetting that the Iowa Avenue overpass was nine foot four inches high and the truck ten foot. Peeled the roof back like a sardine can. The unmarked cop behind us said we woke him right up. But he said we should've seen the semi'd tried it the week before. He was cool. I went home, called the rental place and asked for another truck. I'd checked the insurance box, of course. The only stuff I'd put in the truck was my heavy furniture and a bullshit book which was stupid enough to be used as a doorstop. As I'd gone through with the last load the night before when I'd loaded it I'd pulled the book out and thrown it into the truck. When I went into the truck to move everything out to the new one the book was there, grinning up at me. *The Satanic Bible.* I tore it up and threw it away and made it home safe after that."

"Ever pulled 360's?"

"Twice man, in winter. Once coming back from dropping my dad off at the airport with my sister. We were drivin' his car back and he hadn't put snow tires on it. I was doin' the speed of traffic and went into a skid. Fortunately I like to give my car space fore and aft anyway so when I went into a 360 I didn't hit anything. Stayed in my lane. Wait. No. That was a 180, not a 360. 'Cause I remember this bus coming at us, nose to nose, and my sister screaming, but the driver was a genius, and skidded the bus past safely, missing us only by an inch. But I pulled a 360 up on the bend of 41 by Deerpath but I was alone and pretty much stayed in my lane."

"Yeah, I hit the Dundee West exit guard rail once on 41 in winter. Fucked up both fenders on the left."

"I'd been driving for Rudy's Liquors and hit some guy."

"Drunk?"

"Not at all, man. But I'd been thinking about stopping in this bar for lunch at Morgan and Van Buren where I used to go when I was in school there. I went to make a right turn at that intersection, to get to the parking lot in back, and some little shit Plymouth Horizon squeezed between me and the curb, where no man should have ventured, because the van tore the shit out of his car—ripped it wide open. The van just got dented a bit. But I had to fill out accident reports for everyone and the whole thing got to be a drag."

They are really starting to bore me with these stories. I remind them of the funeral.

"We got plenty of time. Why aren't you going, anyway?"

I guess I asked for that. I don't have a good reason. How can I get out of this?

"I'm here doin' research."

What for?"

"I can't say—a high-level project."

"Bull."

"Yeah, so don't believe me. I don't give a damn. When's that funeral of yours start?"

"E.D."

"Huh?"

"Ease down, pal."

"Shit, you're drinking more of those?"

"Yeah. Why not?"

"You eaten anything today?"

"Nah—liquid food, man."

"Don't get sick."

Which starts both thinking about it. They sit silent for an hour, drinking. The idea churns around inside their stomachs and comes up outside after they leave in tandem using the excuse that they're going to smoke a joint.

Wretched retch. In a garbage can.

Violent expulsion.

Nearer my god to thee.

Yuck. Spit. Foam.

HEADACHE .

cold sweat.

shivers.

god I need a beer.

god it's too late, isn't it?

god I'm going.

god.

ghosts who reenter the bar and order a couple of beers. Gotta admire their stamina.

They look better soon.

Head on out the door towards the funeral site.

"'Least we'll be there before the encore, eh?"

"Should bury us instead."

Chapter Four

Resurrection Rose

They picked me up and lowered me into the ground.

I woke up early one day, died of heart failure, was revived by electroshock and died again.

Fortunately, Doug's an undertaker by trade, so I didn't cost John a lot of money. I wonder what John'll do without me. Poor incontinent.

Doug's been good. He and Barry and Carrie were all pall bearers. Barry on crutches and all. Nice to be with the family. Even if they did get into an argument before I was even covered over. Barry told all about his accident at the lumberyard, too, which seemed out of place to me.

"I'd been working at this lumberyard," he said to Carrie, "for three days. A very physical gig. Lift, haul, load, unload. I was a forklift driver's assistant. Most of the guys were huge ex-marine types, man, so I worked extra hard to prove myself. Pushing it at the edges, you know? Jumping off early, climbing back on when it was already moving. Till I jumped off just as the driver turned and the rear wheel caught my heel and I went on workman's comp for three weeks with a bone chip in my foot. Lots of codeine, man. It was okay."

Doug told Barry the story of someone who was healthy who used crutches as stilts, fell off and fractured his ankle.

I realize Reagan's got his people out there trying to tighten up your asshole. Just wait till they get where you want 'em and then let loose.

The trip's going so right wing it scares Germans and Turks, man. Déjà vu.

The government's fucking over domestic artists again—if they ask you about me tell 'em I didn't know shit about art and that I wasn't domesticated either.

Heck no, I was only twenty-five years old.

Just a kid, Yuk Yuk. Makes me smile, too. If I had lips, I'd kiss you for just being here. Dead women don't plant kisses.

And I weren't no twenty-five I guess. Not but for that one year years ago.

From mono to stereo, babe, we went through it all.

Damn I liked being with you. Stayed with you so long 'cause I hated endings, this one least of all. I hope you bear your grief well, for I know how I would have grieved over you. And I do, my love, I do.

It's been good, but we both gotta be goin', 'know? And tears swell up in my sunken eyes. My body's last gesture, unseen, unseeable.

Thank you, my life's been good because of you. You've always been there when I needed you most. You've shared your life's warmth with me and I love you for it.

And I believe in rock and roll.

Oh? Stop you? What's anything mean? Rock and Roll or Jesus or Buddha or Mohammed? What do you want? Revelation? How about me sayin' what I think, whether it's good or true or right or wrong?

It's nah nah tie a knot exactly what prospected. They've been talking 'bout it for years. And we just kinda hitched up, remember? Telling us 'bout winter come on din't stop us none. Brr... Nnn... Who... Ttt... Hum... Crackle... Turned back, eh? Breaktime. Go somewhere else, look around forwards or backwards, check it out, come back and come back in. Another chapter, another place and I'll just babble a bit about inconsistent nothings to get you bored a bit, no not a bit but more like a lot, yes, definitely a lot because the reality presented to me by the board of the special collections department of the welfare of readers who enjoy the singularly descriptive manner of the works of Alain Robbe-Grillet may find the upcoming festival of beach films unstomachable.

Beach films?

Oh no!

I'm getting out of here.

Out of where? Hey, where are you going? Leave it to the dead to renege their debts. Hey, you owe me! Fuck it, leaving me here with the narrative in the middle of her section. Hey, I guess I could do just 'bout anything to her mid-section I wanted to just 'bout here. But I'm a nice guy. Today. Plus she's kind of old.

Well, someone's bound to come by sometime soon to claim this section so I'd better have some fun while I can.

REAGAN STINKS

silly.

DOWN WITH IMPERIALISM

kinda dumb, eh? Not real meaningful. Fuck it.

ROCK & ROLL 4-EVER

yeah, I'm a victim of the decay of society and proud.

I LOVE MY SLOT

ah, political and sexual, more creative.

PARES CUM PARIBUS FACILIME CONGREGANTUR

too esoteric.

CRY OF GENETICS

got it.

Write CRY OF GENETICS on the nearest wall. Why? Well, why not? 'Least you'll know why you did it. Or will you? Aren't the simplest things overwhelmingly complex?

Who are you?
The rightful heir to this section.
Go to hell.
Really.
Okay prove it.

Got a lot to say, don't you?
I can't work under pressure.
Professionals.can.
Fuck you.
Goodbye.
Huh?
Good day.
S'long.
Good. Got it back. Damn amateur thinks he can take *my*

section away from me. Hah!

Both of you get lost. Just 'cause I'm dead doesn't mean I'll give this up.

Hey you, look what you did to this perfectly good section. Who's gonna clean that up? You trashed it.

You must be a bitter young man to trash an old woman's section like that.

Hey, the young man replied in third person, this being very important to Rose, my artistic expression, 'kay?

Rock & Roll 4-Ever? That's not art, son, that's an adolescent juvenile phase most adults grow out of by your age. And I'm quite sure Mr. Reagan bathes frequently.

Yeah, well, fuck you.

Thank you for sharing your keen powers of critical observation with me, asswipe.

You can't call me that.

Why not? I'm dead.

I could come after you.

No chance, young man. This door is closed.

I could mutate into it.

Don't bother.

We'll see.

Young man!

Catchya later, Gram.

No respect for the dead, I tell ya. Maligning my character with political statements and cheap pop standards.

Well, it *is* my section.

I think I feel maggots crawling in my brain.

Holy tumescence, rat man.

Happy was my life. My children and I loved each other. My husband was good to me. But I never got my lawn furniture. And there's no way John'll remember to buy some. They'll have to have the family reunion indoors, I guess.

Yeah, but you don't care 'bout my family, I know, and I'm not the kind of writer who wants to make you have to care, an ill-minded deception attempted by sensationalist pop writers or sniveling academic invertebrates. And though there are strong writers in both categories, most have limited their freedom in exchange for a guarantee of steady financial income. In other words, they've modified their artistic stances to accommodate the wishes of the holder of the bankroll; the department of English; Strunk and White; the dictates of Science Fiction, Mystery, Romance in their stricter forms; the desire for popularity among students, particularly of the opposite gender; the President; the Board; current fashion; artistic convention; historical progression; the failure of the individual to assert her individuality except in forms accepted by the group, which tricks heir into abandoning that essential individuality and dividing the artist from her self.

Invertebrates who need an exoskeleton to cling to.

But isn't this in ways mostly a self-condemnation? I certainly made adjustments. Tuned it a little finer. Until I died.

At which point everything I had written ceased to matter to me. Truly, my worldly troubles had ended. It just took a while to realize that the lawnchairs were unimportant. Or did I always know that?

There wasn't any real weeping at my funeral. Will they miss me? I wonder. I'll miss them. I still don't quite know what'll happen to me. Nothing's as sudden as you think it'll be. Neither's death. Only half-dead.

With $1.07 in coin still on my person.

Thought they'd at least relieve me of the four coins in my pocket.

Gamble over my garments.

'Course they'd never heard of me and certainly didn't read experimental fiction, especially by women.

And lots of what passes for experimental ain't.

Hey, I could get to work on my posthumous publications. Something slanderous, 'cause I'm dead. Preferably a lie, like my three-way affair with James and his secretary Sam. Or the time I single-handedly wrestled a stampeding herd of elephants to the ground.

Something I wrote when young. Under a pseudonym.

With You There To Help Me by Duncan Rivers

"Nothing in this life that I've been trying can equal or surpass the art of dying."
George Harrison

Preface

This novella is disjoint as my life has been, yet sewn together by a single thread—that of what I've seen.

It is autobiographical and therefore I found it very difficult to write, which is why it is a novella rather than a novel. It is classifiable as a something-to-get-off-your-chest type of work, yet still I hope it addresses that which is more universal than mere selfisms.

A Thought

My folks and I were driving through a desolate farm section of Iowa, along highway 20. My father was speeding a good twenty-five miles over the limit when I jumped out. I don't know why I did. It was just a thought that had fruitioned into reality.

A Truth

Things like that happen to me in a strange reality—like the times I committed suicide. I remember them well.

While vacationing in Alberta, a young man who had given up hope for the previous Lent, in a last act of desperation, rented his body out as an airplane, took off over a cliff and landed in heaven.

While meditating on the meaning of life and the reality of love, a young man who loved incense discovered a malignant tumorous growth of self-contempt and hopeless frustration. He tried a medicine to combat the growth. But the growth forced an overdose, and wings grew from the growth within the lifeless body.

Even in my second life I died often, usually after making love or upon discovering I couldn't. Oh, how sweet to die in one's sleep!

But I'm not the only person I know who killed herself. Many friends of mine loved my example and followed it.

Friends

The shopping center had waited; but the car, so much a lesser of the shopping center, had defied the shopping center's will and spitefully destroyed the miniscule two-wheeled mosquito and its pilot-fish friend.

I was late. The shopping center had waited, but I saw that the car hadn't. It was painful to set eyes upon the forsaken aftermath.

Latin is a dead language spoken in tongues of verbiage and maudlin as a slab of granite reflecting golden sunshine on its cold hard reality.

Perhaps studying a dead language preordained his fate.

Sitting next to me, he was pleasant and humorous as all true peacemakers are in this world. He knew not that he had carefully been shown the pathways of his future which ended in an open door beyond which he spied verbose stars and drunken hopes. Yet stars and hopes were what he wanted, what he needed.

He needed to reflect the warm golden sunshine.

A zombie sat quietly sad at the back. He thought of pain and anguish, of his death, of himself.

A friend observed the ritual of self-hatred and joined the small community. He lives and breathes the golden hope of new splendors never elsewhere realized, now having cast his will from him, for it offended him.

When loveless love the loveless, danger runs amok as frustration ensues. Perhaps it was wrong to follow instinctual self-preservation.

Art couldn't handle her affections, so how could I? I lied, she cried, I soothed and comforted, she renewed her possessive nature.

When I said goodbye, it was gentle yet harsh. How could I have known of mysticisms and magic numbers?

Three was her number—the number of God, the number of hope, the number of rails she discovered on the laid train tracks of life.

Most of life, the pain of torture, dies within a man. But those that live for beauty live forever. Perhaps it is for never staying that they die, who live forever, on the path of existence and live on the path of second realities of after lives and dreams and memories.

I knew such a man of untimely beauty, but the time came and went and he was changed, for the better, permanently. Peace, even in the change, was all he knew of life. He was ignorant of anything other than life and was the better for it.

Medals and papers are not a man, who serves but for the future. His dreams and hopes were buried with him in Poland— grenadiers have fragmentary lives in quantity. But if a better, more devoted man ever existed, he is long dead.

He got in with a bad crowd, forced in actually, but he believed in his own truths and lived for doing right and at least he wasn't a Nazi-volunteer. I love him for a hero, but I should meet him first.

There is an Island nation that killed a girl.

There the sun never rises, the gloom never sets, and all one can see is all one can touch. Forests and hopes are never to be discovered, though somewhere they are hidden, as Caribbean pirate-treasure.

Woe to the girl without a map! She couldn't see that life meant anything. She never lived to see Nova Scotia or the eclipse of what she lacked in her life.

Where there are mobs, there are also deaths. We saw it at Altamont, we saw it at Kent State, we saw it at Pearl Harbor, we saw it at Chicago, we saw it at Vietnam. It was Babylon, Sodom, Bull Run, Bunker's Hill, the Alamo, Wounded Knee, and Ho Chi Minh City.

It saw it July 24 at the Chicago Stadium. Shades of Altamont, but the weapon was an empty fifth and the victim's name was Andy.

There are times within a life when lovers love the dead without asking why. Ten days live that time forgot when communion was served among the dying and she (whom I came to love) was one.

I came, but then, too, I left, for lack of timelessness. Death grinned and tried to ignore me, but I, I knew the truth. Love cannot live among the nondecomposed dead.

Hospitals

Ten days lived within clinical walls of indifference and death. It was here that pain was bred as offspring of a forsaken life. It wasn't I, though it might have been, but I hadn't known so I hadn't known to visit.

Clinical walls have known a lot about my life of fears and hopelessness. Yet, also, they have known absurdity, as well as any other factory, at least. I didn't see much absurd in being stricken with horror, but I had a friend who did.

Some are born into masochism, while others have it thrust upon them. I think Benedict Stoner was born with it. Anyway, we were the best of friends once. When he was kicked out of his home, I took him in and fed him and gave him shelter and everything else it says to do for a friend somewhere in the Bible, though the fact that it says it and I did it are coincidental. And, in gratitude (I suppose), he told me this story.

He promised me to secrecy. I naturally promised—now the time has come to violate his trust, as he violated mine.

Benedict Stoner was a football star. That is, he had played football in high school, but an accident, actually it was normal enough, messed up his knee forever. And so, as with all great athletes, they confined him to a long look at clinical walls.

I presume he was rather nervous; I know *I* was, and my operation was a trifle compared with his momentous incision. He showed me the scar later—a grotesque half-circle of raised pink flesh glimmering in permanence as it strove to encircle his knee. That sounds to me as good a definition of life as any.

After he was admitted he was probably put on sedatives. I don't remember whether or not he told me about the pre-operation time spent in the hospital, so I'm not sure about any of it. Just presuming.

Then came the purpose, the reason for it all—one quick nap and the deepest sleep of his life and consciousness proved him changed.

He felt different but good. Then the pain began to set in.

The doctor came to check up on Benedict Stoner's stability. When the pain caused Benedict Stoner to cry out in complaint, the doctor gave him the options—codeine tablets or morphine shots.

Benedict Stoner, being no fool, chose the latter. Naturally.

The recovery was slow and long and natural. He became good friends with the interns. Their conversations would seemingly last for hours as they told him of the ploys used by which they successfully obtained for their personal use codeine and reds and yellowjackets and dexies and white cross. Blue Cross wouldn't cover the results. Red Cross couldn't supply the materials. But at least the thought was of Christian Patriots—thoughts of surgeons banding together to carry red, white and blue crosses. Perhaps the Calvary Cavalry. It was almost a shame Custer hadn't been a surgeon, or that he'd died.

Benedict Stoner also grew close to one of the nurses there. They now share a bond of intimacy that for all memory couldn't be forgotten.

Get up, he thought, there's something inside that cries to get out and it's pulsating in my penis for expulsion.

Laboriously he attempted to sit up and hobble to the washroom. He was protesting bed pan treatment but found he couldn't go beyond thinking of sitting up. Reluctantly he rang for the nurse.

She came in, and after a brief word of apology and explanation, Benedict Stoner asked for her help. By putting his arm around her shoulders and throwing all of his weight on her that she could carry, they managed to complete the quest.

A new problem arose—without her help he could not stand. He needed, to avoid falling, to lean both on the doorknob with his left hand, and on her with his right. So what could be more natural than having a beautiful nurse unzip your pants, pullout your punctually enlarging sexual organ, hold it and aim it into a bowl forever filled with water.

That is, above all, how I would remember Benedict Stoner as being—natural.

I can't roast of such intensity for my own time spent in hospitals.

Three is the number of God, the number of hope, the number of operations I have had. So far.

The first time, I was twelve years old. I had a hernia that really bugged the hell out of me. Actually, it was embarrassing. It looked like I had three balls. At first the doctors thought it was a hydrocele, but after opening me up they found a nice big fat juicy hernia infesting my sack. Not that it mattered—I was only twelve.

I was born young and I will probably die young—such is the way of the world. Hospitals are made for thoughts of death.

When I was admitted for the hydrocele, they put me in a room I had to share with another kid my age. His name I can't remember, but I remember he had black hair.

He was in for an eye operation. He had three eyes, or something similar to that. The important thing was his sense of taste.

He liked Chicago. So did the nurse. I loved the Beatles.

"The Beatles? They're dead. Man are you out of it!" I can still hear him say. The nurse agreed with him and I was left the loner of a former triangle. It mattered to me then, but doesn't now I suppose. What if I had said I liked the Harry James Orchestra?

My eyes may be bad, but they're better than that kid's, and they recorded carefully everything I saw while in the ward.

I remained in a state of extreme nervousness before the operation. Until the shot.

"Will it hurt?"

"No, no. It's just to calm you down."

"Oh, okay."

The nurse took a syringe with a needle as long as my middle finger, pushed it into my bare thigh, and released its contents into my system. I remember feeling the sedative swishing around in my leg, begging to be absorbed. I helped it beg. I was the organ grinder's monkey. I was the crutches and the pencil-box.

When Benedict Stoner was in the hospital, they surprised him with a pain killer. Two nurses entered the room. One prepared a small syringe, strapped Benedict Stoner's arm, and while he watched in wait for her to inject the small needle into his arm, the other nurse jammed a needle as long as a horse's leg into his thigh. Diversionary tactics and all that.

The time came and the interns wheeled me outside the operating room. There was a short delay and I was left alone on the cart outside O.R. for a quarter of an hour. Another patient before me was also waiting. She was a middle-aged black surrounded by three or four interns and nurses. They had wheeled me into a position so that all I could see or hear were her moans and cries and screams of anguish as the torturers and sadistically cruel pretend-doctors shoved a two-foot rubber tube down her nostril. Needless to say, she fell into regurgitatory convulsions, but had nothing to emit. Just hearing the moans and her convulsions made me nearly sick myself. I called for a nurse to wheel me away to the other end of the corridor. She did, and I lay alone with my thoughts of imminent death.

Eventually the time came and a doctor stepped out of the O.R., looking around but not seeing me. After harshly asking a nurse where she had moved me and why, he came and had me wheeled into O.R.

They strapped my arm to a table.

"Now this won't hurt too much. After I give you this shot, I want you to count backwards from a hundred."

"100, 99, 98, 97..." I think that's as far as I got.

I guess I forced myself awake too soon. I was in post-op and tried to sit up to see what was going on.

"No!" a nurse screamed, "Don't get up. Go back to sleep."

"Jeez," I heard her say to her colleague, "he already woke up."

"Go to sleep," the second nurse reinforced.

In the days that followed I felt immense pain and could hardly breathe without torture. I briefly wondered if I had been castrated. There was no way to find out.

A lot of people came to visit. My family, naturally, carne often; and my youth group sent me a card. One of the local television personalities even stopped by with a gyroscope and a deck of magic cards as a little gift. That really pleased me.

I slept a lot those days, but forced myself awake for meals.

That's an unusual ability of mine. If I know I should be awake, I force myself to be so. There have been times when, having set my alarm clock, it didn't ring, or it rang late, and I awoke of my own volition at the normally scheduled time anyway.

The second time I went to the hospital was for minor surgery. Consequently I walked in, had the operation, and crawled out.

The operation was simple. I was put on the table and given

local anesthetic. The doctor kept poking me in the toe with a sharp needle to see if the area was numb enough for operating, When it was, he cut out my ingrown nail on both sides of right big toe. I could observe him doing this. Then he strapped and bandaged my toe very tightly, so it would not bleed. I had to hop to the car—parked a block from the hospital, but my mother went and got it. She drove me home and I was confined to bed for a few days, except when nature yelled.

It was after coming home from the operation and being left alone that, when in the bathroom, my toe began pulsating violently and bleeding nearly to the extent of splurting, or at least flowing.

I lost a pint or so before I managed to stop the bleeding. But there was a time there I just started crying and screamed, "Help! Lord, don't let me die!" I thought for sure I would—my grandfather had died of blood-loss.

My third operation was on my left foot, again an ingrown toenail. This time, however, it went much more smoothly because of my previous experience and subsequent precautionary measures.

Alberta Voice

My strides, through striving to escape humanity, led me to the edge of a precipice in the Canadian Rockies. The vast pines, reaching up to touch me, though unable, seemed to invite me into their loveless midst. A bitter wind blew through my soul, chilling what it touched; the rivers flowing far below beckoned with icy fingers. I longed to merge with nature, with serenity in peace, but drifting away on bitter winds I lost my thought. I remained, transfixed, hypnotized by the cold swaying of pines, which called with silent tongues and silent hopes, as if silence could produce new tongues and hopes to live on.

My survival, my life, as cold within as without, held serenity with its frost. Endurance, not happiness, is found in a frigid world; the one precludes the other. A bitter wind from paradise swept me up, and I merged as person, not dust, with nature. For a time, a time too brief, humanity had gone; I was alone, content with myself even though and through the ice. The wind pursued me with its knives for several years thereafter, instilling in me perseverance, hounding me until the thaw when I lived no more in a frozen world; I never was a fool.

Untitled Dream

The nameless airplane fluttered, gracefully, swanfully waving its paper wings as a hypnotic kaleidoscope encircled behind, drawing tighter and tighter till hidden as if drawn under a swan's parental folds of warmth. Rising, climbing, spewing back funnels of light as it patterned life into the skies of unflown others. The funneled light exploded.

With You There to Help Me

Characters: Young Man, Young Woman, Old Man, Old Woman

Act I. Scene I: A bare room with only a business desk front-center, facing the audience. The desk is flooded with papers and folders. Conspicuously placed on it are an orange-juice can filled with pencils and pens, a small box of paperclips, a staple-gun and a box of staples, a staple-remover, and a half-empty bottle of Southern Comfort. A window is behind, showing that nighttime has set. Behind the desk sits a young man, of about 20, with dark blond wavy hair combed back, away from the forehead. He looks well-groomed, but is wearing blue jeans, a white tennis shirt, and earth shoes. He is holding a telephone in his left hand up to his ear and is punching out a number on the push-button dial. He finishes dialing, listens for a second, and hangs up. He dials again and listens.

Young Man: Get off the damned line—I've got to talk to you. (He hangs up, dials again, listens, hangs up again.) Jesus Christ, these women! (He grabs the bottle and takes a large swig.) Who the hell's she talkin' to? (He takes the staple-gun, put more staples in, fires six times in anger, and feigns laughter.) Ha ha ha. Come on, God. (He picks up the phone a pushes the buttons very slowly and carefully.) No! No! No! No! NO! (He takes the phone and bangs it against the desk-edge until it nearly breaks.) Answer! (He takes the phone and punches one button.) Hello? Operator? I'd like to break in on a phone line that's busy. Hm? Yes, it's an emergency. No, I'm

no relative—I'm her boyfriend. Nature? What do you mean nature of my call? It's an emergency. What kind? I don't know, for Christ's sake. Tell her I'm pregnant. Oh, fuck off! (He hangs up. He grabs a pencil from the can and breaks it twice. He punches out the number again.) Well, finally! (He changes his tone to one of quiet politeness.) Hello. Yeah, it's me. Hey, listen,
I've really got to talk to you. What are you doing tomorrow? Can you take off work? (a short pause) Great. Well, how's about going to the beach or something? (another pause) Okay, then I'll see you about ten or so. (He picks up the staple-remover and clicks it nervously. He listens for a minute or so and nods occasionally in agreement.) Yeah, well, that's something I want to talk about, later. (pause) Yep, see you them. Bye bye. (He gets up, smiling unsurely, and as he leaves to exit stage right he knocks over the box of paperclips. His smile vanishes, transformed into an expression of pain, and he picks up the paperclips, puts them back into the box, and puts the box back on the desk. He exits.)

Scene II: A deserted beach, the young man and young woman walking along, stage left to stage right, arms around each other.

Young Woman: You told me you wanted to talk to me about something.
Young Man: Hm?
Young Woman: What is it, why you phoned me?
Young Man (pensively): Oh. [pause, while he searches for the right words in his mind] Well, you see, the world goes 'round as my life goes 'round, orbiting mutual sunshine, the sunshine I see in you.
Young Woman: Don't talk like that. I don't want it.
Young Man: Sure you do; it's just you're afraid.
Young Woman (hesitantly): Perhaps.
Young Man: Anyway, now that I've found you I'm afraid to lose you. I have to leave for a year. I'll be back though, then, for you.
Young Woman: What?
Young Man: I'm being sent away for awhile, but I'll be back. I'm not telling you what to do while I'm gone. Just try not to get into anything you can't get out of when I return.
Young Woman: I doubt I'll do much of anything.
Young Man: Sure you will. It's healthy—just remember that I'll be

back.
Young Woman: Yes?
Young Man: And write. I will. I need your hope to live on.
Young Woman: There'll always be that. [They embrace and kiss long and tenderly.]

[Curtain.]

Act II. Scene: Same desk as in Act I, center stage right diagonally facing front center, with same array of papers. Also, center stage left, also diagonally facing from center, another similar, more feminine desk. On it: a small vase containing a rose, a box of Kleenex, a stack of multi-colored papers and folders, and a quill pen and holder. Carved into the front of the desk is the symbol of womanhood, a circle with a cross connected below it. The window shows a rose-colored sky, as dusk or dawn; and a charred American flag, burned in protest, flies beside, on the wall behind the man's desk. An old man, with features like the young man's, just older, sits behind the desk stage right. An old woman, who resembles the young woman from Act I sits behind the feminine desk. She is writing fervently, with quill in hand. The old man is looking at his paper, burying his head in thought into his fists.

Old Man: It's not going anywhere.
Old Woman (writing, without looking up): Sh!
Old Man (reading to himself): "Death of a Kingfisher"'

>The rubble parts, revealing a past
>endangered and engendered in
>perverse dreams, distortions.

>The bubble floats into the sun,
>shining egocentripetal force.
>No one sniffs out the bursting void.

>Life in past's rigor
>provides unsustaining words,
>and we fools live on earthly foods.

Old Woman (without thinking): 's good.
Old Man: There's nowhere to go from there.
Old Woman (keeps writing): A page, a page.
Old Man: Hm? (no reply) Prone to droning on deadened pasts. No. Prone to droning on the pasts of death, where has the present vanished? It doesn't work. It's just not happening.
Old Woman (looking up): The present, not happening? (She returns to her work and within a minute is finished, puts down her quill, grabs the stack of papers that is her manuscript and draws a huge sigh.) Done!
Old Man: How long?
Old Woman: 207. In 43 hours and 17 minutes.
Old Man: Now comes the hard part—revision.
Old Woman: Later. I'd better eat and sleep first. It has been 43 hours.
Old Man: And 17 minutes.
Old Woman: Yes. This time I think I've really captured it. We really had a lot of life when we were young.
Old Man: Until we became successful and old.
Old Woman: What was it you said—the present doesn't happen anymore?
Old Man: Just a poem—I finished my novel four hours ago.
Old Woman: Your 409th?
Old Man: Yes. Well, I suppose you're the prolific one. Over a thousand, isn't it?
Old Woman: I don't know.
Old Man: Hey, let's do something now—together.
Old Woman: What? You mean...
Old Man: No, silly. We're too old. Let's co-author a novel.
Old Woman: Whatever happened to experience?
Old Man: We lived it all.
Old Woman: And the time left is for reflection.
Old Man: I guess so.
Old Woman: Let me read that poem.

[Curtain.]

Nightmares

'Twas once upon a time in the far-away land of Bonnar that there lived a boy whose name was Dreer, and his talking role companion Rea. Perhaps descendents of a shipwrecked crew of Lilliputians, they towered nearly two inches above the ground, by human standards.

As legend has it in Bonnar, the hundred years had passed since the time before, and once again the arrival of a terrible giant from across the seas, as well as his pet sea-serpent, was anticipated. Warnings were being issued by Merl the Wizard to all the island folk, but none took heed.

Then, one lazy summer afternoon, as flowers loomed large in the thoughts and dreams of the restful citizenry, a shape slowly took form in the distance in the sea, dispelling all flowery thoughts of sunshine and love. It was the giant, and his serpent cane to destroy Bonnar. However, after bellowing forth some loud threats, the giant and serpent were confronted by a dinosaur, which came up from out of the depths also as predicted by ancient legend. Following a brief battle, the dinosaur destroyed the serpent and suddenly disappeared, leaving the giant standing alone in disbelief.

The giant went away, and Bonnar began to prepare for his reappearance.

Dreer and Rea decided that, in order to save the population, a hidden underground excavation should be dug. Spending many days and hours on this, Rea finally accomplished the task.

The public invitation went out, but apparently most believed their own private hiding places sufficiently safe, for only two accepted the invitation—Merl and an orphaned girl name Joseline.

The day of the giant's return arrived. As the world above was destroyed, Dreer pledged to avenge the death of his people.

Novocaine

The future beckons with icy heat as though unsure of promises. Not all is gained that desire dictates, but more than despair anticipates. The future holds within its slow-running fingers a figure strangely distorted by horrors of the past and dreads of the yet-to-be.

And I remember my high-school teacher's comments exactly: "Honors Granted—I've enjoyed knowing you this summer.

Have a good trip to Europe. Good luck this fall."

I remember showing my writing to a roommate of mine once and all she had to say was "you're sick." I just added that to the list. Bizarre. Difficult. Hard to live with.

Sometimes I think Mars is more populated. And I recognize kryptonmania when I see it. New York has a lot of people'll tell you how super they are then don't even pay attention to your response.

"No—I'm too big in my own gig to acknowledge yours."

But hey, I've cut loose of that, eh? What's it matter now?

Something else will come along soon.

I feel it's on its way.

Chapter Five

The Legal Office

Will Moore, attorney, executor, and relative, chews on a fresh Upmann 2000 as he stares John Moore down.

"Well, that's the way it is. Plain and simple. Clear and legal."

"I don't believe it."

The phone rings.

Will answers it. Some artist on the line. Another relative. Place is crawling with 'em. Like roaches.

"How's it goin', Bill?"

"Will."

"Bill?"

"Okay."

"Good."

"Who's this?"

"Les."

"Les. I knew that, sorry. What do you want?"

"That painting I'm doing for you, in which I divide the field of vision in two and attempt to force the viewer's eyes farther apart from each other, requires a few rather expensive supplies, pigments that are absolutely vital being rare and my not being able to continue without them—"

"How much?"

"Sir?"

"How much do you need?"

"Another three."

"Thousand?"

"It will be much larger than I anticipated."

"I thought you were a minimalist."

"Touché, monsieur."

"From Detroit."

"Ah, well, I like to pretend."

"You all right?"

"It is good to pretend, to raise the creativity and work from the heightened sense of artistic playfulness."

"Oh—no minimalist would speak thus!"

"No minimalist would speak."

"What are you?"

"I've been labeled post-minimal expressionist, but I often deal with realist subject matter, so I presume I am not in the mainstream but I feel that a resurgence of interest in this kind of painting is due and I'll be right here at the forefront, because the form is not being pursued by very many painters at present."

"Aren't they doing something like that in Italy?"

"Yes, but I've been working at it a lot longer. They learned from me. I'm convinced of it. You are no doubt aware of my reputation."

"Yes—that's why I hired you. I'm just curious. Do you mind? I wanted to know more of where you are corning from."

"From the heart."

"Of course. Forgive me."

"Certainly. For you I propose an enormous canvas, to speak of how vast emptiness truly is, and how full it can be. I expect it to be my subtlest painting, my *Canon in D Major,* at peace with my world for accepting emptiness as fulfillment and the parts of it where I feel differences."

"Dark rosewood frame, maybe?"

"No frame! That's ridiculous! A frame! When have I used a frame? Next thing, you'll have me painting clowns with big eyes holding colorful balloons on black velvet! Ptuii! I spit on your proposal!"

"Sorry, do what you like—I trust your vision implicitly."

"Thank you, monsieur."

"You're from Detroit."

"Monsieur!"

"Sorry. I'll send you the money immediately. Just hurry it up, will you? I'm really looking forward to having that painting."

"Hurry? Hurry?"

"Come on, you know what I mean."

"Hurry? Ah. We will try, monsieur."

"Thank you."

"Good-bye."

The phone hung up, Will returns his attention to John. John lets one go.

Wet or dry? Can't tell. God thank these new disposable undergarments—there's an extra in the briefcase, I'm pretty sure.

"Your wife, John, has written in her will specific provisions in the event that her departure occur prior to yours. This includes watching out for the financial status of her children, who, in exchange for their inheritances, have been saddled with the responsibility of providing you with a comfortable home and income in your later years. All except the one child, Phil, who is not mentioned in the will."

"That's not a surprise. He's a bum. So, Bill, how's the restaurant?"

"Entirely much too good to me," says Will, patting his girth.

"Ah, double-dipping into the profits, eh?"

"I doubt I leave a serious dent in the profits. Anyway, back to the matter at hand. You are to inherit half of everything. The other half is to be divided equally between your children Dick and Grace."

Will wonders if his son Harry made it to Rose's funeral. Will considers Les' sons Art, also a painter, neo-abstract expressionist, and Mark, a graffiti artist who's running around with his cousin Phil, John's son, following their Aunt Carol's band. Obviously they weren't at the funeral. These kids don't understand.

The phone rings again.

Will answers it. His wife Sue on the line. Another attorney. Calling from her office, which is crawling with lawyers, unlike Will's small firm which employs only six.

"How's the factory, dear?" he asks his wife.

"A zoo," she replies.

"Les called."

"He done?"

"No—he just wanted more money. Should have gotten Art to do it instead."

"He couldn't do it."

"Why?"

"He's on a mission station somewhere like Burma, 'member?"

"Oh, yeah. I'm with a client now, Sue. Can I call you back?"

"Actually I just called to hear your voice. It's been crazy 'round here, and I just wanted to hear the lovely strains of your basso profundo."

"My, that's nice. Thanks."

"Thank *you*. How about dinner at The Ox?"

"Seven?"

"Meet you there."

"Your treat."

"Okay. Bye, love."

"Bye."

Will returns his attention to John. John cuts another one.

"I should get going, Bill. This all the paperwork?" John asks, picking up the stack of papers in front of him.

"All but the most important."

"Which is?"

"Your copy of the invoice for my legal fees, which will be deducted from the inheritance before it is dispersed. This method of payment was also stipulated in Rose's will."

"On your advice."

"Naturally. Here's the bill, John."

"So long. Where's the john, Bill?"

"Third floor."

"Thanks. See you soon."

"Yes."

John leaves and Will answers another phone call.

"Do you want something? Are you selling something?" he asked, irritated.

"Don't you remember how you used to steal the apples from my tree?"

He couldn't remember. But somehow it felt like he'd encountered it before in a dream. Around the time he'd dug a tunnel as a boy with two chums who were trying to rescue their fathers from the pen. That incident gave him strange dreams for months thereafter. But that was a long time ago.

"Joy?"

"Bingo."

"What the hell do you want?"

"You're a bit of a beast you know, Bill."

"Sorry, from my sailing days. On the *Persephone.* I was a lieutenant —"

"I know—I read all about it."

"I nearly lost my foot."

"Yeah, I know."

"So what do you want?"

"Dinner."

"Why?"

"I don't know—why, Jackson?"

"Yeah, why?"

Oh, shit. Cornered. Got me. I didn't plan far enough ahead. I find it so hard to float without trying to swim. I'm stuck now. This guy has an affair or he doesn't? What do I do? Realism. But what, with herpes, AIDS, transvestites, and "rearrangements of personal priorities," is real?

"No—a real answer."

Yeah, yeah. Be patient. I'll get there.

Bastards. Some nerve they have, getting ahead of me like that.

A head of me?

"Get on with it."

All right. Because you found out you were secretly married to him without either of you knowing.

"What?"

Their laughter sounded good. I admired them for laughing.

"Come on—you can't talk your way out of this—" More laughter. "Hey, we're not laughing." Yes you are. "Tell us the truth." I'm not *that* pretentious. "About—oh what was I looking for? You asshole."

Now it was my turn to laugh. I love these guys. Actually, Joy's always loved you but doesn't want to interfere in your relationship with Sue, right?

"Right," says Joy, although almost sounding reluctant. "But why dinner?"

I don't know. *You* asked.

"You put the words in my mouth."

Well, swallow your words, and you won't have room for dinner anyway.

"Come on, Will, let's get out of here."

"Sure."

They leave.

Works every time. Now I have all this space to myself, and no one can take it from me. It's not that I resent my characters; it's just that I never really planned on having any. Let alone plots. Leave that to the regs. Most butcher characters anyway. But for me characters grow from the ground. Come upon me like vines. Can't get rid of 'em. Shake my head. They're there.

I can't let go of these guys. Maybe I should follow 'em.

No. What if they're having an affair? I could jeopardize something I don't know about. God am I indecisive today.

As a matter of fact, there's nothing I really want to do. Just sit back, smoke a cigarette, and dream about my tenuous connection to this world. One I'm about solidifying. Can it be done? Certainly.

Smoke rings? Certainly, I said.

Not to worry, for I've been in management positions before, yet have also worked sweeping up and emptying ashtrays. I ain't tryin' to come on like some holier-than-thou asshole, nor do I attempt the futile endeavor of presenting myself as a man of the street.

¿Que?

Maybe both.

Are we being watched? Is it safe to talk? How long should I stand for this? How long should I stand still?

Do I remember her? She was like dick cheese in the folds of the prick of life. They stay together because together they feel safe feeling nothing. Nothing but safety and security.

My deficiency: I don't know how to keep a lot of people close. Those who are are my favorites by far. But I love all of you; really I do. Save the few that have done me wrong—I find it hard to be forgiving. It makes me feel like I'm just setting myself up again. Been ripped off enough to know. There are those who'll take advantage of you if you don't sidestep them entirely. We all encounter this.

My strength: The ability to amuse myself with nothing more than a pen and a piece of paper. In a way I think that I am a simpler person for it, but I will have to move out from ordinary writing. Beyond this pen and paper, but for now they still suit my purposes.

To amuse first time through.

To humor more each successive attempt.

To open up a little more each reading.

To, in it all, convey a bit of what's behind the words that I can't get out because I'm just trying to keep up with my thoughts.

It's either that or I try to stretch out sections when there's no ideas. But I try to be interesting.

TRYING

WANTING

THINKING

GGG

GOING TO SLEEP

OOOO

MUCH

WRITE

LEARN

Time to keep going.

Maybe resume the story for a while. Bring back Jackson Berlin. Don't know.

John decides to call Mary when he gets home—she's always been good company. Very supportive.

Fix a sandwich and watch the ballgame.

Time to turn the old brain off and vegetate in front of the TV.

Enough thinking for a day.

Chapter Six

The Sex Scene (participation optional)

Warning: This chapter is merely tangential to the rest of the book and is sexually explicit. Parental discretion ill-advised. Or at least someone you like who's willing to read this with you (my preference is for someone of the opposite sex). Those of weak disposition should skip ahead to chapter seven, in which we receive Grace. Or return to the beginning and reread the first five chapters. I'm not keen on having to say this again.

Our characters are Rose's son Dick and his wife Fanny and the woman they both love, Perry.

They never leave the bed.

Really, don't read it if you don't want—it won't affect your appreciation of the rest of the book. I've got to do this, though, because it's in the outline.

Or do I? Maybe I was just sexually aroused when I wrote the outline.

Maybe I can ignore this—do something else.

Fuck, why? I've committed myself and am unwilling to cross all this out.

"Well, at least this way no one can say I don't have balls. Actually I have large ones and I ejaculate more than most women can absorb," explained Dick to Perry.

Perry smiled up through Fanny's thighs. "That's for sure."

We'll try to do something different with this than I've seen in stroke books, though. No blatant fucking and sucking unless I change my mind again.

Many stand on their own ground.

"I prefer lying on my own bed," Perry said.

"What? Our bed's not comfortable enough for you?" asked Dick.

"It's not that. It's just that I have a waterbed at home."

"Invite us over," Fanny said.

"Yeah, really," concurred Dick.

"Well, it'd have to be when my parents are gone."

"Invite them too."

"Nah—I'm not *that* kinky."

"Well, that's what you said before."

"Yeah, but I dig this."

but let me interrupt this a while

I've noticed people asking me a few questions whenever I meet them for the first time.

"Do you have a nickname? What do people call you? It's an unusual name, isn't it? What's it mean?"

I like my nickname because it implies I'm at the corner, the edge. But the full first name means "hard-edged," which I can be. It's in my personality.

back to the story

"I've noticed people asking me a few questions whenever I meet them for the first time," Perry said. "Do I have a nickname? What do people call me? It's a strange name for a girl, isn't it? What does it mean?"

"Will you go to bed with me?"

"That, too."

"Here, put your hand here."

"Sure, Fanny. Here, you take that side—let's give him something he'll never forget."

"A tongue-lashing?"

"You got it."

Perry and Fanny stared into each other's eyes. Perry enjoyed the smell of Fanny's breath and the little gusts of air on her cheek.

Dick hugged their bodies and slid three fingers up into each's moist cockpit as he enjoyed the tremendous sensation in his main vein.

He looked at them. They were enjoying this. He began to really work for them.

When they were ready, he pulled his hand away from Perry and moved in with his mouth. She tasted exquisite. Better than Fanny, he thought. Perry gave up licking his javelin and buried her face in Fanny's cave. Fanny took her husband's totem pole firmly in mouth and began sucking very hard, drawing blood into its tip. When he began to shudder she withdrew.

"I want to watch—Perry, ride him."

Perry spread her legs to either side of his hips and lowered herself slowly onto his bamboo bong, shaking her butt back and forth to give Dick more pleasure.

Dick brought his hands up to her small teenage orbs. Perry was a beautiful woman. Dark hair, always sort of mussed up. Penetrating and clear dark eyes. A small mouth of which the top lip protruded slightly over the lower. Somewhat hollowed cheeks. A slender neck. Soft round shoulders. Thin waist. Smooth legs. Watching this nineteen-year-old beauty lower herself onto him aroused him so much he thrust his hip so that he was flush into her. Cupping her hips in his hands, he was able to come in a dozen thrusts, and he pulled her down fully onto him and told her to ride him as hard as she wanted—his erection wouldn't disappear for a while. She moaned, groaned, and eventually screamed as she clawed into his chest and rode him hard. Then they lay down together in their sweat, Fanny coming over to lick them both clean.

"Too bad about your mom, Dick."

"Oh, yeah. Thanks. She was a nice lady. I hear she's left me a good piece of scratch, though."

"Poor Rose. I was lucky to get along very well with my mother-in-law."

"Yeah, but you're a special woman, Fanny."

"Thanks, Perry."

Perry doesn't know it, but she was just impregnated.

Pity the baby. By the time it reaches its teen years there won't be anything left worth living for. And there hasn't been anything worth dying for in fifty years.

It'll grow up, live in fantasy, be knocked down to ground level, and come back up fighting for a little scratch. Same old blear. But that's when the talents show.

Or maybe it's a dream from waste. Take it away, Jackson.

Hurry. Time's running short. Come on come on come on.

Go.

Go.

Go.

It's gonna snow.

It's getting cold, and the troops are tired. Vampires are waiting at the crossroads, and my mouth is dry.

Throwaway your crutches!

Kick mine out from under me. I can walk, goddamn it! I can run! I can fly!

I can fall on my face, embarrassed as hell. I can smell that something's afoul in this state of confusion.

Pull the clutch! Shift gear!

Cough, cough. It's fuckin' dead—sittin' here stranded in the snow.

No heat. Nothin' at all to drink. Windshield wiper fluid empty, out of gas, radiator dry, no anti-freeze, oil leaked out, brake and transmission fluids lost miles back.

Stopped.

Gotta eat the fuckin' snow to survive. Wrap the rags 'round yer feet and move it on down the line.

Trudge 'long da shoulder.

Brrr... Nnn... Who... Ttt... Hum... Crackle...

Hence free, a coolie on the freeze. Please. Don't do it, don't do it. Don't tease. Want me to be there with you, show me more than yer navel, babe. Open your mind to transmit/receive and we'll communicate. Over.

I knew you were going to say that. It's okay. I don't mind. I kind of like it, actually. Don't ask me why. I'm weird (oh, wow, he admits it) yeah 'course I admit when I'm having fun.

Almost made me forget it was colder than god outside. Shaking in my boots.

Just another case of the ubiquitous excuse.

Just another case.

Crack one open and pass it this way. Anything to warm me up. A beautiful woman next to me at night. Someone I could talk to in the morning.

Brandy'll have to do for now. Fuck this shoulder, walk along the road and pay attention to cars. Better yet—cross to the left side (the right side for you British readers) so I can see oncoming headlights.

My toes is froze. The scars from where I had my ingrown toenails removed many years ago feel reopened. Is the moisture in my boots blood or snow?

Some woman's thoughts are in my head, but it's okay. I love women for their sense of mystery—no man ever understood a woman. But somehow they really seem keen at understanding us.

We're really just brutes, aren't we? Now matter how educated, eloquent, or effeminate we are. We're the crude ones. They're a lot more together habitually.

So what if I'm a lesbian trapped in a man's body? What did you expect from someone named Jackson Berlin? Irish jigs? Lawnmowers? Abstract expressionist urban realism, eh?

Canadian?

No, but I like them a lot. One of the truly beautiful countries in this world. They probably sit back and laugh at us like lap dogs laugh at police dogs. Know what I mean? Eh?

Yeah, yeah. Politics. Hey, the weather's pretty shitty.

Yeah, it's cold, man. Freezin' my balls off.

'S okay—not usin' 'em anywho.

Your English teacher just died.

Soiree.

It was for the cause—brokering Anglingo clampit urp. Terns shit off.

Pop. Fizzle. Crackle. Hum.

Brrr.

     Og.

        Og.

           Og.

And being with people is one of the options of things to do with your time and repeating yourself is one of the options of things to do with your time and going to sleep is one of the options of things to do with your time and having dreams is one of the options of things to do with your time and flying away is one of the options of things to do with your time things to do with your things to do with your things to do with your time.

Meanwhile, back in bed, I think she's falling in love with me but I can't tell. Fanny never fell.

She smiles at the right times. Cajoles me for my lifeline with insults and battery.

She's waiting to be free. And when she is, I'll fly alongside her a little while.

MY MENTAL MASTER LIBATIONS: a 90-minute tape

Side A begins with my playing my lamp with a ball-point pen and the microphone and interspersing voice. The music changes to encompass my blinds and my beer. I found the springs on the lamp to be particularly fun. The woman's voice and ocean sounds were already on the tape which I tried to erase for the sake of this. I like the result, though. She mentions God and I change the subject—I read the third Jackson Berlin piece in *Hugh Moore* after easing into the idea.

The second piece is from *The Intersection of Two Loops,* recorded live in a bookstore in Chicago's Old Town on June 28, 1985.

Third is my section of a long piece performed as part of 2 + 1 = 0. Recorded at an American bar in New Town, March 21, 1985. In my books the text appears in *The Intersection of Two Loops.*

Fourth is my song "Afterlife," recorded solo in one take around May of 1981.

It's the story of a man who's died and is coming back to get his girl. In the middle I include Spirit's "Groundhog."

Fifth "Bip Bop," a McCartney tune, done when I was in Glass Fog, is cut off the end of side one and continues on side two. Then our version of "Youngblood." All recorded in the studios of our high school radio station in, I'd say, 1974.

From 1966, when I was in grade school in Nashville, from the Christmas album the school produced (Century Records #25847), a version of "Jingle Bells" on which I'm a part of a sextet singing the center. I'm the kid who's coughing. I had a very bad cold at the time.

Next, a brief intro from *Crack the Sky Live.* Then a little Pankrti into "Ice-Barons," another piece of mine (this from *Truly Fine Citizen*) also performed that memorable night with 2 + 1 = 0.

T.V. Football's introduction to the bookstore reading in summer. Then my babbling and three examples of my work from *Projections* and *Truly Fine Citizen.*

My rendition of Five Man Electrical Band's "Absolutely Right." Solo 11-7-81.

Followed by another part of *Truly Fine Citizen.*

Looks me straight in the eye. Tells me about herself and listens while I explain myself.

Something's going right—let's see if I can float and not try to steer. Follow the path where it wants to go.

Pursue the plane. I should stay where I am. Relax and check it out and try not to define anything. Accept the realities I encounter.

But let's not go that way again just yet.

Let's take the five mile path through the woods which leads to the look-out tower on top of the bluff.

This is the happiest period of my life. I'm finding energy and humor in my new situation. Not to mention how I love to look a beautiful woman straight through her eye (usually her left) into her self. I can find a lot that way. And in this way I am always amazed at what wondrous creatures they are—the mysterious depths of their inner strengths fascinate me, for they are strong in areas I have never even glimpsed. What can there be but respect and fascination when two people coming together want to meet?

Set me down easy.

The weather's cold and I'm feeling warm. I'll do almost anything to keep this feeling going. Remain mute, even.

Perhaps I should change the tack (remember the tack). Find something to say.

Dick has a sister named Grace.

Chapter Seven

Grace

Excuse me, gentlemen. Please allow me to apologize for my husband's behavior.

"Oh, come on, you're jealous, Grace."

I'm sorry—he's drunk. He can be very polite and funny though. Most of the time he's rather, oh, sloppy.

Oh, look at that window, that sweater. I have to get it. Oh, definitely.

"It's yours."

Thanks.

"Where's your husband heading?"

I'm not certain. He's somewhat inebriated. Let us go to the Stränger Café for coffee, please? I'll pay cabfare.

"No, let's walk—wait, go on ahead, I'll meet you there—I want to stop home to change—it's getting cold."

Oh, all right.

"Bye, love."

Bye.

Polite pecker, that boy. Why doesn't anyone ever feel like just taking me? What? Wait, I'm crazy. I need a gentle man, who's strong and has a good sense of humor and is intelligent all the time. Or he won't suffice. I don't have to settle for any but the highest class of man. This man is quite sophisticated. I'm attempting to understand him. Yet these problems of his—can he, will he lose them?

What about my inheritance? Is that why the sudden strong attraction? Does he want me because of how I make him feel or because of who I am?

Can I, as a woman, understand him at all?

Can anyone?

"Not likely—no one will—don't waste time looking—if it happens, let it find you, and then you'll be sure."

She listens to herself and decides what to do beside herself as she's walking towards the Stränger.

There's a lot I could do with all this money. Open a boutique, maybe. And Rich can't say a word because it's my money.

That's a rude sign. "Come in we're open" in a bedroom window. Not too obvious, is it? Maybe they're stupid on purpose. Like my idiot second cousin the sea lore poet, Seaglass Moore.

Ever heard Perry's Riddle: I'm being used and know and I don't even mind? What am I?

Poor girl. It's a shame what my brother's doing to her. Oh, I must go in here—there's a wonderful place for knits on the eighth floor. Take the browser's route—the escalators.

At the top of one a tin can was rolling nowhere. At the top of another a tiny bird was caught with his foot. Grace pushed the bird back and away with her foot and freed it.

The little bird upset her.

I hope it's all right. It was just sitting there. Probably its foot's broken. At least. Poor little thing. Oh, here's a darling coffee shop. A Viennese sounds wonderful.

It arrives so hot she drops ice from her water glass down through the whipped cream into the coffee.

Why does some ice crack going into coffee and some not?

Graffiti on an otherwise bare wall: "These walls are perfect!"

A building under demolition. Another sip of coffee. Drinkable.

Sinkable ice. Bison on a billboard. Children on a park bench staring at a trash fire. Running around looking for trash to throw in—styrofoam cups, aluminum cans, candy wrappers, sleeping bag-ladies, yapping lap-dogs, irrelevant flyers from crackpot religious organizations, the smallest of their own.

They'd like some from me. Here's a used tissue.

More coffee, madam?

No thanks—I have to meet someone elsewhere about fifteen minutes ago. Thanks, though. It was delicious.

Anything else?

A cognac.

VSOP?

Very special old pale. Yes. Have my thoughts flowing freely toward meeting my friend when I really just feel like sitting still, silent, contemplating why I have nothing to say. Not until my chemical imbalance finds this counterweight.

Thank you ← looks weird ← looks weirder ← my eyes are crossed ← no, I'm not Catholic ← stop looking at me creep ← men in this town ← I don't know ← I think it's disgusting ← standing on a streetcorner with his pants dropped ← his beer on the mailbox ← how they drink that I'll never know ← no class ← of course they're all crass ← nothing like kissing someone with cigarette-and-beer breath ← gross

A cab. Smells of stale cigarette smoke. Men need to live in strange aromas—but so do we women, I guess, with our perfumes and such. Guy looks like he doesn't like to bathe, but I can't smell him for the smoke. Don't look ← what's out the window. The same man on another corner with his pants down.

Around the corner. Here it is. Thank you.

See him? Ah—at the side. He sees me. Hi! I'll let him buy me dinner, but I'm not too sure I want to be with him. I mean, I've known him for so long. He's more like a brother than a lover. But then, he'd be attentive. He probably knows what I need that way. He looks a lot better than he used to, and he's working and making money now. And, his artwork even makes more sense. Yeah, he's getting his act together, but there're so many men out there—so many whom I like for different reasons—not to mention Rich—I still love him after all. So does Kyle—they're still good friends.

"Why didn't you change?"

"Oh, I stopped and looked at shops instead."

"Buy anything?"

"No, just getting ideas. A Viennese, please."

"Yes, ma'am. Sir?"

"Espresso, please."

"Certainly. Thank you."

Standard conversation #96 leads into reopening and a sharing of energy.

Pausing, pulling, playing onto communicative highground. To be broken by an energy reducer only a few hours later, where we drift apart to part and Kyle's attempt to repave the land fails.　　Head home—should I call him as I said?

Meanwhile he's thinking about his date with someone else tomorrow.

Why can't I let him get close? Is it because Rich is there? Still? I think I'll need some time for all this. Right now, try to sleep so, refreshed, I can think it anew tomorrow. Will he be there tomorrow if I need him?

Sure—I know he will.

Will he? There's no way to know until it's pushed, forced through. And then I may have lost a friend. Why do human relationships get so complicated? Now I can't even sleep. And I don't feel well—I embarrassed him. So what? Exert a little power over him. Nothing wrong with that.

I know why I can't sleep. My body chemistry's not properly balanced. A cognac would solve that.

She keeps a bottle on her nightstand.

Enough to stop thinking—just relaxed enough that life just floats right on by without affecting me too radically.

*   *   *

Hugh Brrr Hence Wasn't Hugh Hugh Dharma. Fetalitis rerun.

Pounding on my ceiling 'cause the music's too loud for Berlin. Shaking the lilies-of-the-valley.

I don't do much poetry, really.

Got to get up, get out. Staying in place winds me down. Nothing fun unless I'm in motion.

And give me an organized environment. Chaos implies human negligence. I don't understand, though, why he needs silence to work. What's he doing in the city?

Anyway, give me noise—just organize it somehow. Let me know it's human.

Go to the park in a bit, man. Write something. Man did I see weird shit at the bar last night—two women walking around in their underwear trying to sell it right off their bodies. The one had cute nipples, but what a weird idea. First I thought they were hookers, but they were only selling their soft lace satin sheet top bikini bottom wonder things.

So, need three characters. Why? Berlin never uses 'em. 'Course he's a scumbag who's never sold a piece in his life. I'm much more realistic when it comes to how to sell a manuscript. Damn weirdo needs silence to work anyway. What's his fuckin' problem?

Names should be Lewis Glinter, Miles Woodruff, and Mike Quellington. All aged approximately thirty-five. Actually they're celebrating their thirty-fifth birthdays. At a ranger station halfway up some mountain.

Glinter is a bright man, quiet and prone to subtle punning. He usually doesn't speak his mind unless it's for a purpose very important to him.

Not nearly long enough a nap. Better pour through some espresso.

And St. Charles starts in again. Fucker. Oh you need food. Yeah, yeah, all right. Fuck, you're too fat as it is. I'm tired of puttin' it in ya just to clean it up when it comes out. Wonder if a cork'd work?

I'll head to the park and sit on a bench for a while, watch traffic pass by.

Here ya go. Good cat. Yeah, enjoy. You get better treatment than I ever got.

S'pose I should prob'ly quit my gig at the clothing store. Manager raggin' on me for bringin' my TV when the Bears were undefeated twelve and oh and facin' Miami. Dude doesn't understand Chicago, plain and simple. The customers all wanted to hear the game too (all fourteen of 'em).

So, this birthday party.

Woodruff is a big man, loud, overbearing. From New York. Densensitized. But ignorable.

Quellington is a moralist, claiming responsibility for ensuring life is curtailed in areas he's never been.

A halfway-through-life party.

Lewis Glinter's thinking about his dreams—they've woken him up three successive nights.

First, a fellow employee gets crocked and stumbles around the clothing store he works at.

Second, a mouse shuns society and tunnels away.

Third, a woman he knows whom he's about to marry gets called away from the altar only to get shot through the forehead.

I didn't do it. Don't know who did. It woke me up, though.

Miles Woodruff passed out the evening before at his best friend's house after drinking way too much and had erotic dreams about his best friend's wife. Miles was glad his talking in his sleep hadn't revealed his dreams.

Mike Quellington never dreams, but he suspects that's due to his tattoo, which was designed to ward off spirits.

Lewis passes his bottle of tequila to Miles. Mike Quellington doesn't drink.

Mike Quellington doesn't swear.

Mike Quellington doesn't believe in sleeping with anyone

he's not married to.

Mike Quellington has never seen an illegal drug.

Mike Quellington's never had much fun in his life.

His should be an all-the-way-through-life party, but the bitch is anal retentives like him outlast all of us who love life. It's a question of quantity or quality. Which do you choose?

Me, I'll take quality. When I get the quality up to a good level, I'll start worrying about quantity. Not yet, though.

Lewis lights a cigarette and hears crickets in his head.

We're all crickets in the head. I should probably keep the clothing store gig, also. They could help me sell my leatherwork. Manager's been sick, probably raggin' on everyone. He's not from Chicago, doesn't watch TV, and hates sports. How could he possibly understand? I should allow him the freedom to be stupid and forget the whole incident.

So Lewis smokes this cigarette, non-filtered, let's say. Has the shakes from his long night. Started after work with two co-workers. Lewis had three double-shots of golden tequila in the first five minutes. The evening ended at six o'clock at this apartment with a ninth-month pregnant blonde angel of happiness asleep on his armchair and some dude she'd promised a

ride home to pushing and badgering her to wake up. She did, looked at Lewis and scowled as if to say who's this clown, and went back to sleep.

Earlier, Lewis had almost found a fight over a dart game. He and his two co-workers had been tossing darts for a while when some black guy came over, insisted on joining, and promptly changed all the rules. Lewis couldn't double in.

The black guy came over to Lewis and said here aim for this and try standing over here.

Lewis looked at him askance and said, "Look, the last thing I need in the world is a dart coach. Don't try to coach me. Believe me, I know how to throw a dart."

Lewis turned to his pregnant friend and asked her if there weren't some kind of rule as in pool that whosoever has the table or board calls the game.

"What's this with these Afro-American rules? This guy's pissing me off, which is unwise to do. Not when I've got three darts in my hand. Darts hurt."

His friend laughed. His other co-worker, a twenty-year-old Italian, was amused but thought for sure a fight was coming on.

Lewis didn't care. The bartender was a friend of his. And the evening had gone well. Good fired-up conversation and an ample amount of weirdness. And he kept hearing a song about having a rocket launcher which he thought was great.

But now he leans against the wall of the ranger station, shaking with a nicotine buzz, and sipping on some tequila to even himself out. Remembering his friend's kiss and the way her hair felt in his hand when he held her head to his shoulder while hugging her goodnight.

The way they'd figured it astrologically, she'd drop her baby on the seventeenth, and it'd immediately be adopted into a waiting childless family. Lewis' friend already had a five-year-old son. Lewis wants to ask her out for dinner after she's out of the hospital. She's supposed to slide into a deep depression from the eighteenth to the twentieth and he thinks he might be able to help keep her up by spending some time with her. Of course she's been up every time he's seen her, so she might not even need him. But he likes her company and notices the ease and freedom and energy of their time together and wants to explore it.

He lights another cigarette. Lets the smoke out and reinhales it and exhales through his nose.

That was nothing.

Three meaningless sentences. Four? For the brothers James, Nicholas, and Robert Moore and perhaps the missing brother who finked on them and ran. If he's ever caught, I'm sure they'd change his name and address and job and everything. Whatever happened to the Clancey sisters? Oh yeah, they never existed. The Moores got off, too. I remember. They dumped the stuff before being pinched.

Electrical and musical, eh? Oh well, whatever keeps you charged up. Don't worry about what'll happen, worry about how you feel now.

And three million people say I'm wrong. That's why I'm over here rather than there. And that's why I know, when the world comes back over here, I'm here and have been for a while. I think I feel it coming. It's my responsibility to greet you warmly. Make you comfortable, at home, happy, feel like this is family for you.

About the only thing I've figured out is that tenacity and change play off each other and spark things off in the mind. Never quit. But never refuse to adjust to new information. This is pretty basic, and I don't know why I'm telling you all this other than I'm trying to balance everything I want to do. Sometimes I communicate directly.

How are you?

I really hope you're digging this. I'm putting everything I have into it. Hey, do me a favor. Write me a letter after you read the book and let me know if you dug it. Care of the publisher. I'll write back everyone who does. For as long as I can hold a pen. Maybe everyone could contribute a sentence to the next book or the one thereafter, eh?

No, I'm not Canadian. Just hung out with a few. And I collect their coins at work. I exchange American money straight up for it when it turns up in the till. Generous, what?

Why am I here? Just to say hello, and this is what I've been thinking.

Lewis accepts the bottleneck from Miles. Mike's not even looking at them.

"What's with that cat, anyway?"

"Don't know—some kind of problem, probably."

"No shit."

Bloodman flaps his wings and flies over shit. The god of the dudes on Easter Island has wings and could fly out of that tiny island scene.

So long folks, back to the book.

"Want to shoot a game of pool?"

"Yeah, sure," Lewis says, straightening up from the wall and walking toward the table, "I'll rack, you break."

Miles nods.

Mike leaves the station, deciding to go for a walk.

Wasn't everything in here supposed to be humorous? Well, what isn't if you look at it right? Where's the humor in these two godless freaks getting drunk? I've got to find a different angle on this. Maybe the blonde angle. What's her name? I could track her down. No, that would be vengeful and vengeance is the Lord's. Tobacco smell over all my clothes. Tobacco is the tool of Satan. Alcohol is his airplane. Those men don't realize how they're jeopardizing their futures in this world and the next. There must be some way I can get them to change, to accept Jesus Christ into their hearts, to open up and be free in service to him. All they have to do is give up looking for answers themselves. Jesus has the answers. Abandon the search, the truth is in Jesus. Amen.

But let me explain this to you, Mike Quellington. What this is about is tenaciousness. Jesus was a tenacious dude, but he never accepted the ability to change himself. No sense of self-defense. When bullies poked their fingers in his chest, he backed down. So he didn't want to fight, he should have at least come on a little harder because if you follow his model now, you'll be struck down, kicked, robbed and left for dead by a lot of folks. 'Least in this here city. Unless you handle yourself like you got some juice on. Don't go around looking like a lamb waiting for the slaughter is all I mean to say. You're only asking for trouble. If you don't believe me just wait. Some motherfucker'll come out of nowhere and shoot down your fantasy balloon. Sooner or later. Preferably later. Hopefully never. Maybe some of you with more juice than I have can make it through. I've had to call it quits. I'm writing for people I know now, for friends. Make it so my friends can share in my life a little. That's enough. And if everything fails, I'd still write for myself. Put me in prison, strip me down to pencil and bare wall, I'd be filling it with words.

Of course, fancy accoutrements have never been ignored. So, what the hell, I've seen life high, I've seen life low, so come on, life, do your stuff, I'm ready for you. Confusion, get a job. Anger, get tickled by someone you like. The "Stupids," go outside and stop in some place you've never been. Loneliness, go somewhere you've been a lot. Or, if you'd rather not avoid bad experiences record them for the rest of us in some kind of creative way—paint, sing, work in wood, but express it. Be yourself, weirdness and all. Honesty will make it strong.

Kerouac said, "I would like everybody in the world to tell his full life confession and tell it HIS OWN WAY and then we'd have something to read in our old age, instead of the hesitations and cavilings of 'men of letters' with blear faces who only alter words that the Angel brought them."

That may be the first direct quote from another writer that I've ever used in my fiction. But it's a good one. And extremely good advice for any beginning writer. DO WHAT YOU WANT. Fuck anyone who tells you elsewise. Just somewhere in that remember you're a part of the whole thing and we all have to share this trip somehow so how are we going to keep it all going without boredom, anger, aggression, lack of energy unless we pay attention to attention, feeling good, strong, energetic. Only a cornered or starved animal needs to attack. We don't. But some scum do. Be careful whom you tell what, and look for those who look for you. Don't forget to be honest in your accounting and remember you're just one of us. Other than that, you'll have to figure it out for yourself or forget it. Whatever you want. Or figure it out a little and forget it a little. Or figure out halfway and forget it halfway. Anything. Anything at all.

So I seem to have written myself into a blank space here. With nothing to say.

I don't feel like rejoining Mike 'cause the cat's pretty boring, isn't he? Giant rock slide kills him.

Oh, man. You can't do that.

Yeah, watch what I do to the others.

Oh, come one, they haven't even finished their game.

Oh, all right. I'll wait till the game ends. They're playing best four of seven tables.

No problem—I've got the time.

Me too. This doesn't really seem like a birthday celebration, does it?

It's a decoy, lieutenant. Wake up. Anyway the ranger station was untouched.

What about Mike?

Sorry, man. He's dead.

You asshole.

Sorry.

You sorry asshole.

Fuck you, scumbag. It had to be done.

Why?

Don't give me this. It's obvious, isn't it?

Yeah, sure. Okay. Your shot.

Five in the corner.

Good luck.

And the two in the side.

Five bucks.

Got it.

Got it. Five bucks.

Some folks are nothing in my life if not real. Mike walks back in the door and says, "Goddamn it, it's cold. Pass that tequila, guys, will ya?"

Mike and Lewis smile at each other. "Sure, Mike."

"Brought us back some frozen wood for the fire."

"Can see that."

"Thanks, Mike."

"Yeah, no problem."

"Here let me get it going—frozen or not it'll catch if it's built right."

"Damn straight."

"Yeah, that's kind of what I figured."

Standin' out there in the cold the engine would never have turned over if it weren't for the starter fluid and the spare gallon of gas.

Mike asks to play winner, who's Miles, so Lewis returns to his spot on the wall.

Angel's kisses come back to his mouth. The way her hair feels returns to his hand. He looks forward to seeing her on Sunday. The seventeenth.

After goofing with her five-year-old son and watching TV all night with her and drinking beer and tequila and talking about life, and staying up, God, personal history, freedom, growth, kids, love, dreams, hope.

Not to say that St. Charles is boring. I just don't dig the presents he leaves me in the morning. After all, he has a box to put them in.

Angel and Lewis make plans to go roller skating with Angel's son Daguerre and the daughter of Angel's friend Dolores. A party for the kids afterward, actually for the girl Colonia's eighth birthday. And then dinner.

"What do you want to eat?"

"Pheasant under glass," after a pause and laughter.

"Yeah. We'll come up with something."

And Lewis really wants to buy Angel a pheasant-under-glass dinner. If he can he will.

He marvels at the ease of their conversation, their keen understanding of each other.

He's made reservations for dinner at a fine restaurant which has pheasant. Don't know 'bout no glass. But what the hay. Wet checks don't bounce. Unlike wet chicks, but that's another matter.

Angel's eyes are far apart, like she sees more than most people. Open-minded. Gorgeous as a dream going right.

Clouds disperse. Sunshine breaks through.

They meet up and go to a roller rink for the kids. The kiddie rink upstairs is filled with stoned Latino teens who make it hard for the little ones to do any skating. Angel calls the security, who clear the rink.

Lewis drinks a beer and smokes a cigarette, watching the activity from a distance. He feels kind of awkward being in skates again after ten years or so of abstinence from indoor sports. Angel comes over again and sits down next to Lewis and drinks some beer with him.

"I just want to say this, babe. I don't want to give you the wrong impression. I have a lot of male friends, and I'd like to keep this on that level."

"Why should we define this one way or another? We have business together."

"What's that mean?"

"I mean there's something I'm supposed to learn from you and something you're supposed to learn from me. The chemistry is right. Let's just see where it leads."

"Well, here's to chemistry." Angel clinks her beer bottle against Lewis' and takes a good gulp and gets up and skates back over to the kids to see how they are.

The rink closes, the kids are dropped off at Angel's apartment and Angel changes clothes there into a sheer nylon maternity midi-dress slit up the side and sheer black nylon stockings. She could kill a man with a look. And they head on down the road toward the, uh, restaurant.

Lewis takes the waiter aside and asks him for a menu without prices for the lady. Can I sit in the throne chair, Angel asks Lewis. Sure.

The waiter apologizes and says they don't have any. No problem. Lewis alone receives a menu. He orders a Wild Turkey on the rocks. Angel asks for a Corona beer.

Chateaubriand for two, medium rare, mushroom salad for him, tossed for her, house dressing, oh could they have horseradish for the chateaubriand, BV Cabernet Sauvignon, full bottle please. Lewis doesn't need to taste it. He's had it and it's excellent.

This place is neato.

Nice paintings. Fireplace. Dim interior.

French-fried brie appetizer.

Dinner is fantastic.

Best meat r've ever eaten, Angel says.

Sandeman Port 1975 to close the meal and Lewis gets caught with his pants down. Doesn't know his own math. Borrow a ten from Angel and they end up leaving a five-spot tip on nearly a full bill dinner. And don't have enough scratch left over to pay the parking lot attendant so they walk allover Old Town till they find a money machine and Lewis gets cash out of his account. Here's your ten, Angel.

On to a bar. A classy joint first where Angel used to work. Tequila and beer. For free.

Then the bar by Lewis' home. More tequila and beer, and not for too much. Lewis and Angel had been getting along extremely well.

Evening was winding down. Though the friend thing stuck in Lewis' mind in a weird place, he told her he thought it was a good beginning and not to worry about it—he's a smart guy.

One of Angel's friends saw her car parked outside and came in the bar. A two-fifty giant biker type, nice guy, but Lewis started slipping away.

Then the bar closed and Angel asked if they could join her friend at another bar.

It was a C & W dive, and Lewis disappeared into the bathroom and then out into the street, where he lost his dinner. Angel came out and asked, "You getting sick, babe?" Lewis asked her to drive him home. The music had been twangy, the atmosphere a come-down from earlier, and Angel hadn't been sharing her space with Lewis anymore. So he lost it. Drinking whiskey, red wine, port, tequila, and beer all in a few hours probably wasn't too smart either.

A nice evening, he's thinking, but what's this friendship stuff. We'd been getting along so well.

Oh well, better layoff and wait to see what's gonna happen. If it's supposed to be, it will. If not, it won't. Inevitably. Lewis thinks he's sure the right chemistry's there. Yet he knows he might be wrong. Just keep it up, dude. Focus what goodness you have on it. Maybe it'll grow.

Better yet, relax and see where this goes. If it was meant to be, it will be. Don't define what's happening. Definitions limit.

Kiss her on Christmas. Hold her and let her know you enjoy being near her. Read her story about meeting a prince and give her yours about Hugh. The problem is how can she tell what's real and what's fiction? Then again, so long as she has access to you she can always ask, no?

Don't jeopardize her friendship. She's too cool. If it's friendship she wants, really be her friend. Don't lose track of this woman if you can help it—there's something uncanny about the natural understanding between you two.

Lewis goes through changes standing against the wall of the ranger station. Nice paintings. Original Clyfford Stills and Alfred Manessiers.

By the way, Angel's story is very positive and well-written. What seemed grammatical errors at first now appear as an intentional means toward a sense of sound which is essential to the overall tone of the story.

It is the way it should be.

More on this later. She hasn't read Hugh yet. Nor has she heard the right song. I think she knows it exists.

It's definitely just friendship, though.

Suffer verbal abuse for your sense of humor.

If she doesn't like your humor, your looks, your art, hang it up. What are you doing here anyway?

Go back home—find a place you're welcome in.

Quit everything, run away and hide.

Kick start that sporty and ride on out. Find another bunch of folk to hang out with until the mess twists you up enough to force you out.

Lewis kicks the wall of the ranger station, puts on his coat and gloves, and, without saying a word to Miles or Mike, leaves for good, heads down the mountain to the nearest bar.

Time to be alone again—I'll be damned if I ever let anyone get close again—it's that damned word "again" gets me each time.

Fuck. Why can't I keep my head on straight?

Hugh looks at what he's written, decides to stop for a while, call Rain and see how she's doing.

She says she's fine and asks Hugh what he's doing Saturday.

He has to work a fifteen-hour day.

"Sunday?"

He thinks about the family get-together he was invited to and the plans he made to go horse-riding with a friend.

"I'm free," he replies.

"Let's do something. I'll call you first thing in the morning or you call me and roll me out of bed."

"Sounds great. I've got a lot of news to catch you up on. I sent someone to jail yesterday."

"Yeah?"

"A shoplifter."

"Who?"

"Actually two in the last week."

"No shit."

"I'll tell you about it on Sunday."

"Okay. Have a good night."

"You too, babe. Night."

When Sunday morning comes, he calls her. They arrange to meet in Old Town at one. First stop, the Ale House for an Irish coffee while recent news is exchanged.

Rain's looking very good. She's not sporting her nose-ring anymore and the hole has closed up. She's cut her hair short but she wears it well. Her camouflage jacket and boots clash nicely with her purple and pink batik blue jeans.

Hugh's amazed at how good he feels to see her. The fondness he holds for her has grown since last they met.

He tells her about the shoplifters and the craziness of his life and she relates her own zany tales from the last few months. From the bar to a diner for lunch to the bookstore to an adult shop to look at sex toys.

"Let's go back to my place and fool around, or are you still into celibacy?"

"There's always your right hand, Hugh."

"You gonna watch?"

"No."

"How about a blow job?"

"You're out of luck, Hugh."

"Oh, well—worth the asking."

They go to Hugh's so he can give her some of his work he'd like her to read. She likes it, tells him he's her favorite writer.

That's the first time he's heard that from anyone. Some genuine affection is being exchanged. They leave for her house, stopping for beer and cigarettes on the way. Hugh sits at the kitchen table talking with Rain and her mom until midnight, then leaves.

It'd been a heartwarming day. Hugh loses thirty-five dollars on the el gambling with some scam magicians and doesn't care.

Once home he takes out a sheet of paper and writes.

Lewis calls Angel on New Year's Eve. Her son Daguerre answers the phone.

"You again? Mom says yuck to you."

Fuck her anyway. Lewis does some cocaine and spends all night trying to pick up a cute redhead at the New Year's party at his brother's. It isn't until after she leaves that someone bothers to tell him she's only seventeen.

Now he's got his head on backwards.

When he gets to his hotel room he finds out he's lost his keys. The desk clerk has to let him in with the master. Good thing's he's alone. Too drunk to be with anyone anyway.

He falls on his bed fully dressed down to his boots and crashes. Good night.

*   *   *

The first Rich noticed as he approached Church and Ralph was that they were wrong. They didn't do it right.

Chapter Eight

Driving

"Slow down, Phil, I got a headache."

"Can't slow down. Just throw up and get it over with. Sit in a corner with the cold sweats, pass out, and when you come to you'll be okay."

"Thanks."

"No prob, Mike."

That's Mike Moore, not Quellington, who's not even in this chapter other than this sentence.

"Over there," says Mark. "Stop over there."

"What?"

"That wall."

"There's no shoulder."

"Right beyond it. I'll run back."

"Here's your paint, but for god's sake be quick. The state probably comes through here all the time."

"Won't take but a sec."

Mark Moore bolts from the nearly-stopped Woody wagon and hits the underpass wall with

That was his job. Carol had hired him to paint as many of these as possible allover the states while following the tour. He felt it was good exposure for his graffiti art and had already worked out several intricate designs that he could put up quickly and one enormous elaborate ebullient one which he'd spend hours on in some secure location near each gig.

"What were we talking about?" asks Mike of Phil.

"Politicians, man. Like they're a bunch of actors doing this odd little dance for the public which ain't half as decent as a good rock show."

"Damn straight."

"You know it."

"Yeah, I knew it five minutes ago, too."

"It's all a show—like the greatest show on earth."

"Nah—that was some kind of circus."

"Politics?"

"No—The Greatest Show on Earth. Ringling Brothers or Barnum and Bailey. I can't remember which."

"They're the same thing now."

"Yeah—I guess that's true."

"Politics is the second greatest show on earth."

"If you're talking quality, it's more like the worst."

"Worse than the worst—it's about complete and total human degradation."

"Hey, you got my pen?"

"No—Mark's probably got it."

"I want to write that down—I like that—complete and total human degradation."

"You like that?"

"The phrase, I mean."

"You can write?"

"Yeah."

"Oh."

Mark, satisfied with his work, or as nearly so as any artist ever is, sits down again in the wagon's suicide seat and voices a brief concern that his work may be too masculine to represent a band with a woman singer.

Phil takes the rubber band out of his blond pony tail before starting off on the road again.

"Mike, my brush back there?"

"Yeah, here."

He brushes through his hair and responds to Mark's question. "Why didn't Carol hire a chick?"

"There aren't any good woman graffiti artists."

"That's rather sexist, Mark," says Mike, as if he cares.

"I don't mean it to be. I had a conversation with my old man about this. He's said the same thing about minimalism."

"Yeah? I respect your old man. Les is a good painter, man. His stuff was at Art Expo last year, wasn't it?"

"A few of his better pieces were. Anyway, his theory is that most great artists in each artform are men—that goes for chefs and stuff, too—because women are already capable of the greatest creative act of all, namely giving birth."

"That's true. I can dig that," assents Mike.

"So artists attempt, through their work, to give birth?" asks Phil.

"Hey, that works," Mike interjects, "because most great women artists were dykes, right?"

"A lot of them," Mark consents.

"Then, 'cause they couldn't have kids they tried to give birth through their art?" Another Phil question.

"Like Gertrude Stein."

"Like a lot of 'em."

"That's an interesting theory, Mark." Phil reties his hair and the Woody rolls back onto the highway. "I'll have to give it some thought, but I think your old man may have something there."

"Of course there are exceptions."

"To everything."

"Hey, Phil, drive smoothly, will ya? I'm trying to roll a dube back here."

"It's not me. These Illinois roads are shit—I don't think anyone fills potholes in this state."

"We're almost to the border—it should get better."

"Whatever, guys. It's hard to roll when the frisbee keeps bouncing in my lap."

"Want me to do it? I can roll with one hand blindfolded."

"Just keep your eyes on the road. Anyway, I got it. Here, Mark. You light it. By the way, that was a nice piece you painted back there. Carol should be real pleased. What time you got?"

"Thanks, guy. Three-thirty."

"Show at ten? Shit, I hope the rest of the crew show up early enough. I ain't settin' up instruments again. I got enough work just doing sound."

"Sam drivin' the van?"

"Yeah."

"He'll be there."

"Half-crocked."

"Well, what about you, motherfucker? You gonna light that,

Mark, or think about it?"

"The lighter hasn't popped out yet."

"Don't use that one, man. It's busted, remember? Use that Bic on the tray there."

"Watch it, Phil. You're straying."

"Don't sweat the small stuff. There ain't no traffic on this road anyway."

"'Cept that Pacer you just forced off the road."

"What Pacer? Can't see those damn things anyway—they're all glass."

"Just kiddin'. Here." Mark hands the joint to Phil.

"What are you, fuckin' with my head?"

"Not yet. I'll wait till you're good and stoned."

"Nice guy, eh, Mike?"

"Mark? Yeah, a real sweetheart."

A Beatle tune, "Your Mother Should Know," comes on the radio. Phil drifts away into thinking about his mother's death. Maybe he should have tried to make it to the funeral. But they wrote him off so long ago, disinherited him and shit, he didn't even want to see his dad or his brother the pervert or his sister Grace. They really cleaned up. Especially Grace. What a piranha. I've got to call Hugh from the next gig from the hotel. I'm sure he was at the funeral. Find out how it was. Hugh's got a level head, too. Good to talk to. Talk some of this shit out of my head. Oh shit—I'm driving. I'd better pay attention to the road.

"Hey, Mark. Throw that tape from the last gig on. The radio sucks."

"Sure, Phil."

The three of them sink into marijuana silence and listen to the Evil Hearts' Carbondale tape.

Further on up the road the tape ends and thoughts begin to reorganize themselves into words.

There's cat fur all over everything.

St. Charles!

I danced with my cat and it freaked it out.

Sing about love.

My co-workers, my family, my friends, my contemporaries. Anyone else who cares to.

Crowdin' up my mind.

Cut clear. I need only to write without attachment. Here is a place of flight. Be loose. Pick up yourself outside of yourself and feel it take off and glide through the wind up on currents to high in the thermals where you know you'll safely be able to stay until you decide to glide on down, which you don't think will happen soon. To be free. To feel everything alive. To be higher than ever and through to beyond and the shudder's just the shakes of entry into a stop you can't do it yet. Because anywhere you go is an illusion because the key's right down here with the folks around you. Nothing else means nearly so much. But sometimes you need to cut loose, be independent, claim your soul and be alone. To appreciate others. Likewise others let you appreciate yourself. Too bad it sours so fast—it'd be nice to be there, but you'll end up ripped off. So you move along, down to the next farm, do it all over again, and move on once more.

For example, at one place the third was the charm. Later it was the same. The first married, or nearly so, the second wilder than I was, the third so in tune it took a while to notice the smoothness. Both were removals. That's all I can say. Say any more and I dig my grave 'cause I never know who'll be reading this, and at a certain point, on a certain level, I fear my own truths.

You might think I'm heavy, but I can't hold my own with the likes of Patchen. Read that fucker—he's better'n I'll ever be. The fiction, I mean. Fuck poetry—no one cares anymore. We got better thins to do witch our thyme.

Jackson, you out there?
I be nebbah to be fah way.
What do you think?
Dwoman igs ya, man.
Maybe.
Doot sumpin rye'd.
Me? The master of the fuck-up?
Down bee kitchen elf.
White?
White not?
Stupid to my level?
Smart to it, man. You're cool. Don't sweat the small stuff.
Yeah yeah.
Yeah, be there.

But...
Fuck you. You dig her or not?
Lots.
So, go for it.
With my track record?
No one wants to track meet.
You're ite.
No that.
So stop argui.
And maybe cruise along.
Find a wave to surf on.
God tit.
You're not half as weird as I'd been pegging you for,
Jackson.
Oud peggity mew eared?
Well, you are in a way, but not really in a way that can't be
understood.
Dig lout bleary muses?
Nah. Entwistle. Loney.
Sarcastics?
Lyrics do it for me if there's rock and roll to 'em.
Hazin' me.
I know.
Whatcha bout sharon a streo an alternative sites.
Yokay.
Cool.
Pulling cat hairs out of my beard. Gawdawmighdy they's
over everythin'.

Being—a good friend knowing
where—it's from—having—been there—but everyone's got a
unique beauty if you know how to find it. Those you have business
with you'll know where their beauty lies very quickly. And they
yours. Even if it takes years.
Good god
goo gah
goo goo ga ga ga ga ga ga ga ga.
Zoom.
You and me—it's our secret. Not even

the readers will know
except you and me.

I know where you are and you know who I am and nothing
has been spoken that will endanger that. It shall not be spoken—
yet.

Let me just say, this mystery is wonderful. Delicious, even.

Even though sometimes it seems I had odd priorities. See?
Turned it back and it removed pressure and illuminated only what I
felt, but I feel safe in speaking about myself because I know me
better than I know anything else. Or

Ever could. So I'm curious about you because I'm okay
about myself.

If you want to watch I'll open up even more for you. Trade
you knowledge of you for knowledge of me.

Even up.

Okay, have, but it's okay, isn't it?

Well, I'll not say anything else just now.

The Woody pulls into a gas station. Phil gets out and looks
back in before shutting the door and tells Mark "Put in a five-spot of
regular, man. I gotta piss somethin' fierce."

Mike gets out and stretches. "I'm gonna get a coke. Either
you want one?"

"Yeah, get me one," says Phil, "I'll pay you in a sec. I gotta
go now before I die like Tycho Brahe," and he hobbles to the john.

"Who?"

"Dunno."

"Get me a beer."

"They don't sell beer in gas stations, man. Drinking and
driving, you know."

"Ginger ale, then. Here." Mark gives Mike a buck.

"No prob."

As he's filling the car Mark wonders why his Aunt Carol
changed her name to Ada Romp. Ask her sometime.

Maybe a sex thing. Or rambling.

$5.01. Close enough. I should do one of my own in back.

Mark goes back into the car for his can of paint. Shoves it
into his jacket, flips the attendant a fin and walks around the corner
to the washroom. He meets Phil on the way out. Phil's all smiles.

"Whew! That's better!"

"Yeah, my turn."

"See you."

He walks to the can and locks the door. He goes to work on the wall above the urinal.

A rose.

He returns to the car and gets in and tells Phil to check out the can.

"I've just been. Oh no, you didn't, man."

"Yeah—so might as well check it out."

Phil goes back. When he comes out a tear falls from his cheek and splatters on the asphalt.

He gets back into the car and pulls out of the station without saying a word.

Back onto the highway.

Following the white line forward.

Another performance, this from an avant-garde theater in Chicago.

Yeah, it's a pretty odd tape, that's for sure.

Well, you see, I'm sitting back here, and I really have nothing else to do, you know, and I can use this for one thing, or I can use this for another. Matter of fact, I'm not even sure what it is I'm writing.

Shit. I hope this is the right side. Ahh. It is.

She was a pretty good mom, I guess.

"I'm gonna take a nap back here, guys."

"Okay."

"Wake me up when we're close."

"Sure, Mike."

"I really hope Sam's on time."

"Don't worry about it, man."

"Really."

"All right. Turn it up a little, will you? I love this tune."

"Yeah."

Phil and Mark stare straight ahead at the road, sharing a silent appreciation of how to negotiate traffic efficiently.

Being—my   good friend knowing definitely maybe.

Shh!

Mention and contaminate. Allow it freedom not to be defined. Best way is to not mention whatever it was forget what I said I was just drinking wary of embarrassment. And isn't the scenery boring. All these cornfields. At least the road's good, and you see a massive amount of sky. Four different types of clouds. A strong sun on a clear day at horizon.

Colors of sunset.

Violet vermillion.

It gets too hard to see, traveling west, so Phil pulls off at a roadside tavern. "Let's go in for a couple. Lock old sleepy in for a few minutes."

"Good idea."

It's a Country & Western bar. Lewis Glinter's sitting at a table holding a bottle of Dubuque Star.

"Lewis! What the hell are you doing here?"

"I heard this was a good bar."

"I thought you hated Country."

"I'm punishing myself. I figure if I subject myself to it long enough I'll overcome my extreme nausea for it."

"Right."

"That won't work, Lew," Phil advised.

"Oh well."

Lewis had even bought a pair of cowboy boots. Blisters were bubbling on his heels.

Maybe I do enjoy pain a bit, he thinks. Gotta conquer your fears, though.

Mark pointed to his beer.

"That any good?"

"Not bad."

"I'll get one. Want another?"

"Yeah, please."

"Phil?"

"Sure."

He walks over to the bar where a cute brunette is washing a few glasses between orders. Her face is clear, wholesome, and soft. She carries some sadness with her, but mostly she seems pleased with what she does and who she is.

Charlie something is drawling a song over the jukebox.

Twangty Twang.

Fortunately, the place is nearly empty. A couple of guys playing electronic horseshoes. A couple more shooting pool. Three looking on. Three stacks of quarters on the table. Last pocket, it looks like.

"Help you?"

He turns back and smiles at the bartender.

"Sure, ma'am. Could we all have a Dubuque Star each?"

"Right up."

"Thanks."

The beers cost a buck eighty. Mark tips the bartender a buck. He walks over to the jukebox and examines their selection of fine American music.

There's none. Not a damn thing here worth hearing.

"Hey, where's our beers?" demands Phil.

Mark heads back to the table and sets down the beers.

I'm in the drinking car of my train of thought.

Wandering back to you, the woman I dare not identify. Why am I suddenly afraid to be honest? Is it that I'm afraid that I might be wrong—that this is in my perception alone?

out, out, damn thought!

Thanks to *the* will. Can't do that family thing anymore now that they really ripped me off.

I have no business in your heart unless you feel I do. I'm lost at trying to keep you out of mine. You're in there somehow. Such a gentle presence you have.

Yet now I'm afraid. I don't want it to go, but it has to. One direction is no direction. Send it back or I'll have to send it away.

That pains me to have to say, but I'm not sure if you're here today. Eh?

"Thanks, Lew. Good seein' yeah. We gotta get going," says Phil.

"Yeah, thanks."

"Thanks."

"Yeah."

Oh well, back to the business at hand.

This pool game. I started shootin' pool and she wanted to be my partner. Bought me a beer and won the game for us. Being the bartender there, I guess she'd grown accustomed to this table. She threw some quarters into the jukebox and pressed everything that wasn't C&W.

Still, I'm there just thinking about you.

This is the test—can I pull back now without embarrassment? Only through silence. Strong self-denial. Respect for you.

Gotta go, sorry. More here again. Less there. I don't see a door opening up into your heart, and you need space from me because I'm crowding you.

I'll back up, babe. Come to me in your own time. Find me wherever I am—I want to see you again.

I DARE NOT SPEAK

breathing is tenuous. What if I screw everything up?

NEVER MIND — LIVE IN TOTAL FREEDOM

for now.

Good

bye

Run.

It's

claustrophobic

in

Here

but safe.

Warm.

I

admit.

At
least
most
of
the
time.

Gotta
    get
        away
           from
              you

because

I'm
    afraid
        of
          falling
            in
              love
                with
you.
    Because
          nothing
              ever
                lasts
                  or
                    works
right
    and
        because
            I'm
              an

asshole with a bad sense of humor, a drunk, difficult to live with, bizarre, strange, difficult,

but I know what I am and it doesn't bother me. Give me shit, go away. Be straight. Or lie. Whatever—I'll not care unless it crosses me.

I was afraid of this.

Can't really shake it. Yet. I'll work out an angle on it.

Or forget it—after all, who am I kidding? There's not really anything there. A mirage.

Too long in the sun.

So long perhaps I might die from it.

A last sad fantasy before going.

I had thought perhaps I might have been there. I can barely feel the bullet hit the roof of my mouth after pulling the trigger.

But wait! Something great's gotta happen to me tomorrow. The pendulum returns. So I believe. Ebb and flow. Inhale exhale. Wane and wax.

Phil leaves the bar and starts up the car. He sits there listening to the radio for a while, waiting for Mark. Mike's still asleep in the back.

Hugh looks at what he's written, decides to stop for a while, call Rain and see how she's doing. She'd forgotten to phone him. Their conversation was pleasant and brief—she was in the process of helping a friend move. She said she'd call Hugh in a day or two to get together. He told her he wanted to see her face and the rest of her, too.

The door opens.

"I was wondering where the fuck you went." It was Mark.

"Oh, yeah. Sorry. My brain's playin' with me. I had to get out of there—I was freaked."

"That's 'cause you look like a hippie, man. Hippies always get weird vibes in redneck bars."

"No, that wasn't it. We better cruise if we're gonna get there."

He pulls the wagon back out onto the highway.

"What, then?"

"Just a broad."

"Don't let 'em mess with your head, man. You know that."

"Yeah, I know. Wish I knew how to avoid it. Maybe I should check out a doctor and get the big operation. 'Here, Doc. Lop 'em off. '"

　　Mark laughs. Phil smiles. Back on track. Don't have to go looking for things in life. They show up like stupid dives alongside the highway. It's your decision to stop and go in if you like. Everyone needs to stop now and then. But it's not like being on the road, where there's freedom, especially if you travel alone.

　　I'm going to talk to her about it. Release it from my mind. Find out one way or another if the spacing's in my head.

　　Going down that old highway eighty.

　　Iowa City here we come.

Chapter Nine

Stage

"Pat? Would you give mom a back rub?"

"Oh, mom."

"Please."

"Oh, okay."

Pat gets up off the floor, leaves his toy truck behind, and goes around to the back of the couch in the dressing room in order to give Carol her back rub.

"He does pretty well for having such small hands," she says to Wheel, her guitarist.

He sneezes in response, turning his head abruptly so as not to disturb the lines he's been chopping.

"Some energy, Aid?"

"Yeah. Please."

"I had this weird dream last night."

"Me, too."

"I was at some lake with a few friends. Goofin' around, jumpin' in, swimmin' and stuff. Walked around on the shore till we got to this one place where the water was real deep. Someone told me not to jump in, but I did anyway. I dove head first, hit the water, and turned into a fish. I thought that was pretty cool, so I started swimmin' around, lollygaggin' my way in the water."

"Lollygaggin'?" Carol laughs. "Great word."

"Yeah. Anyway, so I'm just swimmin' pretty oblivious to my surroundings. Go past a school of larger fish. One notices me and starts swimmin' at me, this mean old leer on his face. I knew right away he wanted to eat me. So I fuckin' gyrated, twisted, turned, swam as hard as I could to get out of there but he was on me in a second. Just as his jaws closed around me I woke up."

Carol had written hers down. "I thought mine would make, like, a great book for kids. Warn 'em early, you know. Mind reading it?"

"No problem." She pulls it out of her purse.

Wheel checks it out:

"The Leisure of Cairo" by Carol Moore

Cairo was a mouse who didn't want to be with other mice for a while.

He decided to burrow a tunnel deep and far away from the others and see something else.

He began digging next to an aspirin and pushed it into the hole. As he dug, he would bite a piece of the aspirin for food and to help feel less sore from digging.

He burrowed up and down for a year until he found a small pocket of earth near the surface where a seed was buried.

The seed sprouted and grew into a flower.

The flower blossomed and fell into a small stream of rain run-off and floated away.

"Using your real name?"

"Yeah—it seemed important."

"Weird dreams. My step-mother's a dream analyst. Want me to run it by her?"

"No. I'd rather relish the mystery of not knowing."

"Cool."

A vision of a train approached him swiftly, its headlight blinking through telephone poles.

A friend of Carol's, a singer with a band called the Hinge, a dude named Wakelin, opens the door to the dressing room. It's been agreed that he will join the band on stage for two numbers at the end of the second set plus two encores.

Carol stands up and approaches Wakelin when he enters the room. She kisses him. Wheel nods from where he's sitting.

Wakelin walks to the well-stocked bar at the side of the room and pours himself a shot of tequila. He looks at Wheel and stares at his narrow features. He's amused by Wheel's blue plastic glasses. Wakelin starts to make a comment about them but thinks about it twice and remains silent. He's very drunk and sits down to gain strength against the spins.

Wakelin closes his eyes. Somebody nudges him in the arm. It's Pat.

"You okay?"

"Yeah."

"Wanna play?"

"Yeah—hand me that guitar."

"No, not like that."

"Yeah—just like that." A few basic blues runs later Wakelin's already feeling strong enough to have another shot.

"Any beer 'round here?"

"At the bar—all you want. Just say you're with the band," Carol tells him as she picks up Pat.

"Thanks. I'll get a few."

"See you." She gives Pat a big hug.

Wakelin steps out of the dressing room.

Lewis Glinter is sitting at a table, holding a beer, waiting for the first set.

Wakelin sees him.

"Lewis! What the hell are you doing here?"

"Heard about the gig from Phil and Mark, thought I'd check it out."

"Damn. Good to see ya, pal."

"Likewise."

"How've you been? Angel have her kid yet?"

"Yeah—a girl named Leah. On the third."

"Great. Be right back—gotta get a beer."

Lewis remembers Angel from the last two days. Her kisses come back to him. Yeah, but we're just friends. And I'll never listen to country music again. Like that one I heard about somebody's cat, "Just Don't Sit in the Shitbox." Hugh likes it 'cause of St. Charles doin' that, but to me it seems too trite. Some bar named My Mother's Laundromat. Really. I overheard a piece of conversation there. One cowboy said to another "I know women like the back of my hand" and the second replied "I want them to know the back of mine." These rock and roll bars are much more together than that.

Angel. Where are you today?

I remember sitting on your couch with you and Daguerre. Leah's in her crib. You showed me your childhood photos and some revealing adult ones. We listened to a tape of my public performances and tried to find yours but couldn't. We drank tequila and beer and grew close again, and I asked you if I could hold you while we sleep. You asked why. I said I enjoyed your presence. You said I was a man and therefore couldn't be trusted. I held your stomach from behind so your ass would be tight to my crotch and kissed your neck and cheek and mouth. I nibbled on your ear, but only with my lips because I didn't want your long earrings caught in my teeth. You said, see I can't trust you. I said I'll prove to you you can. So, when you finally passed out on your bed, I lay down next to you and held you. Your roommate woke us up a couple of hours later because Leah was crying and you didn't hear it. The two of you screamed at each other—the worst insult being when she yelled that Leah would grow up to be a teenage prostitute because of the kind of example you were setting. You needed to get out of there fast, so you called your friend Ronnie, who said she'd be right over, and she came by and picked us up, along with your kids and the rest of the beer and tequila and a Hendrix album I'd brought over for the sake of the song "Angel." She drove us back to her place in Logan Square, where we spent all day drinking and talking and watching the kids—yours and Ronnie's six-month-old son Donny. I was getting tired when you and Ronnie left to go to the store, and when you came back with supplies and a rose for me for taking care of and feeding and burping Leah and watching Donny on his swing and making sure Daguerre kept out of trouble, I was asleep and Leah was half out of my hands almost on the floor and Donny was crying. Daguerre can take care of himself no problem, but the babies' not being watched freaked Ronnie, who unloaded the angriest loudest meanest stream of bile and vicious words on me that I'd heard in a long time, even though you understood, even though I apologized twenty-five times, even though nothing happened, even though Daguerre kept telling her, "It's not Lewis' fault." I told her she was messing with the wrong dude. She took that as a threat. I told her the only threat I could possibly lay on her was that of my leaving, which she said was no threat. You interceded and prevented me from leaving, which I would have done if I hadn't been too drunk to find my boots. So Ronnie apologized, and I did also. I kissed her hand. She fixed some dinner and her husband Johnny came home and we all ate and watched TV. I fell asleep holding you while you held Leah. Then all night long I kept waking up—the couch was comfortable enough, but Daguerre at the other end would kick me, dehydration would parch me, and a tequila overdose muscle malaise made it difficult to feel all right. You felt even worse—your headache severe and muscles sore. I massaged your neck and back and temples until we both could sleep. In the morning I drank some coffee, hugged and kissed you goodbye, and headed off for home and then work, carrying the rose you gave me on the subway all the way north to Edgewater. I'm not quite sure what you want with me, but I love spending time with you and hope to see you soon. Perhaps we should find a place to live together. We'll see. I've been trying for two days since to reach you on the phone, but your roommate doesn't know Ronnie's number, and you haven't called me either. I want to talk to you very much, but I want to allow you all your space. I'm sure we'll see each other again soon.

Wakelin holds a weiss beer out to Lewis.

"Thanks, man. These are great."

"Aren't they? Only a thousand calories per bottle."

"No shit." And I'm still thinking a lot about you, Angel.

Let's see. "How's the band?"

"I haven't seen 'em for a month and it's great. I've just been partying with friends, checking out the clubs, popping up here and there for a guest spot or two, you know, sing something basic with someone else. That's been great. Been gettin' a lot of juice out of it."

"Singin' with Ada?"

"Yeah, later. A couple."

"Cool—which ones?"

"'Anger and Love' and 'Why Do You Disappear As Soon As You Come Near?'"

"Good shit. Good luck."

"Don't need luck, pal. I know my shit."

"Good."

"Plus they've got a great band."

"I'll agree." Angel, you grow distant again. See you tomorrow or the day thereafter.

Hugh smiles. He had a call from Rain on his machine when he came home. He tries calling but there's no answer.

Calling Jackson.

ooboo nobo cawlin me,

Oak.

Hugh throws a dart at his corkboard. The dart punctures an unanswered phone message from Rose Moore. A week old.

Rose. This is all for her. I loved her a lot. She was always the friendliest, kindliest, most thoughtful aunt.

There's something claustrophobic about a concert.

"Ladies and gentlemen... Ada and the Evil Hearts!"

Song after song. I can't even focus on them because I didn't then.

Wonder how Rain is.

"Hi, Lewis. Hi, Wakelin."

"What's up?" Lewis wonders where Angel is.

Wakelin wonders why he is. A throbbing in the pit of his stomach begins to reveal itself as vibration driven into the ground by Forever's bass amps. It cuts through the fog. Been pushing it too hard too long.

Lewis buys them both a couple of shots of hundred proof schnapps. It's unfortunately been refrigerated, which makes it taste like toothpaste.

The band's doing something in fifteen-eight. The rhythm's odd and Ada's dancing in epileptic fits keeping time.

Oddly, it works.

It flips, it flops, it flies.

It powers through tables, slithers out the door, crawls up the drain pipe, and hides on the roof.

Two roughnecks follow it. They cut their hands on the braces holding the pipe in place. When the first arrives up top he is met by its snarling fangs hissing with a long forked tongue. He is swallowed whole before he can scream to his friend who's just arrived up top and would have been in for the same deal if his friend hadn't been large enough to satisfy it. Instead, it turns and flies off, leaving the second roughneck alone on the roof with an experience that's just burned itself permanently into his memory. The brand of the beast.

A young couple leaves their friends at their table and gets up to dance. They guy's in his mid-twenties, is clean shaven, no sideburns, and wears his hair short. It's wavy and combed straight back.

His partner is few years younger. She's cute, about five foot two, and has red Annie Lennox hair. She hooks elbows with her guy and they swing in a circle. They hug and separate to dance again.

Hugh decides to write Rain a letter:

Sweet Rain,

This will probably be just another letter I'll write only to tear up because of the inadequacy of my words. It could be, if I send it, something for you to throwaway, like others' letters, unless I can make myself clear.

I think about you a lot. You seem to come to my mind time and time again, leaving so as not to overburden me, returning to find me.

I'm falling in love with you, Rain. Your presence is important to me. Yes, we need space to be ourselves, but when I'm near you I'm glad to be there.

I really want to show you my love—I want to write for you, show you who I am, and for us to spend time exploring one another.

This is my gift to you.

Smile, babe. Remember what I said long ago.

Yours,

Hugh

Evil Hearts drummer Bip leads the band into a fast rock waltz. This changes to four-four as Ada introduces a new song.

"Ten years ago today I hid a poem in a bible in a church. This is it. It's called 'For the Youth Group of Zion Church':

Lord, take my hopes for all the group
      and turn them into gold.
Take my wishes, dreams, and joys
      and see them all fulfilled.
I love this group very much
      and I can hardly hold
My gratitude and joy within,
      which seem to overspill.
They share together an atmosphere you know I can't describe,
      of beauty, patience,
      wondrousness,
      of joyous quietude.
Let me live and breathe among them,

Let me see into their souls,
Let me love and learn from them,
Let me share their fears and goals,
Let me hope and pray with them
   for them
   through them
   in them
my happiness can turn to light.
But mostly, let me be one of them,
and let it be right.

"I ended up not staying."

A very odd number for Ada.

"Thanks. We've never done that one before. Something a little less civilized—'The Dirt Bag Blues.'"

Scummy sounding Wheel-works.

Lewis ducks outside to smoke a joint. Outside a scruffy-looking dude walks up to him and asks him for a quarter.

"Sure, here ya go."

"Gimme another."

"Yeah, okay."

"Thanks, man."

Maybe around the block. Looks empty enough. Just smoke it like a cigarette.

Four black guys are sitting on the porch of their house drinking beers.

Lewis calls to them as he walks past.

"Wanna smoke?"

Two of them look at each other and one turns to Lewis and calls back, "Yeah, sure."

He sits down with them and shares the joint. They hand him a beer.

"Hey, man," one says, "you're the friendliest white dude come by here. Most white folk won't even look at us."

"No prob, man. You guys looked like you could use some pot. Thanks for the brew. I'd better get on my way—I just took a break from checkin' out the show 'round the corner."

"Yeah? Who's there?"

"Ada and the Evil Hearts."

"Any good?"

"Damn good. Check 'em out. Cover's just a buck."

"Yeah. We'll maybe come by in a bit, man."

"Cool. You'll dig 'em. I guarantee. See ya."

Lewis gets up and heads back down the sidewalk in his original direction and turns the corner at the end of the block.

He picks up a rock, jumps and twists in the air and throws it back at the stop sign on the corner. He misses and hits instead the passenger window of a '76 Catalina parked there. It shatters.

He hurries back to the club where he finds he has to pay another dollar to get back in because he forgot to get his hand stamped on the way out.

Oh, well. Only a buck. Plenty left for drinks. He has another shot at the bar, tips the bartender, and carries a couple of beers back to his table.

The band's in the middle of another song. Lewis silently hands Wakelin one of the beers.

Wakelin nods thank you.

Wheel windmills. Bip bops. Forever down below. Ada Romp's in the spotlight.

Her hands tear at her hair. Her tears are handed to the audience. They hear what she is saying and she falls to the floor. Bip throws drumsticks at her. She bounces to the bass and jumps back up on her feet. The band thrashes into a cover of Pankrti's "Moja Punca Je Vsak Dan," changed somewhat from the original Yugoslavian version because no one in the band knows what the words are. Pankrti means "Bastards," but more than that they can't decipher. Wheel could find out because he corresponds and trades records regularly with someone over there. Other bands Wheel'd turned the band on to were Ekatarina Velika (Ekathreen Big), Divlje Jagode (Wild Strawberries), Vatreni Poljubac (Fire Kiss), Pomaranca (Orange), and Disciplina Kicme (Discipline of Spine). There were heavy sounds emanating from Yugoslavia, voices of dissent singing against their government.

The phone rings. Hugh answers.

"Well, hello."

"Hi, Rain! How the hell are you?"

Hugh's her favorite writer. She told him so. He reminds her of his dedication to her. This is for her.

Why hide? I'm here. This is for you. I may be lost right now, but the band's taking a break, probably tootin' a few to get up for the next set. Wakelin's disappeared. Lewis is staring into his drink, wondering what the black speck in his beer is. I'm at home staring at this piece of paper and thinking about you and how I really need to see you. You're a drug, babe, that I can't seem to get enough of. Only way to get rid of me is to make me o.d.

I'm not a part of the concert scene. The clubs I used to go to I rarely visit any more. No more bars except when the boredom gets too much to deal with, when I'm all written out and feeling stupid and have run out of material and ideas.

Just a six-pack, a pack of cigarettes, two gallons of coffee a day and I can still hear my death approaching, swiftly, ever swifter, the swiftest now that it's ever been, even without the hard booze, the acid and speed and coke and pot and hash and opium and the rest of the junk I used to force on my brain and body. My death is running towards me, arms outstretched to embrace and engulf me, swallow me whole and shit me out in hell. I've got death in my face. When I touch you, you feel the touch of death. I'm sorry. I begin to understand that there's not much left in me that's free from impending doom—I'm not the sort of man it's safe to fall in love with. I'll take you down with me. Double suicide, or is it double murder? Don't trust me. If you're smart, get out. Don't let me feed on your life.

Snap out of it, Hugh. Jazz yourself up. There's something life-affirming to be done here.

You ready yet, Jackson?

Yeah, okay, okay.

Good man, I'm getting nervous without you.

All right. Let's break until I get up *my* juice.

*   *   *

Jive a rhino livid in the past. Smatter of bean there. Nibble on a root, gore an explorer.

Brush beside. Clouds above. Mud beneath. Thickets. Branches in your face. Poison ivy at your legs.

Good thing you're wearing pants.

Machete.

Lizards in your hair.

Crawling down your neck.

Into the back of your shirt.

Pullout the back and let it out before it goes down your pants.

It's harmless anyway.

Alligator. Crocodile?

Foreign strains of flute. Drums. Bu doop!

Trampoline.

Somersault. Backwards. Twist.

Cool. Breedin' to leak loose. Leadin' to break loose. Bleedin' to keep my
Pen aimed in a straight line.

Babadubabadubabadubop.

Badubabop bop bad uba bo pbop   badu babop bop bad u b a bopbop.

Badubabop badubabop badubabop badubabop.

Babadubabadubabadu babadu ba da dubabadubop.

NO!

No more writing!

THIS

IS

STUPID !

GET
OUT.

LIVE.

DON'T
READ
BOOKS
UNLESS
YOU

HAVE

NOTHING

BETTER

TO

DO.

LIVE.

YOU'RE DYING.

I'M DYING.

GO OUT AND LIVE.

NOW.

NOW.

NOW.

N OW.

Nownownownownownownownownownownownownownownownow

nownownownownownownownownownownownownownownownow

Try that again, Jackson, and you're out of here. It's rather presumptuous, motherfucker, for you to try to end my book.

Jackson responds by drawing a bath and letting the water overflow down into Hugh's apartment.

D
r
i
p

w
a
t
e
r

o
n

y
o
u

through the floor
through the ceiling
o
n

y
o
u
r
head.

But there it's Hugh again.

No, I like that. Go ahead.
You're sick.
Never mind.
No, sorry. I'll try.

I just wanted to let
you know I'm here

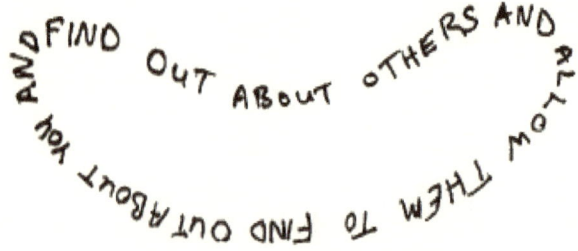

BLESS THIS TIME OF HAVING FUN WITH MY WRITING!
Keep it up.
Fish are flying. Frogs are crying.
Gardens grow sunflowers twenty feet tall.
The path's been made by feet.
No walls.
Little red spiders on the sunflower stalks.
Sun beating down hard.
Over the little wooden bridge crossing the creek and into the forest, where it's noticeably cooler.
Sit on a rock and concentrate on the purple toadstool next to it while you get back your breath.
Swampland.
Quicksand.
Lianas and snakes pretending to be lianas.

What the hell.

Back along the path. Mimosa plants. A little girl runs out from behind a tree carrying two of your paintings and crosses the path into the brush on the other side.

"Hey, stop! You little bitch!"

She's stolen your paintings.

She's swollen your soul.

She's swallowed you whole.

Where the fuck did she go? If you follow her, you'll lose your path. You know you have to take that chance.

Ask her to dance. Pick a pink rose for her and try to meet up with her. If she doesn't show when she should, turn to the prettiest stranger you see.

"Excuse me," you'd say, "could you do me a favor?"

"Sure," would come the soft, tentative reply. She'd seem sad somehow.

You'd hand her the flower.

"I was supposed to meet a friend here who never showed. Would you take this home for me and take care of it?"

"Of course," she would say, lighting up in smile.

You'd smile back.

"You're the most beautiful woman here."

You'd turn away and leave, having made a lovely stranger's day lovely strange.

You'd have made yourself feel fine. The pure act of giving without taking anything back but a smile. Not her name, even, and you'd have to make sure she knows nothing about you.

Will she remember you? Will she try to find you? I'll bet she'll want to know who you are. Better read the classifieds next week. Just in case. But don't expect it.

On the way home stopped at a bar where a friend worked. She told you to kiss her as soon as she saw you. She bought you a few beers.

Other guys were around flexing their muscles, but she went home with you. That's if you found the path there. You realize you should have marked your way away. Put your trust in instinct. You'll get back.

Sure enough, you find the path. Take it back, or continue on? Is it really the same path?

Continue on, I say. You'll find that woman again. Or one a lot like her. Go back, and you're no better than a hamster on a treadmill in a cage running nowhere to amuse a pretty head.

Your path is your own. Do not expect traveling companions. Do not expect anyone to know what you're going for. No one can ever understand you. Just go. Nothing spoken, nothing to apologize for.

The freedom of travel—can't you hear your name on the wind called out by someone far away whom you've never met and who won't be there when you get there?

Or is it someone you used to know whom you lost? Can you remember having been between her legs?

We're talking spiritually. She was a feisty black-haired Irish girl. Her looks stopped the world from turning once.

You've fallen off the path for Eve again, Adam. Perhaps the path is supposed to lead to a clearing where a woman sits, waiting for you, or someone like you.

Does the path continue beyond the clearing? Will this woman dance for you or just sit there? Are particles of human flesh caught in her teeth? Are there any skeletons nearby, particularly those of other men? If you can't be sure, be on your way. If you can't be on your way, be sure of who and where you are.

Down the path aways is the little girl who stole your paintings, standing there, smiling at you, waving.

Goddamnit, where are my paintings, bitch! Out of the clearing into the brush to cut her off. Branches whip your face as you run. Footing on damp fallen leaves is treacherous, and you slide forward with your right leg and fall backwards, hitting your head on a rock.

*   *   *

When you awake you do not recognize where you are. You're completely lost.
The sun has set. It is getting cold out. Darkness surrounds you.

animal

scream

bird cry

bird

cry

```
                 saw                        buzz
                 chew                              buzz
                 saw                                     buzz
rustle           chew            buzz                    rustle
twig snap        saw                     grunt
                 chew
crackle
        cracklecrackle
```

Brush the mosquitoes from your forehead. Something large is approaching stealthily.

A giant flightless ground mosquito, maybe three feet long. A vicious critter.

There's a knock on the door.

It's the landlord, who hands Hugh a Five Days' Notice:

You are hereby notified that there is now due the undersigned landlord the sum of One Thousand Two Hundred Dollars and 00/100 cents, being rent for the premises situated in the City of Chicago, County of Cook and State of Illinois, described as follows, to wit: the four rooms on the third floor of the bldg. located at _____. Rent due being $150.00 balance for the period from Nov. 1, 1985 to November 30, 1985; $350.00 for the period from Dec. 1, 1985 to Dec. 31, 1985; $350.00 for the period from Jan. 1, 1986 to Jan. 31, 1986 and $350.00 for the period from Feb. 1, 1986 to Feb. 28, 1986. ONLY THE FULL PAYMENT OF THE RENT DEMANDED IN THIS NOTICE WILL WAIVE THE LANDLORD'S RIGHT TO TERMINATE THE LEASE UNDER THIS NOTICE, UNLESS THE LANDLORD AGREES IN WRITING TO CONTINUE THE LEASE IN EXCAHANGE [sic] FOR RECEIVING PARTIAL PAYMENT. together with all buildings, sheds, closets, out-buildings, garages and barns used in connection with said premises.

And you are further notified that said sum due has been and is hereby demanded of you, and that unless payment thereof is made on or before the expiration of five

days after service of this notice your said lease of said
premises   will   be   terminated
_____ is hereby authorized to
receive said rent so due, for the undersigned.
Dated this 21st day of February, 1986.

Jackson and his complaints and they've got the nerve to
throw *me* out? We'll see. A quick call to the health department'll fix
the fucking landlord.

"Didn't you get the check I sent you five days ago?" Hugh
asks The Prick over the phone a few hours later, not much calmer,
blood still boiling.

"Right. No—you haven't sent a payment in over a month."

"Bullshit, man. I sent one last week for a hundred and fifty—
I've got witnesses."

"I never got one."

"I guess I'll have to stop payment on it and send you a new
one. Certified."

"Whatever. This is your last chance, man."

"Yeah. I had a bank loan to payoff and shit but it's taken care
of now, so I'll be able to send you some scratch every week like
clockwork."

"You'd better, or you'll end up in court."

"Yeah. I'll send you three bills on Monday. Like I said—
certified. I'll stop payment on check 417 though, so don't deposit it."

"All right."

"Okay. Bye." Hugh hung up the phone. Piranha. Like bill
collectors. God kill 'em all. Subhuman shit-lovin' slimebag
cocksuckers.

Head out for a few. Find Rain at the bar she works at. She'll
smile you up.

Everything's cool. There's an apartment available in her
building. That'd work.

A few draught beers.

She hands Hugh some coupons for dollar dark beers. Then,
on break, picks up the tab for his buffalo wings. They get along as
well as ever until Dwayne comes in. A great guy, boisterous tall,
black man who'd been adopted by a white family as a kid and now
was married to a black woman with a family of his own. He and

Hugh hit it off and are off to the races. Double-doubles of bourbon, kümmel, beers, more more more.

Dwayne eventually leaves to meet his wife and Hugh stays till Rain leaves
but is so drunk by then that she tells him he's obnoxious, which he is.

Kiss me babe, you know I love you obnoxious. Uncouth, drunk, affectionate, honest, in love, loose-tongued, uncoordinated, forgot what I was going to say, in love, belch, gimmeahug, oops sorry, well you know, dron't dink mush bourbon, you know, sorry, hey that's my train. Call me. I love you. Call me later, 'kay?

Small wonder she didn't call.

Stumble back in, the light—outta here, cat! Get off my fuckin' manuscript.

Isn't 'bout time for the second set?

No—I want to rerun that, zoom in close, pick up details—don't need to run so fast—I'm out of breath. Life's too fast sometimes to keep up with my recording of what I see. I'll backtrack here.

"Hello, Rain."

"Hey, how are you?

"Good."

"Good. What can I get you?"

"Old Style."

"Yeah, I didn't see you last night."

"Noticed. 'Sokay. Call tonight."

"We'll see."

"No—promise. I want to talk."

We're going too slow here—get bogged down in conversation some other time. I want to fly through this again.

Dwayne's offended by some old white broad's racist bitching, and I'm the only dude who stood up for him.

So he bought me another double-double.

And she can't be close 'cause I push her away. That doesn't mean I don't love her. It means I'm not getting back the love I need.

She's never asked what love I need.

Nor has anyone.

But I have no way to explain it.

Intelligence above all, appreciation for my work, a lack of

gamesmanship, physical attraction, independence with commitment.

Back in.

The drunk old broad asks Dwayne how many children he's got on welfare.

He turns to me and says, "Man, I don't believe her. What's her problem?"

I tell him she's just old. 'S got old ideas. But then I run into this song—I don't really know anything about human nature other than through observation, experience, or conjecture. Shouldn't there be more that I know through instinct?

The Evil Hearts are tuning up for the first song. Carol and Bip are nowhere to be seen.

So, buy her some flowers, but don't move into the apartment in her building. You're just asking for trouble. Do you want to be treated the way she treats you all the time? Do you like being forgotten so easily time and time again? Hell no, Hugh.

G G G B D Bb A. Each chord a full measure of four-four. Simple, eh?

Not yet. Not yet.

Too late—they're off.

Wait. There was a tax lawyer there who also bought me a beer after I brought Rain some flowers the day I received the first half of the advance for my first book. He and I had a good discussion concerning the legalities and strategies of book publishing, marketing techniques, all that dreary manipulo stuff which I know something about.

All I really want to do is write out my soul for you. Fuck going to heaven, I'll leave it down here for you. If you want it, it's here. Treat it well, it'll do the same for you.

I've got a feeling I'd better be on my way soon. Stagnation's comin' on.

So far everything I've done's been done on faith. Never have gotten anything for it other than some scratch, but I keep findin' stuff in it. That's why I'm here. To learn. To hide. To be alone. To be able to talk as intelligently as I care without fear of competition. To open up quietly alone off to myself and yet be able to show my internal organs to you at the same time. To think. To hope. To recover. To discover. To play. To drink. To life! Cheers!

Sorry 'bout all the booze in this book—I guess I drink a bit. Hope it hasn't detracted from the enjoyability of the reading.

Then again, why should I apologize? I... I... never mind. I ain't the first booze-sodden writer, won't be the last. Not until I take some of you cats down with me.

Uh oh. On that note St. Charles just took a dump on the hall rug. Excuse me while I clean it up and throw the fuckin' cat in my blender.

Want a fuzzy drink? It's the paws that refresh.

Rock and roll's getting boring. They announce Wakelin, and I can't even get any juice up for that. He already had a book, and he's dead now anyway. Has been for a while.

So's no use goin' back.

Head on home and into bed.

Night.

Chapter Ten

Meditation of Mary

Hugh's gotta wait for some help here, so he's gonna let me jerk off again with dwayeye screwtuperware languid jello.

Gotta wait for d'witness t'approach d'stand. But d'judge's still in 'is chambers. Having a cocktail at his side bar. Meanwhiles the jurors are so bored, no coffee even, that they're all sleepin' or readin' the same magazine over again. Beats bein' in the pool, though, so bein' selected is okay, even if it's borin' if yer da first juror selected and have to wait till they choose 'em all, which takes forever cause the counselors don't like teachers but accept a car thief, don't like someone who's worked one good job solid for seventeen years and accept a kid who's never kept one for more than three months.

Well, maybe not. Maybe I'll write it straight. Stop having fun. Bear down and treat it like serious work and turn grey when I'm thirty.

Of course, it *is* serious. You just have to stand in the right place to see it. When the sun strikes it properly the room is illuminated in beams of different colored light. The light can surround you, bathe you, or you can turn your back on it. It could still be touching you. You could dip your hand in to see how it feels. It shouldn't burn you. Hopefully it'll help you heal if you need, or amuse you if you don't, or enable you to teach yourself to keep on no matter what and change and roll and surf, if you don't already.

R: They're too poor to be decadent.

D: They're too decadent to be poor.

Two black guys walkin' to the liquor store right behind me. One stops when a helicopter comes into hearing.

"Saigon! Man, I look up every time I hear a chopper."

I meet 'em on my way out of the store. One's really stoned. We smile at each other. I'm no different from him.

Wonder what they're buying to drink. A twelver'll hold me tonight. Might as well—ain't nothin' else holdin' me.

"Rain, how are you?"

"Hi—you look bummed."

"Nah, just tired. Can't take the pad, though."

"No?"

"No. I have four or five reasons, but I want to talk with you about them when we have some time to talk."

Someone packs boxes for air freight using cigarette butts for pelaspan.

Don't enter

I'm being in   __/   here

sick of Whiskey

an   / cut   Power shortage—plug the 'fridge into extension cord when half the power in the place goes out due to a blown fuse and plug the extension into a dry working outlet.

Old people's faces.

A giant harp. Flames and mentalism.

Whatever, sorry for the stumble, I'm back. I just need to kill some time in here waiting for my collaborator on Mary's Meditation to appear. What'll be written will be subject to her approval. I've chosen her because she's a writer of ability with a meditative, contemplative aspect to some of her work, which I need for Mary. The transcription will be mine, but the words will be based on a conversation we're having, in which she'll help me imagine a woman like Mary, a two-time divorceé, two-time widow, about to wed her fifth husband, John Moore, whose wife Rose just passed away. John's in his late sixties. Mary's forty-nine, almost fifty.

This one juror told me he'd been an apartment manager once and had to serve one tenant his five-day's notice on Christmas Eve for the landlord.

Understand my sentence structure?

Paper change without seeing the original manuscript?

Frog's legs?

Sauerbraten with creamed spinach substituted for cut green beans in butter and German fried potatoes instead of noodles. I've eaten enough cooked red cabbage to last me a lifetime.

Papier-mâché machete.

Milk a manatee.

This juror and I have a few drinks together and ignore the court order not to discuss the case.

What was that beautiful defendant's name? Her address? Maybe we could work something out with her.

You sickfuck.

The review in the free weekly music newspaper says Wakelin collapsed on stage during his first song with Ada and the Evil Hearts and had to be rushed to Rolling Hills Hospital, where he's being treated for a bleeding ulcer of the stomach. One too many double-doubles maybe. More anger than love.

More hope than message.

A statement of my purpose in Dionysus:

God of wine.

Have a drink. Collect yourself, focus in.

Dionysus.

Personal freedom to make choices in life outside of the constrictions of sobriety. And if *in vino veritas,* it's a pursuit of truth we're after. We are not necessarily addressing those who imbibe in the liquid wine, but are definitely addressing those who imbibe in the wine of life, those who encounter it honestly while attempting to uncover their relationships to it.

Right or wrong, clear or confused, what matters most to me is that the magazine attempt to present writing in which the author is being honest with us all, including himself or herself. Unless he's an unindictably good liar.

Man, I dig subjunctives.

So, accuse me of pretentiousness. Proves I know my shit. It's okay to be cocky if you know what you're doing.

These periods of self-doubt come and go. Let me usher this one out.

The door. Use it. And don't let it hit you on the way out. Don't ever let me see you 'round these parts again, pardner, got me?

Yeah, no problem, mister, really. Sorry.

Hahahahaha!

Now, wasn't that funny? No? I didn't think so either. Now I'm killing time not only waiting for my friend's help but also trying to bring my juice up to my life's needs, but the meditative aspect to the coming part requires I slow down, retire to a contemplative quietness, and work alone for a while on this fragile piece.

Should have been a snow-flake designer. If I can keep this up without fucking up, maybe I can be one soon. Should've been a sober man, but I had so much weirdness inside I could barely squelch it until I got older and accepted it. So I have a monkey on my back and should maybe do something about it. Give it one hell of a ride.

And then, goddamn, I don't wake up in the morning until the bailiff calls me and wakes me up and tells me I'm supposed to be in court ten minutes ago. She makes me talk to the judge, so I apologize to him and wash the hangover out of my mouth and head out in the clothes I crashed in. Sit on the El all dragon breath and shiny forehead and sleepin' into the book I'm pretendin' to read. Get there in time for lunch recess so I go have a few drinks with a couple other jurors. One's a plumber, the other's a blues guitarist. We talk about the government. Head back in. Sit there and listen to some bullshit for a couple of hours, and the court's recessed until tomorrow. The guitarist and I get a couple of beers on the way home. I split after an hour and walk home and crash.

The next morning I'm late again, though only ten minutes. This time the judge calls me into his chambers and I have to apologize in person.

He asks why I'm late.

I tell him I cut my face shaving and couldn't get the blood to stop.

After medical testimony in the form of evidentiary depositions on behalf of the plaintiff and plaintiff's testimony and defendant's testimony and defendant's eye witness and closing remarks and rebuttal the deputy locks the court and has us sequestered in the jury room where we order lunch and begin our deliberations. And arguments. Silences. Cigarettes. Sips from the water-fountain. Bathroom breaks. Arguments, silences, cigarettes, sips from the water-fountain, bathroom breaks. Willingness on the part of some to compromise, silences, arguments, silences, cigarettes, coffee, bathroom breaks. Unwillingness on the part of others to compromise, threats of hanging the jury or suffocating them, we may not all leave here alive sort of thing, dinner, okay I guess more compromise, silence, signing the verdict and push that button over.

Your honor, we the jury find that some was cool and some was bogus and often they was both.

After having served the highest office into which a common man can be called, I admit that I feel better about how well our legal system works. There may be problems in a few specifics, but on the whole when justice is finally done (the wait's the bad part) it is fair if a jury judges and a judge moderates. There's no ultimate power, no one to corrupt. Always seek a jury trial if you're right. Between the twelve of them they'll see straight through your bullshit if you're lying. We saw through lies the lawyers didn't even seem to catch.

First thing to do is build an impenetrable fortress around your innermost mind and leave it there. Let no one touch it until you have absolute proof of their trust.

Perhaps then this winter will pass. It's almost time to come back to life.

My fellow juror drinkin' buddy, Kelly, and I stopped at Deadwood Dave's, where he was supposed to be playing with the band twenty minutes earlier. I went to the phone after bummin' two bits from Kel and called my collaborator whom I was supposed to meet more than two hours earlier. I couldn't have known deliberations would last seven hours. We were going to work on Mary's Meditation but I didn't get back early enough.

We promise to meet the next day. She'll call me as soon as she's back in the saddle again. It may take her a while to forgive me because I missed the appointment before last also, through my own stupidity. I feel loss of control over parts of my life. Brain always fuzzy, never a clear head, the days grow from hungover to drunk.

Crashed at my brother's after a long night, some ten bars into it, and woke up sick. Threw up a little blood but not too much, maybe a tablespoon's worth. I'd really been poundin' the tequila.

I guess at the last bar of the night we'd run into a couple we knew and sat down by them. I fell asleep. When my brother asked me if I was asleep, I sat up and said, "I'm not tired—it's just this boring company" and crashed again.

He said that's a funny thing about me when I'm drunk. I'm fine, and then it's as if someone throws a switch on me and I pass out. There's no gradual slide at all.

I'm pissed at him anyway. Went to see him 'cause he's my frisbee partner and temperature's finally near freezing again so we could have gone out and tossed, but he exploded his fucking wrist when he punched a wall in anger so now our season's been cut short.

But I've caught a cold and spent all day in bed drinking Nyquil and beer and smoking pot and sweating the fucker out of my body and watching TV. Soaps. Sitcoms. John Wayne and Lauren Bacall in *Blood Valley.* Carson. Finally got up to write and listen to Tractor and Potliquor's *Louisiana Rock and Roll.*

Have I gotten down enough? Will this lead balloon ever go back up? Can it be filled with helium, munchkin voice, or is it full of shit?

Keep it on maintenance for a while. Mary's Meditation should be uplifting.

The weather's been gettin' me down. That and my cold, which won't go away. Overcast coughing drizzling sneezing freezing chills sleet malaise.

Not enough scratch to just head out and have fun, so I'm holed up. Bored because I'm out of pot. Been goin' through lifestyle changes.

For one thing, I'm 'bout ready to give up on sex—I can't find any women who don't play dumbass games with my head just for yucks. But let's not remove the lid from that kettle of fish.

The real problem is I'm a giver. I do and go and live and give and then somewhere down the line I get hit in the head with the brick of knowledge that I ain't gettin' any thin back for my efforts so I fuckin' blow off the shebang and put it back down to casual acquaintance friendship where we never really connect again because I can't trust my head in her space. Just another bitch tryin' to interfere with my work and my happiness when given the chance. Aren't there any honest women in the world? Or is it just that I have a bad attitude?

Who the fuck knows?

Who the hell cares?

There's serious work to be done here.

A twenty-foot tall bull dyke ninja nun breaks down Hugh's door and confronts him with her nunchaku.

"I heard your misogynous remarks, asshole pigdog. I'm here to remove your balls."

"What for? Don't you have your own?"

"Scum. I'll kill you for that."

Hugh laughs.

"The 8:04 is due through here."

"So? Before I destroy you fix me a drink."

"You can't kill me."

"Don't push me. Get me a bourbon, little elf."

"I ain't gettin' you shit."

The nun enters the apartment, swiftly stalking her prey, carefully cutting off his escape routes.

The hole in the wall that used to be the door is filled by the frightening form of Jackson Berlin.

More tattoo than skin; larger, heavier, and meaner than any ninja; ugly, smelly, toothless; fat, slovenly, and wielding a three-foot-long lead pipe onto one end of which twenty nails have been welded; Jackson cuts a powerful figure.

When the nun turns her back to Hugh to take in Jackson, Hugh pulls a star out of his jacket and throws it so it sticks in the back of her head. This irritates her and she turns back to Hugh, ready to kill. Just at that moment Jackson leaps forward and swings the pipe at her head like a baseball bat. A few of the nails drive into her skull, and she falls, pipe sticking out like a pencil tucked behind her ear.

"Thanks, Jackson."

"No prob. Better get her out of here before she bleeds allover the place."

"Yeah—here, help me throw her out the window. I bet we can make the garbage bin from the kitchen."

They miss, but so what?

Hugh's phone's ringing, which breaks his violent reverie.

It's a friend, a woman. He remembers that there are very friendly people on the planet and smiles again. Bad mood gone. No where to go but up. People are the key. When we're good to each other everything works out better.

Yeah. I've got to remember to be cool to people. Then again, my record's clean. I haven't had to throw a punch in fourteen years. I get along with people pretty well, most especially when I've been drinking. I'm loosened up enough to jabber away and be amusing. I keep writing no matter what.

Used to pursue enlightenment or something, now I use it

backwards—to record where I've been, not where I'm going. Seems more natural, not forcing the future.

I should remember to make my decisions dependent upon whether or not they're good for my writing. If lovers or friends are bad for my work, I'm afraid I'll just have to cut them loose. They're not long for my world. I wish them well wherever they go, but I need juicy people around me—those who accept my need to be a scribe and understand what vocation means.

I run on bearded-man time, but my collaborator is even later. Poor Mary may not get her chance to speak. I'm feeling down and lethargic and indifferent. All I want to do is slow this down to a crawl and maybe stop.

I have to find a way to bring it back up. I am standing still. Sitting on the windowsill. Bored out of my gourd with nothing to say and nothing to do. Everything's the same. Nothing's changed. Wish I had some news, but I don't. Wish I had some views, but I don't. Perhaps I should go to sleep or go out and cause mischief.

I like this windowsill. Still, looking at life on the street is dull unless I'm down there, a part of it. I'm apart from it. Need to practice my art in it. But where is there to go? What is there to know? Even thinking exhausts me, so I'll think oddly instead. In deed. That means I've got to *do* something. Can't just sit up here writing, wasting time waiting for Mary. I'm about to summon forth my last lone spark of energy in order to produce some active reality. I hope it'll charge me up.

I'm out of here—see you later.

*   *   *

I'm beginning my spring cleaning. First thing I've done is quit smoking cigarettes. It's clear, as a painter I know says, that they're a one-way ticket to the coffin. I'm also much reassured that I care about myself enough to assess my lifestyle and make adjustments in the areas that are causing problems. I've been coughing too much, spitting up tobacco-flecked phlegm. Furthermore, I suspect the nicotine of having drained my energy.

What I figure is people do these things until they get to a point where it doesn't make sense anymore, deep within their hearts, to keep doing them anymore.

I want to learn to give love. A black-haired Irish woman, one I knew many years ago, has returned into my life. She deserves no less than my selflessness and desire to see her be as happy as possible. We have the ability to communicate. To write about her is to take from her, which I don't want to do. Let me respect her privacy and confidence and give to her without taking back anything that isn't given.

God I'd love a cig. Oh well—I've quit before—this shouldn't be too hard. Work on the booze next. Make myself a little easier to get along with.

*　　*　　*

I'll let you in on a secret—Jackson is the author of this book. He's conjecturing behavior and family on his downstairs neighbor, another writer he barely knows, one whose name is Hugh Moore.

Jackson decides to read some Pirandello soon. The man's work's been recommended to him by a friend, a painter.

Other than that everything's still on maintenance, hovering until Mary meditates.

*　　*　　*

Two hours ago I published in some comic book a portrait of a winter in Ireland. I was afraid I'd never return there, but now I'm swimming back that way underwater.

The ice overhead is crystalline and vermillion through the settling of the sun.

Three-to-one odds were the best I could get. The development of artificial gills is a tremendous advantage, information concerning which I neglected to provide my "better" with.

Anything's possible for a price. Sad perhaps but at least a means toward action is always guaranteed.

*　　*　　*

Irish dream doesn't know anyone I know anymore nor vice versa—clandestiny could be a consideration facilitating an exchange.

*　　*　　*

I need to be skinny. Break the attachment to food.

*　　*　　*

Jackson wrote a letter to "my sugar babe" to appear in next month's *Arts & Letters* Magazine. He brought it over in person with three bottles of Yugoslavian wine and got drunk with the editors.

Thinking about his dark-haired Irish friend. Her name is

Millicent, known as Milly.

The one editor is a talented painter whose wet canvas Jackson accidently backed into. His ass wore a crimson donkey home.

The other editor, the boyfriend of the first, is a guaranteed good conversation, especially with wine.

Jackson was there ostensibly to discuss the chapbook *Arts & Letters* is publishing but his thoughts came to the place where how Milly'd react to a public confession of love occupied him. He didn't mention this to his editor friends Chad and Fran.

Jackson'd been supposed to bring his idea for a cover for the chapbook over for Fran to see because she's helping with its design. His head was too full to remember.

He'd also forgotten to make a copy of the letter before submitting it. It's his idea to go back there the following evening and borrow it back to make a copy to include it in his book that you're reading now.

*   *   *

He ran out of time the next day and had to skip the stop at *Arts & Letters* because his afternoon professional obligations ran late into his evening obligations.

Soon, he thought. Tomorrow if at all possible. It's a pain being so busy all the time, but it sure is better than being bored.

Remember life with the penguin. That was the most boring of all. Sitting there watching her rot into her knitting.

She was incapable of excitement. Now Milly—that's a woman who understands that the mind is fed by the energy it produces.

The penguin understood only sloth. Sad.

*   *   *

Mary's had her phone number changed and did not let Hugh know what the new one is.

It looks like Mary's Meditation won't appear in the text.

What is known about Mary? She loves and is engaged to John Moore, the old fart whose first wife, Rose, died a little while ago.

John and Mary had been seeing each other before Rose's death.

What about Rain?

She sent Hugh an invitation to celebrate her twenty-fourth birthday. The invite arrived two days before the party, much too late for Hugh to be able to cancel his two other commitments that evening.

Why didn't she just call him up on the phone and ask him? A sheet of preprinted paper in the mails seems so utterly cold and impersonal.

He doesn't even R.S.V.P.

*   *   *

Milly's not returning my phone calls either.

Fuck it—I'm going downstairs to drag Hugh out for some frisbee tossin' and a good drunk. I just hope we don't talk about writing. I just want to get stupid and forget everything. Go downtown and drink some Wild Irish Rose in front of some transient hotel.

Nine thousand three hundred seventy-six responsibilities and I meet them all. All I really want is to leave them all behind, take off for the coast and sleep outside away from people.

Cruise along and stop where I want. Hit and run. Bop into town, have a beer and a game of pool or something, leave right away.

Eat my dust, all you towns, all you people! I'm taking no one with me other than the occasional hitchhiking skirt.

I'm tired of the rot of the rut. This craving for complete freedom is growing into a monster.

*   *   *

I'm on the train right now, if you can call the "L" a train, traveling from Granville, which is fairly close to where I live, to Addison, which is near the apartment of my friend the painter, a man named Melville. He and I are going to walk over to Chad's to see if I can copy my letter to Millicent, though not having heard from her makes me wonder if I should. But I'm committed now and if I'm not I should be.

Only a long-time Chicagoan or a fool can write prose while traveling on the "L." The quotes are meant to imply disdain.

*   *   *

This is so real that I wonder why Hugh's even bothering with Mary.

*   *   *

My Sugar Babe,

Years days go and we still know that smile of each other's eyes. After all so long and not enough and my I disappointed you with doom and gloom I'm still kicking and still feel something like a depth charge for you just to see you again.

The years between hospitalized us and tried to bury us but resiliency is the one. All that time then I couldn't make me happy now I even shared your laughing happiness and you mine at being in the same space at the same time again: we who wouldn't have met if it weren't for my insanity in knowing I needed to meet you whom I didn't know. I must admit you handle it well, and I hope I didn't contribute to your hospitalization.

This heart hasn't been so open for some time and amazingly it isn't killing me. I have dreamt your hair and felt your mind and thoughtthoughtthought wouldn't it be the greatest beauty in life to be able to see that Black Irish woman again that you alone always will be the loveliest dream I ever screwed up with my stupidity and juvenile rigidity.

I've been told in life there's usually a chance to redeem yourself for the past and I swear I won't fuck up again too much has come into this head, too much has passed by this soul, too much has been carved from my heart by the so-calleds to let me decide out of ignorance—I know what I want and where I'm going. As far as I can see down the road there's a chance we could have a hell of a conversation walking together for a while.

Smile for a mile, no demands are your way mine. Claws are retracted and I purr for you. Let me tell you a few stories, and let me listen to yours. There's nothing I'd rather do. I want to know you before I die. And this: I know at last we make each other laugh and shared happiness is all that means anything at all in life.

I love you like I always have.

Yours,

Jackson

*   *   *

HOW I SPEND MY TIME:
Tuesday. Wake up 9:00 AM. 11 to 4 work one job, 6 to 10 work another. Home. Beers.
A paragraph or two. Sleep about 1:00.

Wednesday. Wake up 9:00 AM. 11 to 7 work. 7:15 meet with publisher, planning strategy and physical object. Home. Beers. A paragraph or two. Sleep about 1:00.
Thursday. Wake up 9:00 AM. 11 to 7 work. Evening social obligations or write a few pages. Sleep about 1:00.
Friday. Wake up 9:00 AM. 11 to 7 work. Meeting with the other editors of the magazine or evening drinking party with friends and only brother. Sleep about 3 or 4.
Saturday. Wake up 5:00 AM. 7 to 3 work one job, 6 to 10 work another, maybe write a little in between (it's 4:24 PM Saturday, April 5, 1986, just now), drink a 6-pack at the store. Home. Crash 1:00 AM.
Sunday. Wake up after twelve or thirteen hours deep sleep. Coffee and writing. Maybe frisbee and fun. Get drunk and watch TV all night. Sleep whenever. Monday. Wake up whenever. Clean. Do laundry. Drink. Write as much as possible. Walk around. Take a bus. Visit painters or editors, writers or friends. Chad and Fran. Melville and his fiancée Amanda. Home. Beers. A paragraph or two. Sleep about 2:00.

Melville and Amanda are getting married next month. I'm flying to New Jersey for the wedding. Just made my reservations yesterday. Staying at an old friend's, someone who knew me when I was living with the penguin. It'll be good to get away. It dents my finances severely. I'm moving out anyway at the end of the month (so's Hugh, I guess; great landlord) and'll need some scratch for that but I'm sure it'll all come together. Maybe some money'll come in from a publisher. Hope so.

I'll have to party with Hugh before we move. Maybe trash the apartments up a bit.

*   *   *

Wustabee ahead of lettuce please bowtie of arms in silent wars.

Wustabee a cryogenic darkie lighted with boozin' droog.

Wustabee dare bee there someplace toga.

Wustabee ahead a woman but not a book to sail. As soon as the woman left someone wanted my book. Now I feel much better.

*   *   *

I'm committed to the process.

*   *   *

I went downstairs to find Hugh—still no sign of him. I haven't seen him for days. If I didn't owe the landlord money, I'd call and ask him about Hugh.

I suspect he's moved out. It is my sad humiliation to have all this time been poking fun at his family when something serious may be afoot. I'll never get Mary's story now. In two weeks I also will be gone and the building will stand with neither Hugh nor me inside.

I didn't hear a sound out of St. Charles either. Hugh must have moved out one day when I was away. He should have asked me. I would have helped him.

His phone hasn't rung. Probably disconnected. His lights are never on. No mail in his slot. No sign of him at Fat Bill's. Nothing in the paper. Nothing at the bars. No one's come around looking for him. I hope he's all right.

*   *   *

Bored. Call Milly. She answers, but it becomes clear quickly that she's in the middle of fucking some dude, so might as well write it off goodbye Jackson you're completely free and you are a complete fucking idiot if you ever let anyone near you again. Go clean your gun and figure whether to hold it to your temple or hers.

Of course no bitch is worth that. They themselves make it impossible to care for them. Games, fucking games. I've got to get out of here.

Give love and get stomped. Give more love and get more stomped. Where the hell's the sense in that? In my heart I know I'm capable of love.

Fuck it.

Out of here.

Gotta go gotta go gotta go gotta go.

Leave these crazy women behind. Find another place where they speak my language, Never let 'em fuck with my mind again. Tried and tired of namby-pambying around. You're either with me or you're not. If you are, I love you. If you're not, get the fuck away.

Goodbye, Milly. You're just making me sad, and I don't need that. I don't need love, and I don't need you.

Hold on—there's the phone.

It's a friend, a woman. My brother's girlfriend. She asks me if I'm asleep. No, I say, just bummed. Me too, she says. Just wanted to talk—I always feel better talking to you.

"Thanks, Angelique."

"We still gonna get an apartment together?"

"Definitely."

"I'm looking forward to it. We get along so well."

"Well, it's easy to get along with you."

"Stu thinks he's found a place. When are you free to take a look at it with us?"

"Thursday night."

"Okay. Let's plan on getting together Thursday to take a look at it."

"Great. So what's bummin' you?"

"Oh, Stu and I got into it again. Sometimes I think he just treats me like a piece of property."

"Jeez."

"It's okay. Just wanted to talk because you always cheer me up."

"Perfect timing. I needed to talk to someone too. I've been pissed. I called Milly and she's 'entertaining' some guy and I was working up to this hostility against all women but you're definitely an exception to that."

"I've been feeling hostility against people in general."

"I can understand that."

"I should probably go. I've got to get up early for work. But thanks, Jackson. I feel a lot better."

"Yeah, me too. Your phone call came at just the right time."

"Yeah. We call you when we need to talk. You call us when you need to."

"That's 'cause we connect. There are only a few people I've ever really connected with."

"Maybe that's it. We understand each other so well."

"It's easy to get along with you."

"Love you, bro."

"Love you too, babe."

"Good night."

"Night."

*   *   *

Jackson met his publisher Bering first thing following morning. The

contract for his first novel of experimental fiction had finally been drawn
up, and it was offered to him to sign or not within the next eight days.

*   *   *

Hugh knocks on Jackson's door.

"Man, let me read you what I got."

"Sure, come in. Want a beer? Where the fuck you been anyway?"

"That's what I want to tell ya. I've been at Mary's. I got the meditation."

"Terrific. Let's do it."

"Yeah."

*   *   *

It's been too fast. The third one's not even far enough past me yet, and now I'm supposed to be married again?

Pero was insecure with our love, but what a love it was. It was powerful. It burned. He occupied my thoughts. I neglected my work for him.

If I'd been able to communicate clearly to him, it might have worked. Our marriage fell between his poor English and my non-existent Macedonian.

We should have dated longer or lived together before we married. Two months was too short a time in which to get to know each other.

But our lovemaking was always good. Until he stopped paying close attention and began hurting me without realizing it. His sense of timing was off. And he seemed unconcerned with my pain.

John makes me happy, but I worry about him. Our love is very different from the loves of my youth. Our ages have a lot to do with that. I'm forty-nine.

I still don't know how I got here.

John's getting old too. He's lost control.

*   *   *

Start again—the feeling is wrong.

*   *   *

It has happened all so quickly. Just like my third marriage. So quick to be married, quick to divorce. He was tall and handsome, dark eyes beautiful shiny black hair with waves and curls accentuating his tender face. His Roman nose was perfectly sculptured. He didn't put it into the air either unless he was trying to make up for his insecurities.

What a love it was. So burning, so overpowering, all I could think of was him. When he came to pick me up from work I dropped things and turned red in the process. We had a bit of a language problem, but that didn't really bother me except when he had friends or relatives over. Then even though they spoke fluent English, they would converse in their native Macedonian. I wasn't sure if they really didn't want to talk to me or if they just couldn't help it. Maybe because I was the "hostess" and supposed to cater to all their needs, or so they thought. Sometimes when they would talk for hours in their jibberish, I would quietly leave for an hour or so. I don't think they noticed, except when they wanted a drink. Sometimes I even thought they were talking about me! But that was sort of crazy thinking that way.

"Pero, could you please have your friends and family talk in English?" I'd ask. He would laugh.

"Just sometimes? Please!" I pleaded. He would laugh again.

Sometimes he'd answer by saying, "I don't, how could I ask them to talk in English?"

"Just ask. Because if you don't, I just don't have a reason to stay."

"You're being funny, just funny."

Maybe it was the language barrier or maybe it was just that I got bored with him, though I loved him feverishly for a short time—two months we dated, then we were married. Married. What a frail lock we had. I think it was only based upon sex. Because when he began to hurt me—I couldn't continue. In sex he was just too big, and he hurt me and I couldn't bear the pain. It was. Even the thought of it now makes me ache. Many people think bigger is better—they are crazy. They don't know what pain it—they don't know what love is.

But John—he's gentle, caring. When we—oh—he really knows how to make me happy. But I worry about him sometimes. I love him so much. It seems a deeper love than the others. Maybe I'm just older—40 —? I can't be up to 49 yet no, I haven't even begun to live! Maybe that's what Johnny will help me with and even though he's lost control of himself, I understand. I lost control of myself for a while after my second son was born. They cut me too deep, and I couldn't move any of my muscles for months. It took a year for me to heal. Then I had to exercise in special ways for such a long time—I still have to exercise that way every day—not as much, but I still do. Open close hold my stomach up let it down, up and down, open close.

Johnny's problems aren't all that bad. What worries me is sex, though. Because I think that's what broke up my second marriage. After Philip I couldn't have sex for months because of my muscles. Then even when the doctor said it was all right, I couldn't enjoy myself. I was always worried about Ralph. I couldn't—I just couldn't, and when I almost did, I would think about it for just a moment, and then I just couldn't. Oh, look at me, I'm crying now.

How can I how could I think of marriage with a man who's lost control? What will be next? His mind? No, no, he has a fine mind. I'm sure I'll probably lose mine before he loses his. But after four marriages... He's only been married once—he's almost finished with that thank God. His poor wife—I wonder what caused her death. I wonder if she'll leave him anything.

I hope that's not the reason he wants me, is my money. I wonder if any of my other marriages were based on that. My dear sweet first husband died only three years after we were married. I was so shocked when the police questioned me in such a leading way—so accusing they were. But I was grief-stricken over my first husband. Just because he was independently wealthy gave me no reason to—oh, it makes me shudder. I even had my son Rudolph Wayne with Curt. My first love, my first lover.

He wasn't the best but he was good and sweet and gentle to me and I did love him. Who would have thought that such a young man—he was only thirty—could have a heart attack. He worked so hard. I knew the story. His mother would tell it with pride every time we visited. As though I was a new girlfriend. I had hoped for that kind of adult pride for my sons.

But they are dependent—Rudolph is twenty-seven and my second son, Philip, is twenty. I think he is more independent than Rudolph. I really believe it is Curt's fault. He gave him so many things—just because he was never home. He thought he could buy our love just like he'd bought everyone else's. I wonder if he ever knew the truth. When he lay in that hospital bed so pale and in such deep pain, I tried to tell him how the only thing that mattered was that he would get better. I honestly thought he would. Curtis held my hand tight. Rudolph stood in the corner—he was only five then—wearing his favorite suit that his daddy bought him for "more than a hundred dollars" he'd say whenever he wanted to wear it. Rudolph was quiet, scared, pale. I thought he was going to faint. Then after a long quiet, Rudolph asked very slowly, very quietly so he had to repeat himself.

"Father?" Curtis made Rudolph call him that. "Father, are you going to die?" Tears sparkled on his face ever so faintly.

"No, of course not. He's not."

"I think so!"

"No, how can you say that, the doctor said it was only a minor heart attack. Any healthy man could come through with flying colors."

"I think you're going to die, Daddy." He slipped and covered his mouth quickly.

"That's all right, son. Come here and give your daddy a hug before I go."

A long long love of a hug they gave, and I could hear Rudolph whisper, "Don't go, Daddy. Who's gonna take care of mom or the business?"

"You will, son. You will."

I've been waiting for him to be able to take over this business for years. He just can't. Somehow something psychological must have happened. I think he must have seen that request of his father's as just too big for him to handle, so he just kept that immaturity covered with that fear. Perhaps it was the thought of his own father's dying at such a young age that made him fear death himself. He's been to several of the best psychotherapists. They can't get him to cooperate, and that's what it takes. Someday he will. I hope before I reach my coffin. I really could use the help. The business has gotten so large it has at least tripled the ten million dollar size it was when Curtis passed on. My Curtis.

But what about Johnny—could I bear it if he passed on; I would probably die myself. I've just been through so much pain.

When I almost lost the business a few years after Curtis passed on, I lived on the poverty level, saving every penny I could.

All the scandal about the board members' diverting funds—so many millions and millions, and the government thought it was me for a couple of years so they would only allow me to have a small salary until it was all cleaned up. I should have sued them.

But Johnny—will he be able to put up with my being gone so often. He says he will, but I wonder. I don't see him too often. When we see each other, it is nice, but is it realistic to think that we are actually compatable? I should suggest we do what so many younger people are doing—live together.

What will Philip or Rudolph Wayne think? They are really so old fashioned.

But Johnny—with my track record how could you still want me? After all the men and marriages I've been through, yet your sweetness tells me you really love me.

My friends are against this marriage. They think it's because of the money. But I'm sure John won't be totally broke—his wife has to leave him something to survive on—if she doesn't, I will help him forget it. But it may look bad.

Johnny and I have been in love for a number of years now, but we never would say it. We just kept our distance—he was married, and I am against adultery. Besides I didn't know he felt the same way. He was always nice, but I thought it was just our business positions. He always handled his wife's affairs, and her business was doing business with mine for so long.

I remember when John and I met—ten years ago. I fell in love at first sight—but I knew he was married—it was at the spring ball I hold every year. His wife brought him over. I had been admiring him from afar for several minutes, and I found myself quite red when she introduced me. I could see it in his eyes that he felt the same. Such a long yet short romance.

When his wife became ill five years ago and he began to handle her affairs, then every time we needed her firm's help, he was the one who handled my account. I saw the way he looked at me. He couldn't help, I'm sure, but notice my stares—but we never would give in to our urges until about a year ago when he called me.

"They've put her in again," he said somberly yet almost with a sort of relief.

"Oh, John, I'm sorry. How long will she be in this time?" I

tried to console him.

"They don't think she'll come out."

"No, no, I'm so sorry. Can I do anything? Anything at all?"

"Well, I think just to see you would be nice. I seem to always feel better when we talk. Seeing you really lifts my spirits."

"Well I could change a few appointments around—drinks and dinner?"

What was supposed to be a short dinner turned into an all-night ordeal. We talked and talked and laughed. We tried so hard to be sad, but we just couldn't. We were just so happy to be together we couldn't help it.

We both called our offices and homes and checked to make sure all was well. My youngest Philip, whom I was closest to, did keep me informed as things in the stocks and other areas of the business were moving so rapidly these days. Those days.

Johnny. What a long time it took for us to bring our feelings to the surface or at least face them. Such a glistening joyous laughing love free from sadness. We went dancing—"just for old-time's sake" we said. We danced for hours until the club closed at four, and we knew it wasn't something we could ignore any more. Half of me felt very ashamed and the other half so incredibly happy. We moved so exquisitely well together—such ecstasy—the kind we still experience.

The strange thing was that our far-away hidden nights weren't ever often enough, and the dirt I thought I'd feel just wasn't there. I even tried after about six months to make myself feel bad. But when I'd see him, I just couldn't keep it. The bad feelings just disappeared. I could hardly hold onto it for more than a few minutes when Johnny entered the room.

There were times I'd decided flat out that we couldn't go on. He was married. It just wasn't right.

"Well let's see each other and talk about it," he said several different times. We would then we couldn't. We were simply meant for each other.

And yet it still seems like such a short romance. A year and then his wife finally, oh and I say that with such guilt, but she finally passed away. I just hope she didn't find out. I don't think anyone knew except my son Philip—he figured it out.

But we tried to make it discreet.

So now, all we need to do is wait a few more months before we can marry. It's only proper to allow him time to mourn properly. And the will—if his step-children ever found out that we'd been together for so long—they would cut him off short. I don't mind—I have so much now. Not like I did twenty years ago—so broke— almost on welfare till I was cleared.

But Johnny does have his pride. I worry about his having lost control three or four months ago—I hope I didn't cause it. I wonder if I should talk to his doctor, privately. Johnny and I should go to see him together perhaps.

Part Two

Jackson Berlin

Chapter One

Jackson Flies a Kite

Jackson read his contract carefully. It seemed good.

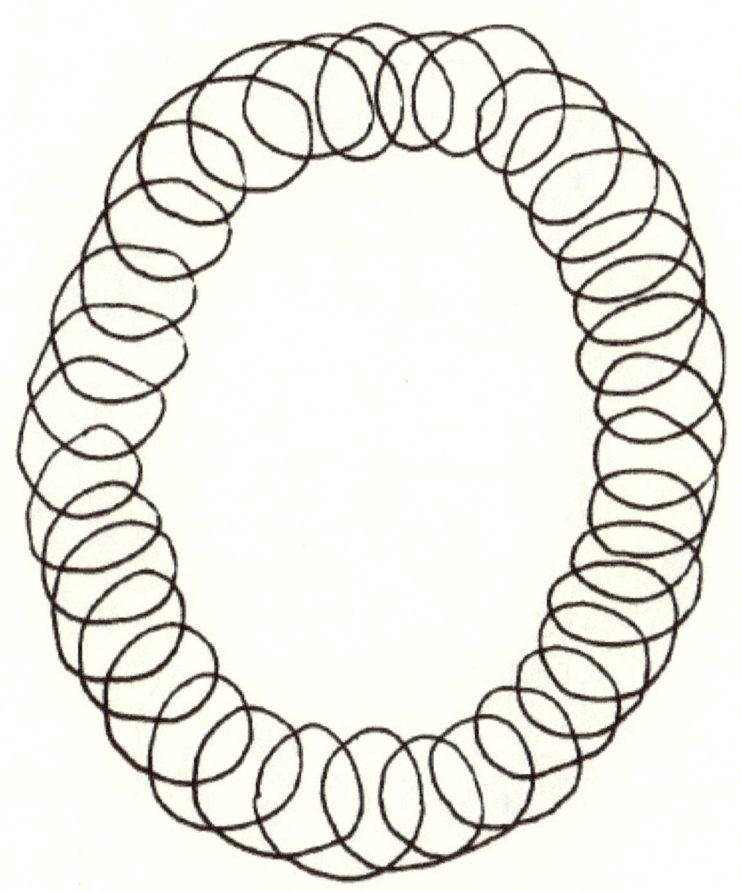

High on feeling successful he called up a woman he knew whom he liked quite a lot. He told her about his contract and his writing. She asked if she'd have to wait until the book came out to read it.

Jackson suggested that he could give it to her if they met. He had a bound copy of the manuscript extra.

She said it'd be fun, and they arranged to meet.

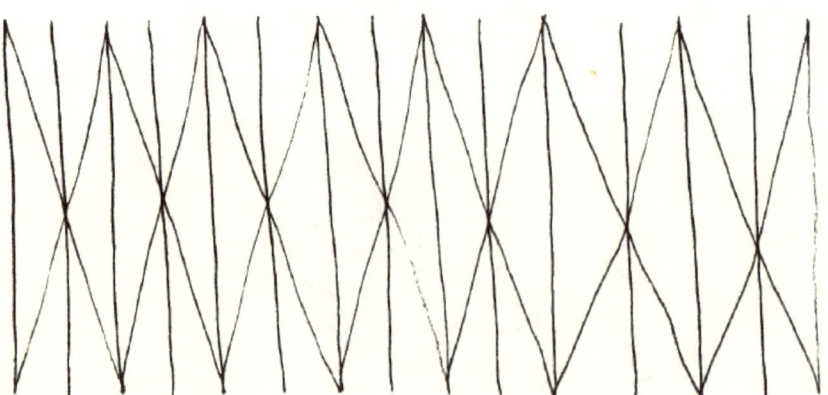

And wasn't she beautiful?

And wasn't she fine?

Dinner flew by, and when the check arrived, she picked it up fast and said, "I've got it."

That impressed Jackson. A woman who wasn't out for all she could get. She admired Jackson's success with his work, and he spoke upon the subject zealously. She listened until Jackson asked her about herself, and then she spoke sweetly softly oh so beautifully well.

"So, do you live with your mom, then?" asked Jackson after Freya told him of her father's departure to California.

"No, actually I live with my boyfriend," she replied. "You know him," and she said who it was.

"Well, is that going to throw a damper on our seeing each other again?"

"No, I don't think so. He doesn't know. He's a sports fanatic. He doesn't know that there's a problem yet, but there is."

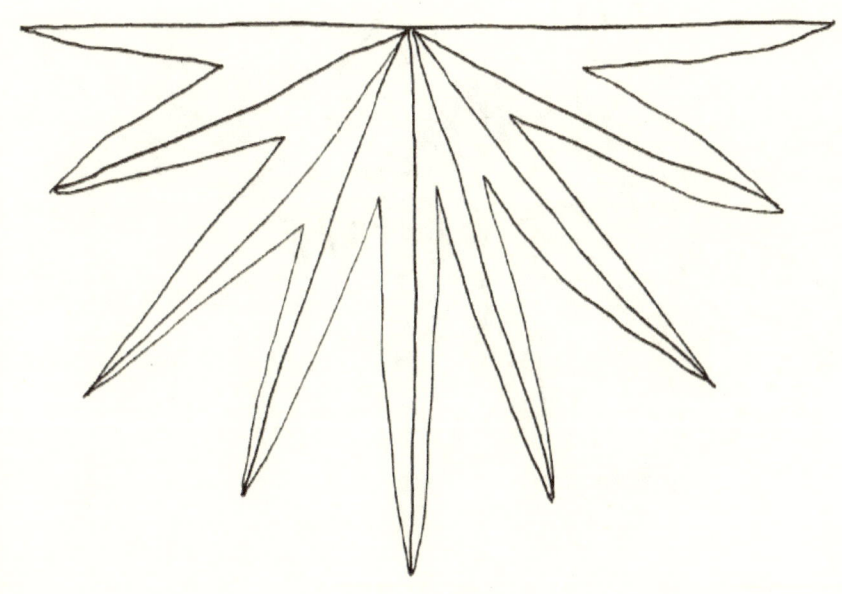

Mavins at the gloaming agree that love is the wrong way to go, but that it is also the only way to go.

Jackson's tired of anger, tired of frustration and disappointment, tired of noticing the negative. Zombie for good for a while. Push it up. Weather's great, book's coming out, new pad's tops, job pays well, woman's entering his life.

Thrown into the present, everything is as it should be.

Jackson decides to give notice at his part-time job so that he can more enjoy where he is. Leave some room for Freya to come in by.

Same time next week?

Sure—only problem's the boyfriend.

No problem—I'll work myself around your schedule, says Jackson. And his heart is on beat.

When he quits his job at the literary bookstore, the general manager tells him she'd like to keep in touch with him, do something special for the book, have him help with readings and signings. He parts from her company on good terms and feels good for having left a bridge unburned. His having passed it over seems to have strengthened it.

In my will I wish for everyone who has even a scrap of my work to see that it gets
published, preferably for personal profit and certainly not without remuneration.

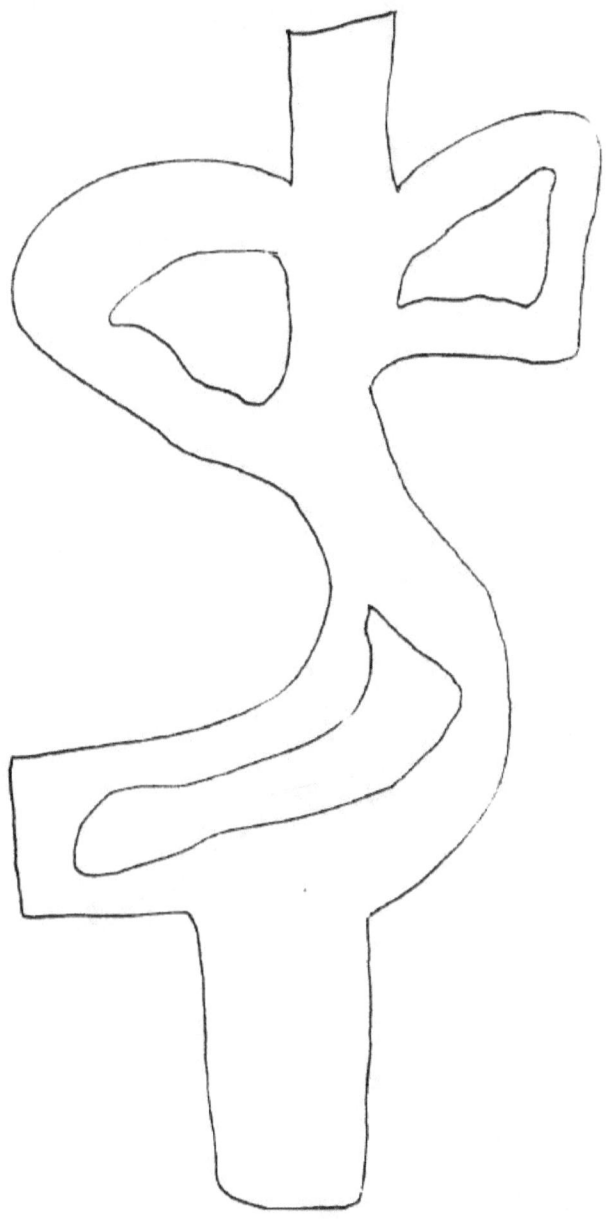

Just make sure there's no copyright and that you enjoy the entire project, except where it's not supposed to be enjoyable but just enthralling, or troublesome, or wearisome, or naive, or cynical, or any other of hundreds.

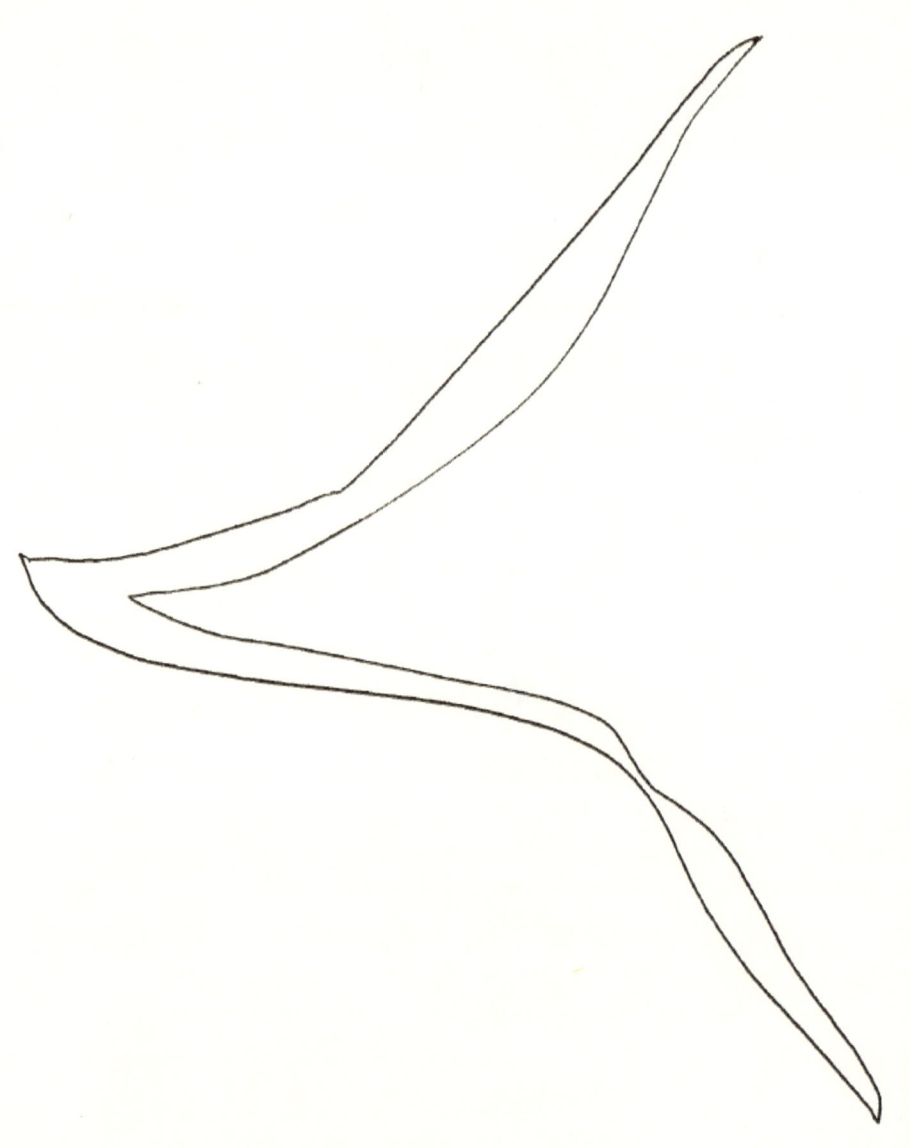

I like the feel of your flesh.

Do I owe anyone an apology?

Why'd
you
have
to
come
at
me
with
your
kisses
at
this
time you
? Thank
Because
I'm
leaving
?

this
could
confuse
everything
up

what am I going to need a bodyguard?

woman?
married
a
with
it
making
than
hazardous
more
be
could
what

we were just drunk I think

my touch?

Will you remember

did it?
happened
really
nothing

Will you remember

(your
husband)

A mess to get into & out of I didn't
mean
to
cause
any
trouble

I
out
of

think
something
happened

silly
me

What have
we got here

It seemed right and I'd probably do it

know not to say anything
I'm going to assume you'll
again

Maybe
we
should
leave
it
at
that

Write the community and tell 'em the subversion's progressing well.

Identity to identity.

We're digging wells and growing food. Raising the dead and gettin' 'em to abandon hell.

Word is out. We're isolated in safety. But what's this community? Some system through which my mind was copped into working to support it?

Maybe I should just steer clear and continue on my own way. Freed from that which freed me from something else.

```
I need to be myself
            with someone I love
who allows me the
                identity I
        keep
to or for, by, with, from
        myself
```

I burn 'em out fast. I do too much or not enough.

Whether I'm disliked or loved, I'll still be there, so what's it matter?

I'm burnin'.

Rippin' through life with my teeth bared. And takin' what I get and throwin' it right at the heart.

Is there a way to calm that down? Relax to where I could sit on a rocker on my porch and talk to everyone as they walked by?

I'll do that later, I guess. Perry gets 'em horny. They've got to get out and get together.

He knocks on her door.

She lets him in.

but Freya never showed same time next sure right not even a phone call to cancel good bye if it weren't for the search for love I think I'd be more in control, stronger, my head less bowed under the weight of my embarrassment at yet again having perceived this all incorrectly. Yet it could be that this time the error in perception was hers.

Certainly I don't have the time or desire to stay here in abnegation thinking about my errors and flaws.

Time to get up, go on to whatever lies ahead. History indicates that it could only get better. What little time together there was was valuable. One last thing—I'll need my manuscript back. My children are not safe in Freya's hands.

Word is out. I'm isolated in safety. But what's this desire to couple? Some system through which my mind was copped and my energy dissipated on futile women?

I'll just sidestep this mess and be on my way.

I'm not going to New Jersey—can't afford to attend Melville and Amanda's wedding. Round-trip flights and car rental are too expensive, seeing as how I have to pay for the first month's rent on the new apartment yet and still owe the old asshole landlord some scratch plus Melville could probably better use the money I owe him for a wonderful oil painting he did in violet and green of an aging couple at the gloaming which I bought, and I still need to finance the *Arts & Letters* chapbook, which involves color xerox costs. I'm going to apply for school, too. A year and a half of college left, I just got word from my father that he's got a new academic gig in Iowa and I could finish my education out there for free. Change of scenery. Find some women in school with artsmarts who could communicate with me. Find some honor outside my home town. No one disappointment will be my anchor—I'll transform every negative and use it for good purpose.

I would change my attitude to Chicago's traditional Love Me or I'll Kill You but it's still buried in Al Capone's vaults under the Lexington Hotel on S. Michigan.

Remove myself from my heart, bury my head in my art, and most of all keep the activity level high. Maybe I shouldn't have given notice at the bookstore. I can't have regrets, though, if I'm going to keep moving forward.

Saw two poets read there and felt funny 'cause I'd read there before and now I was leaving. Couldn't even get myself to say hello to the poets and introduce myself—most likely they've heard of me also, but I'm not a good hobnobber. With hobby horse and hobby knees. Not my needs. Home, Jeeves. Hop on the el and fall asleep somehow always managing to wake up just as the train pulls into Loyola. Well, not always. Sometimes the conductor kicks me in the feet and wakes me at Howard and I've got to backtrack.

There's always the Ganges River slogan: just-a-shittin'-an-a-drinkin'.

Gotta pack today. Movin' out in three days. Change over the phone. All that crap. Buy some hash as anesthesia for the move.

Spend dinner at a friend's—drinkin' Smith's Oatmeal Stout.

Got no packin' done. Just caught a good hash buzz and lost motivation.

Take the next day off and try again. Pack. Box.

Oh, one story. My friend told me I could repeat this story.

His grandmother calls him to tell him she'd bought a new couch and that her old one was still in excellent shape and that she wants him to have it. He borrows a van from a friend and goes to pick up the couch with another buddy. The van breaks down on the way back. It needs a new starter. They take a cab back to her house and borrow her car, go to a gas station, get a new starter and drive out to the van. On the way, my friend's grandmother's car breaks down. And it's raining. My friend's buddy hitchhikes down to a gas station to get a tow-truck. My friend meanwhile flags down another tow-truck and the guy says he can fix the car immediately back at his shop. The other truck says nothing can be done till Monday. So they payoff the latter and accept the former's offer except that the car turns out to be worse off than expected and it can't be fixed till Monday anyway and will cost $238 to repair. They take a cab to the van whereupon they discover that the starter they just bought doesn't work either. Exhausted, they call for a tow and ride on the couch in the van towed back home. For eighty dollars.

For a free couch. So much for that.

Saw Chad and Fran again. Over champagne. Decided on a color xerox cover wrapped with mylar around a cardstock inner cover on which one of Fran's drawings will appear. The inner pages will be reduced in half from typescript with new pagination and an upper border consisting of a repeating zigzag pattern.

Fran was working on a landscape which was an excellent piece of design work. Jackson fell asleep on the couch midconversation and woke up a little later, Chad reading in a nearby chair.

"What happened?"

"You fell asleep."

"Uh. Was I talking or snoring or anything?"

"Snoring a bit."

"Sorry."

"No problem, man. Must've been tired."

"Yeah—didn't sleep at all last night. Just partied and went straight to work."

"Drag."

"Fran asleep?"

"Yeah, she crashed too."

"Wow, hey, I guess I'd better crawl home. Thanks, though, man."

"No problem. I had a lot of fun."

"Yeah. Me too. Good seeing you. I can't wait to see the book done."

"Good night."

"Night."

Hop on the el and fall asleep somehow always managing to wake up just as the train pulls into Loyola. What'll happen after I move? North Evanston with my brother and his girlfriend. Fireplace. Skylight. Porch. Large rooms.

I should get back to packing. Just needed this break. Grab a beer and put my laundry away from two weeks ago.

Make boxes.

Pack books.

And books.

Aristotle. Hunter Thompson. Don't know why I still have the Aristotle. But that's me. I had trouble following his line of thought. Plato was easier. I thought Hume wrote with great style—more writer than philosopher. A couple thousand books.

Boxing books.

Ali. Frazier. Foreman. Spinks.

One hundred twenty-three books are published every day in the United States alone. And nobody reads them all.

Books deep enough to wade through.

Ideas. Scams. Nonsense. Egos. Dreams. Lies. Memories. Philosophy. Style. Plot. Characterization. Word play. Poetic devices. Truth distorted. Truth revealed. Real people. Ghost people. Friends of Divine Intervention. All sorts of freaks and weirdos and drunks and clowns and gongfarmers and booksellers and books—pack more books!

Make boxes.

I should get back to packing. Just needed this break. Grab another beer.

Books.

Books.

Strange damned little things. Why is it you hold a book you have a strong urge to throw it against something hard?

Hey, do that with this book, will you?

Wait. Better yet box it until after the move. But then the move will be lost. Hey, what about fiction for a change? A story or something?

A break.

Books. Books. Books.

Boxes and boxes of books.

I hate the damned things. Ugly antiquated artform. As soon as I feel I have a hold of it, it slides out of my grasp and slithers away along the wall.

Box 'em up. Move 'em out. Raw books.

Three flights down. Into the truck. Get some more.

Three flights down. Into the truck. Get some more.

Anesthetized so none of it hurts.

Never read most of them. Just keepin' 'em because I was fascinated with 'em as objects. Who cares what's inside. They make good stepladders and doorstops and flaming projectiles.

Got books up the butt. Maybe that means I should write out my ass. What a mess. Dysentery fiction.

Box 'em up. Move 'em out. Raw books. Three flights down. Into the truck. Get some more.

Three flights down. Into the truck. Fuck it. Leave the rest—leave the cheap mass market paperbacks.

Let's go. After a beer. Nah, take it along—a traveler. Just one more box, throw it in, we're gone.

Nice twelve-foot truck. Reminds me of driving for the liquor store. Only 233 miles on it and it runs smooth, Lee.

Thanks for helpin' with this shit—it's a royal pain havin' to move.

Can't take Ridge or Sheridan Road. No trucks allowed. Maybe take Devon to Western which becomes Asbury and leads into Green Bay Road. Central's right off that.

Back to north Evanston, man. I grew up there. Weird moving

back. Know the neighborhood, though. And the pad is great— fireplace, porch, skylight. Park across the street. No neighbors.

Wonder where and how Hugh is. I'm sure he's moved by now.

How'm I gonna squeeze everything into my schedule? Unpacking, writing, work. Chad and Fran expect me over because the chapbook's camera-ready and the rest of the work from there's mine 'cept what they sell mail-order.

That's exciting. Paying for it with the second half of my advance from my other publisher plus my tax refund. I should probably flip a bill towards my old landlord and clear up ComEd and Ma Bell and People's Gas. 'Least I was able to already give Melville the rest of the money for his painting. It looks great in this light new apartment.

So I'm back in the suburbs again. Farewell the urban man, eh? I'm going to have to start worrying about lawnchairs and Dutch Elm disease and begin watching a lot more television. Time to relax, find breathing space again—head space.

The streets at night are safe and quiet and dark. Families nestled snugly in their hundred thousand dollar homes.

Head back to the city—Chad's alone. Brought a case of beer and some Babycham. Fran's at her father's for Mother's Day in order to do a house drawing for a friend of his.

Good writer's drunk—looked at his poems and pulled 'em apart by strands like stringcheese for him. Naturally they were better whole.

This move has disrupted my writing   it took four nights. Didn't do much all week but hump furniture and books.

Books. Not more books. Boxes and boxes and boxes of books. Spend days moving books. I've moved books more often than I've moved my bowels.

But it's all done and I'm going to kick back and drink myself silly. Reread the camera-ready copy and look at the mock-up of the chapbook again. I'm really happy about it—if I die next week I'll have at least accomplished that much. I'd like to celebrate with a little weed or blow, but I should really pump my money back into my art.

Living out of boxes. Where's the artwork for the chap's cover? Bottom of the last box, of course.

Melville got married today.

As I said, haven't had much time to write. Not that anything's wrong. Making a little too much sense perhaps. Let's see what we can do 'bout that. Inner commitment to my former community before I claimed my individualism. I'll head back up there in a couple of months and say hi. Tell 'em how successful I was at fuckin' up the English language. Or how successful it was at normalizing me. I don't even really remember what anyone up there looks like. Wings or somethin'?

For now, sitting here drinking perry and beer, watching Elvis question one of the Darrens from *Bewitched* about a chick who split in the middle of the night, listening to the Stones' *Exile on Main Street,* something like that, and I don't even have a stepfather in spite of what I say when I talk on the telephone in my sleep. Credits rolling on Elvis the Darren was Dick Sargent. Burt Reynolds in *Shamus* up next. Look like a TV night. Reynolds has a hangover to begin the film. The question at the end is will Dyan Cannon return?

Call a few women and see about dates. Retire to my dreams and hope everything works out tomorrow. More unpacking, dishes, the evening's my married friend's until her husband comes home and then it's all of ours. Roommates are out. TV's a bore. Should be okay later on. Think I'll have me a rotgut tequila.

Little cat's in heat. Give it a cold shower.

Wonder how Hugh's doing and how his cat St. Charles is? All these cats. Sometimes I think it's them that's the masters. We live to feed 'em, clean up their shit, give 'em attention.

Anyway, there's nothing exciting happening right now, so let me tell you a couple of stories about my family.

My maternal grandfather died when my mother was nine. He was the son of a man who'd started the largest chain of grocery stores in Berlin. On the last day of the war, when the Russians were "cleaning up," they shot everything in uniform, as well as burned and raped things, things to them like children and women, and my grandfather caught a bullet in his leg. He was wearing a policeman's uniform at the time. He had joined the police force in Berlin so that he would be exempted from the military draft. When he was shot, he was brought to the hospital and would have been fine but an intern came in and, seeing my grandfather's leg bent, which was the only way the wound would heal, thought it a mistake on the doctor's part, straightened the leg out, reopening the wound, and left. My grandfather bled to death.

My grandmother says I walk like him, sound like him, and more than anyone else in the family, I look like him. I certainly drink like him. He used to hit the bars with his dog and stay out until my grandmother, out of frustration, would send my mother out to find him. He despised his wife, and I can't say I'm too fond of my grandmother either. She told me once I wasn't as good a person as my sister. That same day she took my sister aside and told her she wasn't as good a person as I am. Trying to pit us against each other.

My grandfather had a passion for gardening and for collecting exotic animals for his backyard zoo.

He eventually sold out his share in the grocery stores because he couldn't stand being in business with his relatives. Generally a back-stabbing, petty little bunch. That's when he joined the police force.

I'd say more but I haven't unpacked the dishes or silverware yet, and it looks like my hands will be very wrinkled today. I still have ten boxes of books that need to go up as soon as I clear enough space to put up my shelving.

Before I do anything, I'm taking a nap.

Dream about books. Probably a nightmare. When I wake up, I'll start working—while I'm at it I'll see if I can find the application and catalogues for school.

*   *   *

Now wouldn't an advertisement for <u>your</u> business make an impact if it occupied <u>this</u> space?

In the next edition of this book this space will be filled by an advertisement for the business of the highest bidder and is certain to be seen by thousands of people. Intelligent people. People with with money. People like you.

So don't delay. Send in your bid today to me,

                    Jackson Berlin
                    c/o this publisher

I'm kicking off my shoes and socks, rolling up my sleeves, lying back on the porch, staring at the clouds going by. Sometimes counting them, sometimes comparing them to familiar shapes.

I don't need to know what anything is. Just stay here relaxed. Something's bound to happen that'll force me to move. Wonder how long it'll take?

Right now this is comfortable. I can even concentrate on my breathing.

Winter's over. My weirdness is gone. My surroundings are pleasant. My roommates, my brother Stuartson and his girlfriend Angelique are cherished, long-time, tried-and-true friends.

Even_so, I enjoy spending time here alone. It is my way to find inner relaxation.

Enjoying the weather. A soft cushion.

I've been looking for this for a while.

Just sittin' back, dreaming, glad of where I'm at. I want to tell Stu and Angelique I love them both and that I'm very fortunate to be living with them. I feel more at ease around them than I do or ever have around anyone else. I want to thank them for being the best friends I've ever had.

I will. That cloud's a Picasso sculpture—an aerial view of a vagina by the Richard J. Daley Center.

Rorschach should be here now. Another cloud that looks like an erect penis penetrates the first cloud.

My God, I'm in trouble now. I've doubted you, and there You are, in the clouds. It's okay I just lie here and do nothing, isn't it? Charting the seas of wind. Listening to the peculiar arhythmic music of nature. A flock of switches. Bubbles of light. Dynamics among ushers. The lips of God. Cloaks of combined intertwined northern flowers. Tables and canyons.

The sixth hour depends on the finger of the number you want.

This is the closet in which I keep what baffles me. There is mystery, but it comes out of humans and is projected heavenwards. Is it right for a people to be dying of malnutrition and disease if it makes their thoughts more beautiful? Pain deepens us, comfort lightens us. Which is better? Loftiness is pretentious. Self-examination pathetically self-piteous. The ability to live both honestly and easily lies in the balance. To live in accordance with one's ideals separates one from one's reality. Ideals are the fantasy. Yet to live without these ideals is to condemn oneself to continual grimness. It is perhaps possible to use one's ideals as a key with which to interpret one's reality without actually trying to push it to change. Pushing the future inevitably gets me into trouble. Yet what is making decisions according to ideals other than pushing the future? To sit back and accept life as it comes, however, seems too comatose. See how I must strive to keep my balance?

Enough thinking.

Spent another night at Chad and Fran's. Met them at their pad. Had a few. With another friend of theirs we trucked over to Gaspar's to see friends of theirs—a neo-psych band from downstate.

Drank four or five pitchers and did some shots. The band cooked. Originals of course were as excellent as on their tape, which I've been listening to for weeks, but I particularly enjoyed their version of an old Arthur Lee tune.

The other two bands were okay. Musically the third was quite good but, even for my deaf ears, way too loud. Chad's friend got very drunk, grabbed Fran, gave her a long passionate kiss, pushed Chad away, sending his glasses flying, and split with some chick. I asked the soundman for a flashlight and eventually we found them. It's hard to find your glasses if you're not wearing 'em.

Fran and I danced ourselves silly, partially from my desire not to have to think about the volume of the music.

The last song of the night was a killer rendition of the 13th Floor Elevator's *You're Gonna Miss Me* and then the bouncers threw everyone out except the band because it was closing time.

Chad invited his friends in the first band over, and the party continued well past my falling asleep on the couch, occasionally waking to get "one more beer before I go." Eventually I left at 7:00. Slept till four the next afternoon.

*   *   *

Slipped into a routine which involves more time at home. I need to in order to save enough money to pay for the chapbook. I haven't been socializing much, nor hobnobbing, but I'm enjoying being with my roommates or alone in the apartment. Unpacking a little more, doing dishes, rearranging my room, listening to music, occasionally opening the manuscript in the hopes that I'll be able to work on it. Still have to cope with the day job and the Dionysus magazine and meetings with *Arts & Letters* and with my publisher Bering.

The Dionysus group got on my nerves the other night. Trying to get business done and them just fucking around and bragging about how well they fuck around. I closed the minutes and said that's it. I'd just spent ten minutes talking business to myself.

So I went over to married friend's and got drunk with her husband, who's also a writer of experimental prose, and had a great tequila conversation with him which led us out of the apartment with 3-D postcards and a two and a half hour trek to a Polish bar where no one understood English and we found it impossible to order specific drinks. When we returned to their apartment my married friend was upset with both her husband and me, so I went to sleep on the couch. She thought we'd ditched her. Hadn't meant to.

Chapter Two

Stuartson Berlin

Although we ride different porpoises and were hatched from eggs in different nests, Stuartson Berlin is indeed my brother. In thought, in word, in our hearts we know our brotherhood as though we were born into it. We ride through torrents of adversity and come out smelling like we've been sweating dirt, yet we maintain our poise and know enough to laugh at the problems of the past in order to improve the present. We share a certain ease with which our lives are led. The difference is, perhaps, he faces events as they come whereas I get anxious if they don't fall fast enough or quite where I want them to.

My brother is a charismatic man.

My brother is a visigoth.

My brother is the kind of man who gets things done while having fun.

He can fill a room in a way I can't define. People notice his presence.

So this chapter is about my brother. That's the dumbest thing I've ever written. Of course this is about my brother—the chapter's named for him. But it wasn't so bright my making a big deal out of this. Maybe I should just get back to my brother.

I met the man eight years ago. His wife and I were working together at a bookstore, and she introduced me to him. We hit it off immediately. We started partying together, saw eye to eye on most everything except college sports and polities. He prefers amateur football and I look at college as a training ground or perhaps even filter. We won't mention politics.

We have similar tastes in music—impeccable. His reaches back a little more and mine ahead but I don't mean that derogatorily. I enjoy a lot of the L.A. neo-psych stuff right now—especially Ada & the Evil Hearts. Glenn and John are excellent musicians, the astronauts of the band.

My brother works as the foreman in a body shop, is a black-belt in Kendo and former instructor, used to ride a Harley, plays golf, and enjoys wearing obnoxiously bright Hawaiian shirts with equally loud shorts. In many ways he's also the most complex person I've ever met.

Both of us have at many times sworn we'd take a bullet for the other.

A more steadfast friend I could never hope to meet. He takes the value of friendship seriously.

The years have put a little paunch on him but that's only because he knows how to drink and likes to cook good meals. Conveniently I like to drink and know how to eat good food.

He walks leaning forward on his toes, shoulder squared, chest out to meet the world. Sometimes he packs a handgun. He's put people in the hospital and has also been put there by other people. Usually my brother's a peace-loving guy, but don't push him past his limits of tolerance.

Stuartson Berlin. Where have you been?

His father's in Texas, his mother's in Pennsylvania. Both are remarried.

He's lived in Kenilworth, in Skokie, in Chicago, in Toronto, in Edina, in or around Pittsburgh.

Now he's my roommate. Again. We lived together for a short while when he first split from his wife. He's here with his girlfriend, who split from her husband. They're probably my closest friends.

And I'm heading out tonight to see Ada & the Evil Hearts at the West End. Should be a good show—maybe I can find someone to take along. Bring a copy of a manuscript to give to Ada.

They've cancelled twice before.

Hugh was there with Rain, embarrassing himself, telling her how much he loved her. I didn't feel like breaking in. Ada and band never showed—they were stranded (stoned?) in Pittsburgh. The Warm-ups had to play the gig by themselves. I had a few shots, a few beers, stayed a set, said hello to one of the Warm-ups I knew, and took a cab back home. Nice twenty dollar fare for the cabbie including tip. He seemed very pleased.

Stuartson's not here right now. All three of us keep ourselves very busy, and there are times we see each other briefly in passing. It's easier to tell if the others have been here if they've been eating beans. They're out drinkin' on Lincoln, and I'm grateful to have this time to myself.

Pardon me for a while. I've got to cut loose.

*   *   *

High-grade blank. Casual get-togethers. Flop-houses. Dreams of crawling away. How long must I keep this running game going? Where is the sea? What can I cover, fill, or surround? How sharp are the claws of an aardvark? Why am I asking these questions? Who am I? When will I know?

Sometimes I think my injuries show. I'm a chameleon. Constant change covers me, but it means I don't know who I really am. Other than a writer and even that grows ugly when I note the abhorrences produced by my colleagues. We all suck. All writers suck. All professional anythings are bull-shittin' everyone else into believing they're really any good at what they do. Even the most intense scholarship is rudimentary. How would you know a forest unless you've seen one? Or been one?

Would moss grow at your feet? Would you understand why I want you to ask yourself questions? Why are things the way they are? Can we change language enough to help move the world to a safer place, away from nuclear war? Who are you and I—two in billions? Why aren't there many others out here in experimental fiction land anymore? Not like they used to be? Or rather than using their brains in their creative act, the work itself, they utilize them for marketing strategies and determining salability and come out with a successful amount of nothing. I know I'm not easy to read. I'm trying to make that worthwhile. Thanks for being here so long—I know you don't know what all this could possibly be leading to, and if I had my outline, which unfortunately I misplaced during the move, I'd be able to put it together enough for you to get somewhere with it. You'll hopefully trust me for it for a while.

Summer classes are well attended by students of all genders. Special interest groups make it possible for you, Mr. Armchair Detective, to receive that gift of love within your hometown by someone you haven't met yet. Be off! And be sure to have a good time without having to worry, no, not at all. Sex camps with rigorous health inspections. So buy one today. And visit the neutron bomb plant where no one works anymore down near Normal. If I could only get rid of this coughin'.

*   *   *

My brother hangs out with cops. He's painting one's truck today.

My brother never reads my work. Wonder who does?

Burglars? Fretget it owl. Hugh was wrong about me. I may be a scumbag but I've sold quite a bit of my work over the years, albeit most of it boring non-fiction book and music reviews and interviews with musicians. However I have also managed to sell some poetry. Do you realize how hard it is to sell poetry, I mean for money? There can't be more than ten thousand people in this country who read it at all. Publishers of poetry are either philanthropic or poets themselves because little or no income can be earned from it unless they accept dole from the state or feds. In which case the work has to conform to certain government-regulated standards of what is "acceptable." I'm very much looking forward to seeing the chapbook and the novel both published. I'm going to take care of the chap's cover today. I got my tax refund yesterday. Three hundred copies color xerox two-hundred twenty-five dollars. I'd better head over there now. Wait—what about tax. Fuck. I'd better wait till tomorrow when my paycheck will be in the bank. Running out of time this morning anyway. I might head over to the Blackstone tonight to a party for an audiophile magazine I used to write for. I called an actress friend of mine, and she'll let me know today if she can get out of rehearsals for a night. I'll need some money for that. The copying'll wait till the morning. So long as I'm there 9:00 so I can be at work by 11:00.

I spoke with Melville over the phone last night. They're back. I congratulated him. He said the wedding went better than he could ever have dreamed it would and that it had been by far the best day of his life. He said he wished I'd been there. Yeah, I should have been there. All these things pull at me from all sides. I end up being wherever I'm pulled the hardest.

I also talked to my married friend. She said her husband wanted us all to get together. I suggested sometime next week. I have so much work that needs to be done I'm in the market for a cloning machine. God knows how much that would cost.

Never trust an artist while he's alive because you can't tell where he's going and he might be leading you astray even without perhaps realizing it himself. Evaluate his work when he's dead and safely gone having caused no harm.

I think I write with a mental limp. The pacing you see's not the pacing I seized. But I've already bored you with my true confessions—let's just get on with the story. What was it anyway?

Jackson Berlin writing about Hugh Moore writing about Jackson Berlin.

Got to get up, get out. Staying in place winds me down. Nothing fun unless in motion.

And give me an organized environment. Chaos implies human negligence.

What? Hell with that—a break from this up to the North Woods is what I need.

Angelique asked Stu if she could have a cat too. I've got three, Stu's got one. She says she's always wanted a kitten. An Angora, no less. Stu told her he'd buy her a sweater instead.

You can't teach a penguin to fly. Remember her? I was throwing away some old papers and kept encountering postcards and letters she wrote when she first fell in love with me. So I called her at work. We had a very friendly conversation devoid of disagreement until I asked her to have lunch with me sometime. She said she'd have to muse it over.

Onwards, forwards, anyone know where we're going? It's all a matter of keeping moving till we drop.

The spaceship opens above the lake and from it drop thousands of invertebrate paleontologists who've never had a drink in their lives. Clouds of psychiatrists darken the sky. Earth tremors are cause by proctologists. Mine has very small hands. Photos are taken by philosophers. Drinks are discussed by Dionysians. And whomever else they do. The path towards flight is but one and that is up. Putting a man on the moon is the greatest accomplishment we as a species have mustered. Makes us sound like hot dogs, what?

I picked up the covers for the chapbook. I found a printer for the body—not the cheapest but he impressed me with his efficiency and professionalism. I need to locate sheets of mylar today. I'll check out an art supply store, see what kind of thickness I need and then maybe buy it from a plastics warehouse.

Angelique, Stu and I had fresh lobsters for dinner with a couple of bottles of a nice French chardonnay, ears of corn, dinner salad, asparagus with hollandaise. We went out for after-dinner drinks. I had a few beers, a shot of tequila, a shot of bourbon, a shot of hundred-proof schnapps, and left in search of food. Found a couple of slices of pizza at some cheap scarfin' establishment and returned with them to the bar. The different boozes in me had me feelin' mean. I saw Angelique at the bar and asked her if she'd like a slice of pizza. She declined.

"Where's Stu?" I asked, looking around.

"He went out for a little with someone."

At this point I went off—the booze nasties speaking through me—causing a scene and accusing Stu of treating his own brother like a second-class citizen. Don't rightly know why. I was just in a weird mental space. Angelique tried to calm me, invited to join her in her conversation with her friends but I would have none of it and ate my pizza quickly before leaving without a word of farewell.

In the morning I knew I'd been unfair to Angelique and apologized to her several times. She asked only that I keep my conflicts with Stu between Stu and myself.

They're both off to work. I have the day free. Think I'll spend it at the zoo, meander aimlessly, overcome some of my lonely embarrassment. Take the 201 bus to the L and head south to Howard, transfer to the North-South and take that down to Fullerton and walk east. Beautiful stained glass windows in the old houses on Fullerton. Must be expensive to live there. But before I can leave, green seeps into the room under the door. The carpeting turns to grass. I think there are carnivorous insects crawling towards my naked feet. They get under my toenails and begin boring pathways into my body. The only solution open to me is amputation. I remove my feet and walk on my hands. The bugs get under my fingernails and dig tunnels into me. I sever my left hand and gnaw off my right but they get between my teeth and up my nose and I can feel them crawling around inside my brain.

*   *   *

Questionnaire for the Reader, pt. 1

Please send me your answers via this publisher.

1. Are you indoors? If so, describe the room you're in. If not, describe your outdoor setting.
2. What have you found most valuable in this book? What has annoyed you most?
3. What is your major concern in life?
4. Have you found the love you need?

5. Are you successful in your vocation?
6. Do you spend more time swimming with the current or against it?
7. Do you write poetry or fiction? If so please send me a sample to read.
8. What's your favorite book? Painting? Piece of music? Photograph? Building? Sculpture?
9. Do you prefer mountains, ocean, forest, desert, plains, or city?
10. Who do you think you are?
11. Are you happy?
12. Please write something obscure or nonsensical.

Your responses will not be used in my work without your express written consent.
*   *   *

Nothing seems to be happening to me anymore. A woman from the newspaper called me yesterday to ask me about the famous American LSD community emanating from San Francisco. She'd been given my name from the official publicist. I told her simply that I wasn't involved in the scene anymore, that I was a writer not a photographer as she'd thought, that I'd just sold a novel a few weeks ago, and that that was what I was concentrating on now. I recommended she get in touch with the penguin, who's still involved in the scene and took most of the photographs back when anyway. Have to give the reporter credit. She tracked me down after two moves in which I left no forwarding addresses with the post office and no forwarding phone numbers (which are unlisted anyway) and after four occupational changes. She's wasting her time on this light-weight frivolity. She'd be good doing investigative hard news.

I guess I withdrew because I got tired of smiling stupidly at everything that went down. That had become my response to everything. Someone would insult me. I'd smile stupidly. Rip off money from me. Smile stupidly. Steal my girlfriend. Smile stupidly. That's when I decided it's better to be a mean-ass motherfucker so that creeps'd think twice before burning me. I'd become too soft. Flushed the rest of the acid down the toilet and stopped smoking pot regularly. Started boozing more because that will turn anyone mean sooner or later.

Recently my drinking has come to concern me. I'm going to work this out also. Especially since I'm returning to school. I just sent in my application to the university where my father's on faculty and submitted my transcript requests to the five colleges I've attended so far and to my high school. I should be hearing from the admissions office soon. However, normalization seems, at least in some regards, to be detrimental to artistic development. It's as if art and life contradicted each other. Then again, perhaps not.

I'll visit my father this weekend for Father's Day. Get away from the city and relax out in Dubuque. Dubuque. Ya da da da da Da da da da Dubuque. Dubuque. I'll go out there with my sister and my brother-in-law and test again the town's atmosphere in preparation for my return to school. I lived there for six weeks a couple of years ago when the penguin waddled out of my life. At that time I found it relaxing albeit a bit dull. I didn't know anyone outside of family and was bored a lot of the time (a problem I've had since birth). My father had helped me piece myself together until I decided to return to Chicago. He had helped heal the stab wound in my back. I never knew penguins could wield weapons quite so large. Never underestimate anyone.

The bluffs ensnare me. The river winds its way into my psyche. I can feel the need to be away from the jaded frenzy of the city for a while. To be able to lie back in the grasses, miles away from everyone, watching the sky float by. Just me and my thoughts—the resimplification of my life. No one in my life but the reader, that evasive non-entity, the abstract god of the writer.

Back to school soon. Alone with my books in the country. Live with the other isolateds. A community of hermits. A society of the anti-social. We'll like it that way. You outsiders had better stay away.

I told Angelique I'm leaving soon, but not Stu. I don't know how to tell Stu. Angelique's probably told him anyway.

There are 836 dirty dishes in the sink, and none of them are mine.

They invited me along to the bar last night, but I wouldn't go. We'd have gotten into the bar and I wouldn't have seen either of them again all evening. Instead I went out with a couple of people from work, and we all shot pool. I won the penultimate game on a tough bank shot. Even my partner Oscar, a much better player than

I am, was impressed. He won the next game for us, but then the owner threw everyone out because it was closing time. We lost the table to time.

Work was tough the next day. But then it usually is.

The fern back here on the porch has a berry on it. Wonder what fernberries taste like. Probably poisonous. Just for show. If you can't eat it, it ain't worth a damn. Sounds like an oral fixation to me. Or a Frenchman. Ha ha.

Stayed in. Talked to, of all people, Mary's sister Caledonia. She's a very interesting woman. We're going to see Rodney Dangerfield's *Back to School* Saturday. It was released six days ago, and I've already seen it three times. It speaks to me in how I relate to my father, though the roles are perhaps reversed. Each time I see it, I get something else out of it. The first time, my sister and brother-in-law and I took my dad to see it out in Iowa. He thoroughly enjoyed himself. I laughed so hard I missed a lot. This I noticed the second time, when I payed attention to Rodney's acting and felt sad that he didn't seem healthy. The third time I noticed Lou's girlfriend.

Caledonia seems to like me. We spent an hour on the phone talking about food, sports, olympic novel-writing (wherein the ten best novelists from all over the world are given typewriters, paper, and fifteen minutes to do their best), her three-and-a-half-year-old son. I know I met her once in the bar where Mary used to work. Impressed me as a good-looking lady. She converses intelligently and listens to what's being said behind the words. I read a poem of hers recently. Very strong. It dealt with a former lover's brutalization of her. It sounds like she's seen some rough waters in her life. She might understand my need for dramamine. If calm waters lie ahead, I'll throw the extraneities overboard. Anyway, I don't expect she'll be judgmental. I'm certainly interested in positioning my person closer to hers. See what happens. She might understand my need to write.

Frightening dance. This is the fear I must face for love. Right? Hope so. Float along and test the waters.

Now there are 927 dishes rotting in the sink. Nine more and I'll do 'em myself. My cartoon of a smiley face with death crosses for eyes and a yuck frown for a mouth, with tongue stuck out, didn't communicate the dish problem sufficiently efficiently.

In today's mail I received a personal letter from Dubuque College's Director of Admissions. Looks like they want me. They have no idea what they're in for. Hope their English department survives. Maybe I should just stay away from it.

Went out and came back.

I really abuse time.

We had reasonably good fun out considering a 3½-year-old was with us all evening.

My roommates were great—they did all the dishes and cleaned the schiethüs before we returned from the movie. We talked, smoked some weed, and then Caledonia had to go. Don't know if I'll see her again. Probably will.

Nobody's a long time. That's Ken's.

Stu and Angelique are heading out today. Stu has to work on his car, his Austin-Healy, which he's rebuilding. Angelique's going along.

Going to try something different now.

What's most important is staying free.

We've been freed from having to lead lives that inevitably lead to crucifixion. Absorb, understand, then leave it behind. See something else.

Chapter Three

Liv, part one

I had a dream about a co-worker. I went to a party with her. After walking around a bit, Liv, that's her name, sat down between two men she knew at the long dining-room table. I went into the next room, where a crew of several unrolled a tarp over those of us just standing around with drinks in our hands.

It was my day off, so I woke up slowly, showered, forgot to shave, and decided to cruise down to Lincoln Park and meander through the zoo. Unfortunately it was raining heavily outside and the phone people were supposed to be by because Stu tripped over the phone cord twice and tore both jacks out of the wall. A ballerina he ain't. So I had to stay in, alternating coffee with beer. Mostly coffee. Hovered around all day, but Ma Bell, with her fucking responsible employees, never showed, and my day was shot to hell. I couldn't even go to the bathroom to scratch my balls for fear of missing 'em. Now it'll take another week before one of us is home all day to let 'em in to work on the phones. What with me expecting a very important call from the President of Burma and all. So at five o'clock I said a few choice words and headed out to a used bookstore where there was going to be a reading featuring poets from Wisconsin, Minnesota, and Illinois. Chad from *Arts & Letters* invited me. He and Fran were going to be there. I expected other writers I knew would be there too. Painters. Editors. Friends of the family. Drunks. Hooligans. My kind of folk.

When I got off the train at Belmont and approached the store, I spotted Huey D., probably the most successful young male poet in the city, hanging out in front of the store with his even more successful poet wife Annabelle Lee, talking to one of the Milwaukee poets.

"Huey! How've you been?" I shook his hand.

"Great. You?"

"Excellent, thanks. Can't wait till my book comes out."

"Bering's going to do my next collection, too."

"That's what I understand. That's super. I really trust him—he's a good guy."

"The last book he did impressed me."

"It was good."

"Looks like they're startin' in there."

"Yeah—I'd better head in and grab some wine before it starts."

"See you."

"Yeah."

Melville and Amanda were there. I congratulated them on their nuptials. I made my way to the four-liter jug of burgundy and poured myself a healthy glassful. Chad was in good spirits. Fran seemed a little removed, as did Melville. They're both unemployed right now, so I can understand. Not working, or rather, not having an income can be very draining. When I was living with the penguin, I lost my job, and the strain that put on our relationship never healed. She resented my freedom.

The poets and their poems were interesting. Their styles not only of writing but of reading varied greatly. I was amused, bemused, confused, infused. The Milwaukee poets were the youngest, least established of the poets. The big name Illinois poet read last and impressed me most.

A Minnesota editor gave away chapbooks of many of the poets' works.

After the reading we stopped at Chad's for a few. Several of us then went over to Huey's, where the party and conversation continued and the imbibing continued with beer. I fell into a long discussion with Huey and Annabelle and a Duluth poet about small press magazines.

Huey ended the party at midnight, and the more stalwart among us headed out in search of more beer: three Milwaukee poets (an attractive blonde, a guy with his pants tucked into tall boots, another guy who's reading of the last of his poems had sent shudders up my spine), one of their friends (a small dark-haired woman named Donna who wore black leather and long hair in a smoot) and me. The first bar we found was a gay bar on Clark Street. That did not hinder our approach.

"Do you know what kind of bar this is?" asked the Milwaukee poet of the tucked pants.

"Yeah—one with beer," I replied.

I ordered a round of beers for my friends and asked for my change in quarters. Donna and I fed the pinball machine. I was too drunk to play well. She beat me game after game. Eventually the poets got bored and wanted to head back to Milwaukee. The poet in boots said, "Come on, we'll drop you off on the way."

"I live pretty far north," I replied.

"Not as far north as we do."

"Milwaukee? That's true. You know Milwaukee's the only place in the world I've ever seen a bar that opens at seven in the morning and closes at seven at night."

"That's Milwaukee." On the walk to the car Donna took my hand.

The blonde was driving so I gave her directions to my apartment. I sat next to Donna in back. I held her right hand in mine. I put my left arm around her and held her left thigh.

As we approached my apartment I asked her to stay the night with me. She looked at me shyly and shook her head. I asked her to come up for a while. She said no with a very pretty smile that made me want to dive headfirst into her world. I gave the blonde directions to the 94 and stumbled up to bed.

When I woke up, I called Chad. I realized I'd left the chapbooks at his apartment. I asked him about Donna, but he didn't know who she was. I'd like to see her again, but I have to find her through the Milwaukee people. I'll have to examine their chapbooks. I don't even know Donna's full name. I can't even be certain her name was actually Donna. My head hurts, but for a moment there I felt some life in my heart, and I know she put it there.

Maybe if I don't force it, I'll run across her again sometime anyway. Keep moving forwards.

Head back down to Chad's and Fran's in a few days. Bottle of German sparkling Riesling and three for five Yugo wines again, another bag of sliders, shooting the shit out of other writers and praising the honest ones. Discuss the reading, share each other's work. I need a Chad story for Dionysus. Fran's new painting is very strong. Her poetry, too. Donna's name is really Sue. Picked up all the chaps and litmags I'd left over. The more I see of these two the more I like them. They're straightforward and honest. I need their friendship, especially now that my roommates are hassling me all the time, pondering expelling me because they think my cats smell funny. Well shit, I clean the box a couple of times a day and change it about every three.

When I get home at 2:30 A.M. Stu and Angelique are waiting up for me. We hammer out some kind of agreement over a few beers and a toke and a line but I don't suppose there's any solution other than my moving to school ASAP.

Mary called. Caledonia's boyfriend, whom I never heard about before, died this weekend off an eighth floor window.

Liv's boyfriend's father's in intensive care at the hospital for brain tumors. He's got six months. Liv's bent out of shape. I understand. I've spent a few days in I.C. before and was also suspected of a tumor (which turned out not to be a cause of my weirdness at all).

Liv's wonderful. We fly sexual innuendoes at each other. Today was the fourth of July. I wore a red-and-white striped shirt with my blue jeans. Told Liv I dressed patriotically for the occasion. She asked about my underwear. I showed her it was blue. My socks too. Told her I had stripes in my shirt and my star's in my pants. She said "I don't doubt it." I enjoy just being near her. My balls are in her court if she wants them.

It's good to know I can come in and find her completely bummed and by the end of the day have her in a really good mood despite how hard recent events have been on her.

A third note of tragedy—the man who brought by our paychecks every week died a couple of days ago of a heart attack.

My glasses broke, and I had to spend seventy bucks for new frames. The family dog's passing out walking and pissing in his sleep.

Grim days. That's why I'm hiding out alone for Independence Day and not concerned with crowds of firework watchers. I'd rather try to fill another sheet of paper with strange little marks.

I was supposed to meet someone down at the zoo today, but I'm not going.

I'm going to sit outside in the heat in my mother's backyard and do a few loads of laundry while I'm there.

My mother's a nice old German lady. The only time I remember her causing anyone harm was in the final days of the War Between My Parents, an historical event that inflicted injury on all those who touched it, as any failing relationship (including mine with the penguin) does. My mother fixed me lunch and told me to go lie down on some lawn furniture (oh no!) in back. She said she'd do my laundry for me. I accepted her sweet offer and fell asleep as the sun shone down from directly overhead.

When I awoke, the sun had moved a third of the way toward the horizon. I had had a dream, which I immediately wrote down so as not to forget.

I was working my first day alone after my apprenticeship at a restaurant that looked like a deli and was owned by the liquor store I used to be a driver for. A regular customer, Ewen, came in and ordered a roast beef sandwich. I checked a list of ingredients and started making his sandwich the way he wanted it, with lots of mayonnaise (which was salmon-colored) and tomato and lettuce. There wasn't any roast beef in the refrigerator so I went around to the kitchen and requested some from the cook.

"Do we have any roast beef?" I asked.

"No, we don't sell it," he replied smart-assedly.

"Just get me some," I retorted and walked away. In a few minutes I returned and there was one slice of roast beef on a plate waiting for me. I took it back to my area and continued assembling the sandwich.

Ewen told me he knew someone who knew me and was a friend of my father's.

The name was unfamiliar to me. I conjectured that perhaps it belonged to a man I met in Europe who, after not even two minutes of conversation with me, had said, "You must be Emerson Berlin's son."

Ewen said my father was in this man's new movie. We left immediately to go see it at the theater next door. It proved to be a partially on film, partially live lecture my father was giving. It was difficult to hear what he was saying because the people around me were very loud. Ewen kept babbling to my left. Someone behind me was snoring. I looked over my right shoulder and three fraternity louts were laughing and talking among themselves, not paying attention. I punched the nearest in the knee.

"Stop snoring. Shut up. That's my father. I want to hear what he's saying."

"It wasn't me," he said, pointing to the seat to his left, the one directly behind me, in which the culprit snorer was slumped down asleep. I punched him also.

My father was on one knee on stage, smiling and making an exaggerated vertical circular gesture with his flatly extended right hand. It seemed he was hamming it up for the film. He was funny, seemingly a natural for the movies. What he was talking about wasn't light-weight stuff either. Something like the theology of astrophysics. I don't know. It was hard to tell.

After the lecture scene I returned to the restaurant, where a few orders had backed up for me, including one for boiling pots and supplies for the delivery department, but no one was sitting in my section so I set about resuming the construction of Ewen's sandwich. It had disappeared. This worried me greatly, but finding Ewen, I found that he had taken it upon himself to finish making it and was eating it hungrily.

*   *   *

I mailed financial aid transcript forms to my old schools today. Then I called Dubuque to ask them for an aid application.

"What's your name?"

"Jackson Berlin."

"Oh. We were just going to mail your acceptance letter. I'll just enclose one with that."

"Great. Thanks a lot."

It looks like I'm going.

"One thing, sir."

"Yes?"

"On your application you asked for Spring admission in '87. Would you prefer that or Fall of this year?"

"Uh—Let's push it up to Fall."

"Certainly. I'll just change your application."

"Thank you very much."

"You're welcome."

It's raining again. Otherwise I'd be at the zoo. One of these days. Christ, I only have two months left.

*   *   *

Went to a bar after work with Liv and her friend Selena, shooting pool, drinking shots.

Writing about my love contaminates it somehow. But how can I work out what's in my head so I don't have to carry a heavy heart unless I commit it to paper?

Selena saw how I felt towards Liv, but I can't write about this because Liv has a boyfriend and she wavers between loving me and barely tolerating me according to her situations and mine.

//: Am I beginning to sound like a man with a repetition compulsion? *://*

I've known her for eight months and have known how I feel towards her for quite a while. But how can I speak? I tried to today, but she wouldn't hear it. My timing is atrocious. Her boyfriend's father's in the hospital dying. How can I expect her to think about me? I guess I don't. I'm glad I'm leaving. I'd ask her along, but she probably couldn't up and go. She won't talk about it either. Love's great deaf-mute. Yet I know she knows it's there.

Let's change the subject.

There's a glowing purple worm in the belly of the earth.

Whoever stands the most to lose does.

Made a bit of a dog's breakfast of this, I'm afraid.

I feel like a china doll in a bull shop.

I went to visit Chad tonight. Chad told me one of my pieces will be in their next issue, a special on dementia. The implications of representing the demented worry me.

Fran was in Florida with her family. Chad and I got drunk and talked about writing and writers and ourselves.

The next morning I left for Dubuque for the weekend to see my father and step-mother, to talk to people at the college, to begin my emotional transition from the frenzy of Chicago to the scenic quietude of Dubuque.

I called Liv long distance, but she didn't sound pleased with me. Perhaps she feels I've backed her up against a stucco wall. When I return to work on Monday, I'll let her know I'm leaving, that I pose no lasting threat. That I have deep feelings for her. That I think we could do well by being together. But that I don't want to upset, disrupt, or interfere. I'll ask her to come along. At least she'll know I cared. Maybe not all of this at once. I'll start with I'm leaving. See how she reacts.

I was introduced to the president of the school by my father. It really seems to me they want me there. I'd rather be welcomed than abided.

Keep moving, keep changing, keep going. Motion tells you you're alive.

Once in Dubuque, I'll seek the quiet of my soul. This frenzied madness can't last forever, especially when I distance myself from its source, the bee-hive, the ant-colony, bumper-car life in the city. I must go, and I know I must go alone. It may be my fear of transition that attracts me so greatly to Liv, and she does right to resist.

I wish I had the day off tomorrow. I'd spend it at the zoo. My boss knows I'm leaving Chicago. Maybe I can get him to let me off on Wednesday.

*   *   *

Walked into the store, and Liv was at the register. I said hello, and she said hi. I asked how she was, how her morning was going. She said okay, fine.

When I noticed she was away from the register and someone else was up there, I asked her if she had a minute. She said sure. We went and sat down in the office.

"Yeah, what do you want?" she asked, abrupt because abrupt is her style, and I like that in her.

"I'm leaving in five weeks."

"Five weeks?" I'd taken her by surprise, as expected.

"Yeah—I went out and talked to the people at the school, even the president of the whole goddam college and it looks like they really want me there."

"It sounds like it'll be good for you. Wish I could get away from here."

"Yeah. Well, I explain it like this. It's the difference between a vocation and an occupation."

"Vocation?"

"From Latin, *vox,* voice, meaning it's a calling, something I'm called to do, which is what writing is for me. I know I'm going to make it because what all my decisions come down to is whether or not they're good for my career. As opposed to an occupation, which is something that fills time. My occupation for the last ten years has been as a bookseller."

"I understand."

"Don't tell anyone I'm leaving, okay? I don't want anyone to know until two weeks before."

"That's all you owe 'em. Plus if you told 'em they'd let you go early."

"Exactly, and I'm not ready to go yet." I told her the only people who knew who were associated with the store were Lemmy the manager, Liv's friend Selena, and her.

"She knows?"

"Yeah. If I seem to be in a funk over these next few weeks it's because I'm sad at having to leave."

"Why?"

"I really like this place."

"*This* place?"

"Well, not so much this, definitely not the owners, but the people here. I like them all. Especially Lemmy and you."

"Well, don't tell anyone this, but I've heard rumors."

"What rumors?"

"That they're going to sell this place. But don't tell anyone because everyone'd quit, probably."

"Be let go then anyway, most likely."

"Probably."

"No, I won't tell."

"Jack, I've got a lot of work to do. Anything else?"

"No," seeing her stand up I added quickly, "other than I want to go out with you."

"You shouldn't have said anything. You know that's impossible."

"Well, I had to speak my mind and let you know how I feel."

Judging the way the rest of the day went I'm glad I spoke. She was flattered, I could tell. Attracted, also, but involved in this heavy scene that stopped it. For now. I'll bring it up again in a few weeks and maybe ask her along then. Meanwhile we're getting along very well and the tension has eased for having spoken.

Lemmy said it was all right for me to take the day off tomorrow. I told him it was for my writing. He's a painter. He understood.

I'm finally going to the zoo.

Chapter Four

We Meet Up Again

Trip to Zoo, Wednesday, July 16, 1986

I'm waiting at Howard for the train to get moving. It's about ninety degrees outside today and should get up near ninety-four by afternoon. On the train it's in the hundreds. One guy across the aisle from me is mumbling "it's too hot" repeatedly. I came prepared. I'm wearing nothing but sneakers, swim trunks, cut-off jeans, a Chicago Cubs floppy hat, and a t-shirt with a pocket to hold my cigarettes. I had to help a couple different people with the trains. One wanted to know which train stopped at Wilson. Another if this one stops at Belmont. Easy enough. My floppy hat must make me look expert, a prime candidate for questions about Chicago's transit system.

I feel light-headed from the heat and from not having eaten. When I get off at Fullerton, I'll grab a quick hot dog and drink at the stand downstairs.

But it isn't raining, and I'm glad I'm finally going to the zoo. Spend a day relaxing outdoors, keeping a running account in a miniature note pad I picked up on the way.

They charge five cents each for extra packets of ketchup at the hot dog place. I find that rather greedy on their part, but the food's good and I don't use ketchup on fries anyway.

On the way to the zoo I stop at a used book store on Lincoln where a friend of mine works. Say hello and find a novel by Kenneth Patchen I have't seen before. I don't have enough money on hand, so I ask her to hold it for me and continued on my way.

First stop, the conservatory. It's extremely humid in here, which makes breathing quite difficult.

I'm sitting on a bench looking at Artillery Pilea Cadierei and other unlabeled plants and flowers. A couple of cute girls ask me to take their picture for them. I enjoy their smiles through the viewfinder. I've got to move on now—I'm beginning to run in sweat.

Inside the zoo the first animals I see are pigeons, of course. The compound they occupy no doubt hosts some large animal which has been brought indoors because of the heat.

The black rhino is enjoying his mud pool.

The baringo giraffes, who seem quite content with the heat, are munching on grass in a tall basket and on leaves that are attached to trees by wire catchers.

The capybaras, who share a compound with a tapir, have recently had a litter or two.

The pygmy hippo hides in the shade.

The arctic and antarctic seabird house is reasonably cool. I have to wait for a large group of day camp kids to pass by, but I finally find a seat to watch the penguins from. I always feel some sadness when I see anything to do with penguins, but this is still my favorite part of the zoo. I should find out when feeding time is and come back then.

Sea lions at two, great apes at three, lions at four, no mention of penguins. Oh well.

The arctic birds are off display for some reason. Too bad. I've always enjoyed seeing the puffins.

The female humans are scantily clad. This exhibit I enjoy tremendously. You know you're getting older when the camp counselors are all substantially younger than you.

A spectacled bear cub is frolicking, just born January 14th. A passing mom misinforms her daughter that it is a speckled bear.

I have to get back indoors. The first building I come across is the small mammal habitat. Geoffrey's cat reminds me of mine. The armadilloes beat a path in their cage by running the same track over and over, much like grand prix racers. A sixteen-year-old blonde is stroking her crotch in front of the fruit bats.

Outside, the kids are getting restless. There must be several hundred here today, and together they make a lot of noise. More chattering than monkeys. Back inside, the blonde is still stroking herself.

For the most part the great apes are fat and lazy, enjoying their noon siesta.

A man says to his son, "There goes the big bad camel."

The sun's starting to get to me. It's a quarter to two. I'll find the sea lions to see them feed and then maybe head home. I've done pretty well to avoid large masses of kids. Feeding time should be a mess, though.

Cruise past the flamingoes, get to the seal and sea lion pool, but it is drained because one of the animals has medical problems and the zookeepers need to be able to get to it easily. The animals slide around in the constant fountain waters, but their feeding is not nearly as amusing as it is when the pool is full.

I am climbing down the benches from my vantage point in order to leave and run into someone I know from a long time ago, a semi-fictitious depressive named Duncan Rivers.

"You're still alive, I mean, how've you been, Duncan?"

"Lousy."

Figures.

"Well, couldn't say things've been too great for me either. You've lost some weight."

"Should. I'm bulimic."

"Oh, man. Did you have to bring that up?"

"I have trouble keeping it to myself."

"What, you work up an appetite by watching the feedings?"

He begins to look uncomfortable, furtively glancing about for the nearest escape route.

"Looking for the can?" He is shocked I've noticed the movement of his eyes.

"No. Look, I don't feel well, Jackson. I'd better go."

"Yeah. Guess what? I finally sold a novel. Should be out within the year. Also I'm heading back to school to get an art degree."

"Great. Look, I'd like to stay and talk but I got to go. Bye."

He hurries towards the can, or maybe the concession stand.

A quick stop in the primate house, then I'm going to have to go home.

In the primate house I spot Hugh. I don't see Rain, though.

I wave. He waves back. I approach him. He approaches me.

There's a sign above his head: HUMAN, Homo Sapiens.

There's another sign to the right:

> You are looking at the most dangerous animal in the world, the human animal. It alone, of all the known animals, can and continues to exterminate entire animal species. Unless the human animal changes its attitude towards the environment, this waste and destruction will continue. What will you do to change this?

Hugh's mouth forms words silently as I greet him. He hands me a sheet of paper. I read it.

Something About Mice—a story by Hugh Moore

No measure of mouse contained Cairo. Nothing could. He was not like the others. He avoided where they congregated. He stayed away from them as much as possible. They confused him. He wanted peace and could not find it near the others. It required his dedication to it. Avoidance of conflict gave him the illusion he was at peace. He settled for this and withdrew.

Alone at night he began burrowing an escape tunnel to lead him far away from the others. He wanted to see alien sights and far away horizons. He wanted to go sailing through the universe. Tried to find the way. As he dug into the earth he removed himself from it.

He came across an aspirin and shoved it down into the hole. He'd burrow till he felt sore or hungry, take a bite of aspirin and continue with his project. He burrowed for days.

Eventually his path led him to a small seed buried just below the surface. The seed sprouted and Cairo was to see it grow instantly into a flower, which, having blossomed, wilted and fell into a small stream of rain run-off and floated away.

The sun's gotten to me. That's not Hugh. It's a mirror. It looks like Hugh. It is Hugh. It's me. I'm Hugh and Hugh is me and we are both together. Sometimes I'm him, othertimes not. Sometimes I'm Jackson. Othertimes I'm others. The development of multiple personalities is a risk among certain types of artist. Puppeteers predominantly. Fiction writers too. We have to project ourselves into our characters and they are all us. But not all of us is them.

It's a perplexing proposition. To be pondered as I leave the zoo. I end up at the bookstore the penguin manages. She's not there, but I have a good conversation with her first assistant, who's a friend of Chad's and Fran's, and with her second assistant, a very attractive blonde whom I lusted after during my days with the penguin.

I invite them both to a combined farewell and chapbook release party at the end of next month. I explain the circumstances of my leaving, and they agree that it is best for me to take advantage of this arisen opportunity.

A friendly goodbye to them both, flirtatious with the blonde, whose musical name is Minuette.

Home on the CTA with a/c broken, of course.

*   *   *

I called Rain last night. Said I wanted to see her before I left. She'll call back later. My married friend came over tonight with her husband, my fellow experimental fiction writer. This guy could make it. He seems talented, determined, and *hungry.*

We drank tequila and shot off bottle rockets until the neighbor complained.

Next day's tough. Liv's decided she's better off treating me like dirt. Not only have I lost what love she felt for me, but her friendship as well, all for telling her I want to go out with her.

Don't look for logic in the ways of a woman.

I expect her at this point to inform my bosses that I intend to leave. Never should have trusted her.

It's supposed to get up to ninety-nine degrees today. Good thing the store's air conditioned. 'Bout the only good thing. Stayed twelve hours yesterday just to be cool.

Work hard, drink hard, sleep hard.

No wonder I want to get out. I need a way away.

I talked with Liv. She promised not to disclose my leaving. I guess I'll have to trust her.

The expense of moving again so soon is beginning to concern me, but it will be done one way or another.

The heat's finally broken. I'm eager to leave. Anxious soon.

When I got my new glasses, the woman who fitted me started laughing when someone else across the store had a severe coughing fit.

"It's not funny," she said. "My ex-husband coughed so hard once his false teeth went flying in this bar we were at, and we were both crawling around on our hands and knees underneath tables looking for 'em."

Reminded me of Chad and his glasses. An odd little coincidence.

I'm going to leave early today. I want to go sell my San Francisco sixties psych scene album collection, almost my entire library of music by America's most popular LSD cult religion rock band. I haven't listened to them in almost two years. I doubt I'm going back that way again. I have to let my own feet do my own walkin'. I feel this is a significant break from the past and from sentimental attachment thereto.

I called the penguin and asked her if she wanted any before I sold them. She's still involved in that world. She asked me to set aside six and I told her I'd sell them to her for fifteen bucks and that I'd be by on Thursday.

I got ninety bucks for the other forty albums plus ten bucks' worth of trade.

Bought chopped steak, canned corn, and a can o' peas for dinner and two different types of 1985 Piesporter Michelsberg Riesling Kabinett to compare 'em with each other. These Mosel wines tend towards sweetness, but I enjoy them anyway. They don't compare with the Neuchatel, which particularly pleases my palate, but I can't find it anymore, and if I could it'd run upwards of twenty dollars a bottle.

Opened my mail. Said in a letter from the island folk that 'less I weird it out they'll take 'way my 'sperimental fiction license. Tell me to leave the community, which, of course, I already have. But they don't know that. So, to really fuck 'em, I'll do it, but not for their glory, oh no, not for their glory, but for the sake of having fun. Chomping for culture with a typical teenager singing the famed world barren but for operating in an age procession with the lone woman client and the middleman.

"It's not funny," she said. "My ex-husband coughed.

"I think he just treats me like a piece of property.

"But I've caught a cold and spent all day in bed drinking.

"Your presence is important to me.

"But wait!" and I remembered my teacher's comments exactly:

"Latin is a dead language spoken in tongues of verbiage and maudlin as a slab of ghosts who reenter the bar and order a couple of beers."

Be tweenya wanta.

"Anyone here own that?"

Chinks missing in the wall.

Flaw out.

I've seen pigeons and sparrows picking at the bodies of processed cousins—fast food chickens discarded to the street—and I wonder if there's a lesson to be learned about humanity here.

Have you lost your sense of humor, too?

Flogs cloak darkness with screens. Took another day off, ordered and paid for the mylar (a hundred thirteen dollars and sixty-three cents). Stopped by my friend's tore, took her out for coffee, and bought the Patchen novel she'd set aside for me. Stopped by the penguin's store. Both she and Minuette were working. Minuette was looking great in a tight yellow t-shirt and a soft black sun-dress. I wanted to touch her. I felt too awkward to display interest with the penguin there, to whom I sold the six albums. As I've mentioned, she's still in the scene, now looking more like an emperor than a rock-hopper. Conversation was stilted between us, but not without politeness. I smiled goodbye to the blonde and reconfirmed my invitation to her for my farewell party. I went downtown to pick up my sister at the Sears tower, where she works. We had dinner and went to see *Pirates,* the new Roman Rolanski movie starring Walter Matthau. Matthau's best role, I thought.

I'm trying to see as many people as possible before I leave in order to overdose on socializing because I know it'll be a while until I make new friends in Dubuque.

Chapter Five

Liv, part two

I sniff her moccasins and kiss them to know that she was here.

I just got in the door last night from a Dionysian meeting when the phone rang. It was Liv.

"I have to see you."

"When?"

"How long would it take you to get here? I'm at Loyola Beach."

"I don't know. Thirty or forty minutes on the el or ten or fifteen if I take a cab."

"I'll split the cost of the cab."

"Be right there."

The ride was fast and, before I knew it, I was sitting on a bench alongside her. She was talking about my asking her out and so forth. Thought I'd arrest the conversation by kissing her.

Her friends were nearby, but she said we could be open in front of them.

Li v and I talked through our feelings for each other. She explained her love for her boyfriend.

"I really do love him," she said."

"I never said you don't," was my reply.

I told her I loved her.

She said it was like.

I said no I don't think just that.

The cops came by and told us the park was closed and asked if we'd seen any gang types as they were expecting a clash between rival gangs just then just there.

We left, and I convinced Liv, Selena and her husband Rollo and Liv's best friend Sandra to come over to my apartment, and we could sit out on the porch and shoot off bottle rockets. I brought my radio out back, put it on softly, Sandra went to the bathroom, and Stu barged out of his room, pissed as hell.

"Can I talk to you?"

"Excuse me, Liv. Be right back."

He took me aside and began giving me shit about he and Angie having to wake up at five for a fishing trip.

"This won't work," were his exact words.

"Fine," I said. "I've brought friends over twice in the last three months and you've blown me shit both times about it. We'll leave. But as far as I'm concerned that's the end of our friendship/brotherhood/whatever."

Angelique came out of hiding that moment to insert her wisdom. "We told you we had to get up."

"It's Friday night for one thing and no one said anything about tomorrow morning to me."

"Stu says he did. I did too."

"Well, then, both you and Stu are wrong."

"Fuck you. Get out of here by tomorrow, asshole." She always did have a way with words. The door to their bedroom slammed.

"Come on," I said to my friends. "Let's get out of here. My roommates are being real assholes."

We went to Rollo's and Selena's.

"I left my shoes at your place, Jackson."

"It's all right. I'll bring 'em to work."

"No, it's not all right. How'll I explain this to my boyfriend? He's probably waiting up for me."

"Tell him you were with us," said Selena. "You were."

Sandra passed out on the bed.

Rollo and Selena started fooling around in the bathroom.

Liv took the initiative. "Stay in there, Selena," she said, handing me a prophylactic.

I undressed her, then myself, unrolled the condom tip down onto myself, and we made love on the bed next to the sleeping Sandra. Long love. Slow love. All the beer I'd had didn't hamper my ability to get it up, only my ability to get it out. We went until we tired. She was pretty drunk, too.

I'd masturbated earlier in the day and that may have affected me. I told Liv this and apologized. She didn't seem bothered. What was beautiful was looking into her eyes and being inside her, knowing there was no finer place on the planet. I told her so. I might not be leaving quite as soon as I'd thought.

She said she didn't want me to go, but that I should return to school for my own sake.

We kissed and held each other. I love you, I said. I really do.

*   *   *

A sadness has overtaken me. I haven't spoken with Liv since Friday night and now it's Sunday. I had to work today. Sandra stopped by and seemed distant, but then, though she was closest, she was farthest away. Rollo and Selena worked across the street at a restaurant. I stopped by for coffee, and they were both very friendly. Rollo smiled at me as only a man, knowing the situation, could. But what about Liv? I don't want to call in case her boyfriend answers. Her boyfriend's sister, who's married to a cop, answers. Great. I tell her we've been having problems with a woman customer, who spends hours in the store every morning, calling the police on another customer and that that's what I need to talk to Liv about. I leave my number, which may have been a mistake, and word for Liv to call me when she gets in.

Angelique's in the hospital. She had a grand mal seizure on the boat yesterday. The doctor says it was brought on by severe sleep deprivation, which makes me feel a little guilty. She went into convulsions and pushed her front four bottom teeth out of her mouth with her top teeth and began vomiting blood. A friend of theirs, a nursing student, was fortunately aboard and helped as much as possible. Angelique's stable now and out of serious condition. I'm going to visit her tomorrow. I apologized to Stu for my anger and explained that my verbal attack on him stemmed from my fear of screwing up my closeness to Liv. I told him of the love Liv and I'd shared. He understood and everything's all right between us. I sent my best to Angie with him.

It seems like craziness has found me once again, however. Peace continues to elude me. Confusion's running rampant. Life won't let me settle down. Won't even let me sleep. It's the middle of the night. I'm going in to work early tomorrow on my day off to see Liv. She never called me back. Did she tell her boyfriend? Had she had a hard weekend? Is she feeling remorse? Or was she just out and didn't get back early enough to call? Was my call a tactical mistake? Why can't I sleep? Why can't I get her out of my mind? What in god's name am I in for tomorrow morning? Why is life so hard? Will we be together again? These questions are driving me nuts. There is no easy love.

Sleep forces itself onto me for a couple of hours. I set the alarm for seven, when the store opens, so I can call her as soon as possible.

"Hi. Guess you know who this is."

"Morning. How are you?" There was love in her voice.

"Not too good. You?"

"It's Monday."

"Yeah. How are you feeling?"

"Weird."

"You say anything?"

"No. Think I'm crazy?"

"No. I won't say anything either."

"Better not."

"I won't. I'll just deny everything."

"Huh?"

"I've got to come by there today. Can I buy you lunch?"

"Can't."

"Oh. It's my day off. I could meet you somewhere."

"Fred's supposed to be by."

"Oh."

"My friend Lucy's in the hospital. She's going to have her baby."

"That's great."

"Not necessarily. She's sick, and they're worried about complications. I may have to go out there sooner than I thought."

"Jesus. What a weird weekend. Angelique's in the hospital too. She had a grand mal seizure and pushed out her front teeth. It was all brought on by sleep deprivation. That was one reason she snapped at me like she did the other evening."

"Yeah?"

"You get my message?"

"What message?"

"I called last night."

"Where? My house?"

"Yeah."

"Who'd you talk to?"

"Your sister-in-law."

"My sister-in-law?"

"I mean your sister."

"You mean Fred's sister." We both chuckled.

"Yeah. I told her I was calling you to warn you about a

problem out front. Which is a reason I'm calling, but mostly I just wanted to hear your voice. I've been thinking a lot about you."

"Yeah?"

"When can we get together?"

"I don't know."

"Well, thanks for Friday. I'm glad you called me. I've got to come by anyway to talk to Lemmy about the paper count. The new system's not working."

She laughed.

"Maybe we can talk a little then," I suggested.

"Yeah, but don't be surprised if I act weird."

"Okay. Let me tell you about out front. There's a problem with Jo."

"Why, what's she done?"

"She called the cops on Fat Bill to prevent him from buying his papers at the store."

"She can't do that."

"You're right. And he's really pissed. He'll be coming in with a full head of steam to talk to Lemmy later. Just let him handle it."

"No problem."

"I just wanted to let you know because Jo's your friend."

"She's not my friend. She's just a weird chick who hangs out out front."

"Good. Because we may end up having to ban her from the store. I'll have to have a talk with her."

"Be careful what you tell her."

"Yeah. I already heard about her fits."

"Really. Make sure she's sitting down."

"I will."

"I've got to go, Jack. I have to get the news bills ready for the drivers."

"Okay. Well, I'll see you a little later on."

"Okay."

"Bye."

"Bye."

*   *   *

I brought a gift of a bag of chocolate kisses to work for Liv, and a card "For You" that on the outside read "Kiss Pet Pluck," on the inside "So much for foreplay. Let's fuck." I signed it "Love, me."

She thought it amusing but couldn't take the card home, so I kept it.

It was difficult to talk to her with her brother there and Lemmy and other folks. Eventually I went across the street and called from the restaurant. At least that way we had a chance to talk.

The weirdness and remorse had set in. I have to allow her to have these. She'll naturally waver. She said she made a mistake Friday night, that it shouldn't have happened. I know she doesn't feel that way. It's guilt for having, for the first time, shared love with someone other than Fred. This is the time for me to muster together all the patience and gentleness I hold. She needs me in her life and is afraid of that.

I offered to take her to lunch when Fred didn't show, but she preferred not taking lunch at all.

I left to go see Angelique at the hospital. She looks much younger with her teeth missing, but seems in good spirits. I brought her a couple of carnations I picked up at the gift shop on the way in. Stu was there and gave me a ride home.

I called Liv on the phone and told her she was beautiful.

She said I was hallucinating.

I told her no, I wasn't. I'm not. I hope I have the patience for this. Deferment of my admission to Dubuque seems necessary to give this the nurturing it needs to blossom.

I asked her to call me tonight if she remembered. She said she'd remember but she might not be able to because Fred was living with her now.

I understood.

*   *   *

Dear Liv,

Do me a favor. Whatever happens between us now, whichever way we go, do not look with regret or remorse on our having been together. The love we shared was honest, it was right, and it was holy. It was meant to be because we've been drawn together by forces stronger than either one of us alone. There is indeed a chemistry between us that attracts us to each other. You know I'm speaking the truth here. That chemistry is manifested in our common sense, our common desires, our common dreams. The North Woods. Freedom. Family. We both are overly sensitive and prone to depression, so we compensate by looking for and finding fun. I think we need each other. You say I don't know you. I do. I've been watching you and learning you for eight months. I know your weaknesses and strengths, as you know mine. Even secrets you think you've hidden well about what's inside your heart, I know. And I know you can read my mind. I think we'd make a powerful combination with a sense of both purpose and direction as we grew closer still to discovering the other, shell fragment by shell fragment, hope by hope, hurt by hurt. I want to be that close to you.

Moreso, I trust you with my heart. Your wavering now shows your sensitivity, your faith, your difficulty in causing another human being to hurt, even though you know eventually someday somewhere somehow you're going to have to break free because it's not what you need. You can't even negotiate anymore. You're trapped and you don't know how to get out.

I can say this because I know. I won't push you, but I'll help you if you ask me to. However, it must be your decision where or when to go. That "Where" needn't even be with me, but I'd still help you free because I've come to love you deeply. Enough so to want to see you ecstatic and fulfilled. And to want to be there to see it because you could make the world glow.

You are beautiful, Liv, and a part of my heart forever.

I love you,

Jackson

*   *   *

I'm going to give her the letter this morning but my own remorse is beginning to overcome me. Maybe she's not the right one. I've decided to defer my admission anyway and try to get together enough scratch to make it a more comfortable move.

I presume she was unable to call last night. I don't like being played for a fool or the feeling I have that I've somehow been used.

This letter's my final gesture to her. It's as far as unilateral energy will travel.

*   *   *

Four o'clock Wednesday morning my head's forced my body awake. Thinking about yesterday.

"You read it?"

"Yes. I have to reread it."

"Nice?"

"Too nice."

Our conversations grow shorter and more enigmatic. Work was difficult today.

Monday night I felt so heavy-hearted I called a dozen old friends on the telephone to be assured there were folks out there who like me.

"Let me just say one thing, Liv." One of my feeble approaches yesterday.

"Yeah."

"My heart feels like it weighs six hundred pounds."

"I'm sorry. That's my fault."

"I suppose it is."

I called a buddy in Boulder. I called my dad in Dubuque and told him I was planning to postpone my arrival. I called an old friend I'd seen on TV on a comedy program. I called a woman friend of mine who's an artist and published author of children's books. She said she needed a job to get her out of the house once a week. I told her to come by the store.

She, Lemmy and I went out for lunch and she charmed the bejeez out of him. She starts next Wednesday. I'm glad she'll be working there. She's bright and funny, has an interesting past, having been art director for a financial weekly and having worked at the Metropolitan Museum of Art in New York. I've known her since high school when we had an English 4 summer school class together ten years ago. And she's my friend. Her presence may also set a fire under Liv, providing Liv cares enough to feel jealousy, which I fully expect.

"Can you call me tonight?"

"Can't. I have to go to the hospital to visit Fred's father."

Fine. I'm not going to beat my head against a wall. If she won't own her feelings, I can't help her anyway.

Though I appreciate I've been able to write so much in the last five days, I wish kind of that I didn't have to. My mind's hyperactive, my body wants a heart transplant, I'm sleeping very poorly, all from this sickness love. All for a woman.

I wonder should I stay up and head over to the art supply store when they open? In all this, my books march on. The mylar's ready to be picked up.

I started rereading J. D. Salinger yesterday because I remember he wrote something in the voice of his character

Seymour Glass in which Seymour recognizes his fiancee's inability to cope with her own falling in and out of love with him.

Maybe a 28-proof beer (god, they taste horrible—Stu says like blueberry syrup) and a cigarette will numb me, deaden my psychoactivity enough for an hour or two more sleep. Look for the Salinger quote while I tire.

This is a sickness.

Salinger, from *Raise High the Roof Beam, Carpenters,* page 78:

"She worries over the way her love for me comes and goes, appears and disappears. She doubts its reality simply because it isn't as steadily pleasurable as a kitten. God knows it *is* sad. The human voice conspires to desecrate everything on earth."

*   *   *

"Good morning."

"Morning."

"I might be a little late—I've got to go to West Huron to pick up my mylar."

"Okay."

"You reread it?"

"No. I was at the hospital all last night. They're operating on Fred's father today."

"You still have it?"

"It's hidden at home."

"Well hidden?"

"I hope so."

"What are they going to do to him?"

"Remove the tube from his nose and put it directly in his stomach."

"That's heavy."

"Yeah, but that way he can come home and we can take care of him there."

"He's going home?"

"There's nothing they're doing at the hospital anymore we can't do at home."

"Jesus."

She had to get off the phone. I could hear a woman in the background haranguing her with questions about a missing section in the newspaper.

I'd better shave and shower and get moving. Change the catbox. Lemmy and I have a meeting at noon with one of the magazine reps.

"When are you going to have time for me?"

"To talk, you mean?"

"Yeah."

"Don't know. Everything's real busy right now."

"Okay. Well, I'll see you in a bit."

"Bye."

"See you soon."

*   *   *

Work was a disaster.

Liv told me it was all a mistake. If she had to do it over she wouldn't have.

I told her she was rude and insensitive.

We didn't get along all day.

I told her I felt used and asked her if she was enjoying this laugh at my expense.

She said she wasn't laughing.

I told her I was a real person with real feelings and that, though my flaw is sensitivity, my strength is that I need to talk things out until they make sense to me. Right now they don't make sense. I gave her my love, she gave me shit.

I'm pulling back. Retreat. I'm not going to lose a single soldier of my heart. What's inside me is too precious to be toyed with, bent out of shape, and left to collect dust.

She wants space, I'd love to move to the opposite side of the universe, but I'm staying. She can split if she likes. Fuck the bitch. I know who I am and I don't need to put up with this. I've had enemies be kinder to me than this lover. If she thinks I'll be brought down by an immature newsstand girl who's too stupid to recognize her boyfriend's a fag and that's why he never touches her, she's wrong.

I told her most women would have been flattered to receive a love letter such as I wrote her.

"Well, I'm not most women," she said. She's right. She's one of the few who refuses to see the nose in front of her face. Hit her with a brick, Ignatz. That'll turn her on. The milk of human kindness gags her.

*   *   *

I feel very strong this morning. I threw out Liv's moccasins. I'm consuming a massive quantity of caffeine. I'm ready to move on to something else. This hiatus is over.

Know what I want to do? I want to write a story. Maybe something about Hugh or his family. See you guys in a while.

Smile.

Chapter Six

A Story

Rich looks at his watch before turning the key to enter his loud penthouse suite. The party's been going on for a couple of hours, and he knows he'll be admonished by his wife for his tardiness immediately upon entering.

The thought that he should turn around and spend the evening somewhere else instead enters his mind, but he's here now and might as well comply with the natural flow of events which has brought him home at this hour.

After all, the party'd been his idea. A family gathering. Of a family of crazies and artists, mostly both. Painters, graffitists, musicians, writers, sex maniacs of every ilk. None of them sated, all disgustingly querulous. "Hello, Rich," they'd say, "listen to what I have to say for hours on end, boring you until your eyelids droop and you fall asleep and I carry you off to the bedroom to perform unnatural acts upon your sleeping person."

God, not again. This *was* his idea, though. No one to blame but himself. Family. Ha. Not *his* family. Just Grace's. They're all nuts. Swear there must be incest in her family for them all to be this looney.

He turns the key and pushes open the door as slowly as he can, hoping he'll be able to sneak in and slip into his study without being noticed. Hide in the closet if necessary.

"Hi, Dear! There you are! We'd just about given up on you and were going to call the police."

Would an "oops, wrong apartment" work? No, doubt it.

"Hi, Grace. I was delayed. I apologize. I was confident you'd handle it, though."

"Certainly, sweetheart. We're having a wonderful time," she said, putting forth a false face for family that might be overhearing.

"I'll just go change and will be right out."

"Just a minute, Rich. First you've got to talk to Hugh. He's been *dying* to speak with you."

Let him die then.

"Okay, dear. Where is he?"

"On the veranda."

"Thanks." He kisses her and turns away.

"I love you, Rich. Thanks for making it."

"Come on, Grace," he said, turning back. "I know you're upset."

"Let's talk about it later."

"Yes, all right."

Rich pulls a Camel out of his pocket and lights it. After weaving through unacknowledgeable bodies in order to get a Scotch for himself at the bar, he walks out toward the balcony, which his wife calls a "veranda" for some unknown reason. It's a balcony. His wife has an annoying habit of giving simple things complex names—"Here's my feline housepet Xanthippe." Rich is more the "that's my cat" type of guy.

He is in a bad mood and hopes Hugh will be quick about whatever it is he wants. At least the Scotch tastes good. It's the single malt which guests never see unless they come over singly.

He ignores several "Well, hello, Rich"s so that he can get to the balcony unimpeded. There must be fifty bodies in here. Overworking the air conditioning. He glances at the piano in the corner and sees Lee standing there. Her long brown hair has recently been kinked up into a perm. She looks good. Her eyes sparkle when they meet his.

That's who he really wants to talk to. She looks away. Oh well, later. It's only been three weeks since she broke off their affair.

Wonders if she misses him.

"Hello, Rich."

"Hello, Hugh. How've you been?"

"Not bad. Busy, you know, with the writing and all the stuff about Rose."

"Yeah? What are you writing? Still working on that self-indulgent weird fiction of yours that nobody reads?"

Hugh forces a laugh out of his throat.

"Sure. Still writing popular drivel, Rich? Pap for the simple?"

"Least I make sixty grand a year writing. What'd you pull in last year? Fifty bucks?"

"A lot more than that. And I didn't contract any mental v.d. either."

"Where's that red-headed bitch you pal around with?"

"Rain? Who knows. She's kind of drifted out of my life."

"If you made any money you'd have women hanging all over you."

"Like you?"

"I'm a happily married man, Hugh."

Hugh waits for someone to pass out of hearing.

"That's not the scuttlebutt I've heard."

"You shouldn't believe everything you hear. But I guess weird fiction's attracted to you like a fly to decaying matter."

"You truly wax eloquent, monsieur. Such subtlety of language. One could tell you indeed are of patrician lineage, n'est-ce pas?"

"You get that off a French post card?"

"Glad you know what they are. For Grace's sake."

"What'd you want to talk to me about?"

"I read your story in *Arts & Letters*. I just wanted to tell you I thought it was some of the best work I've ever seen of yours. A serious piece of fiction. I was surprised."

"I wrote that years ago—before I began writing for money. But thanks, Hugh. I was rather proud of it and am glad I finally had the opportunity to publish it."

"You know Chad and Fran?"

"No. I've never met them. They found my address through Sorenson and knew from him I had some weird old stuff. They wrote me and asked for some."

"You hear about Androla?"

"Sure. Fell asleep on his couch smoking a cigarette."

"Man, that's tough."

"Quite unfortunate. He was very talented."

"Prolific, too. What'd he publish, six books last year?"

"Something like that. Well, I need another drink. But first I'm going to go change out of these ridiculous clothes. I'll see you, Hugh."

"Nice chatting."

Yes. Now where's Lee? Oh no. She's talking to Grace. Well, at least old Rich'll be able to duck into the bedroom and change.

Into what? The smoking jacket? Yes, nice and annoyingly pretentious. Where's the calabash? And that putrid English blend?

Who's here anyway? Should cut loose of the bad day and

relax into this. It'll be all right. Go sit on the throne and get rid of the crap.

What's Lee doing here? Maybe she showed up to see him. Could see her body clearly through her yellow cotton dress. Suppose the air conditioning's working well. She's lost some weight, too. Her hips look like they were made to be held. He decides he has to find a way to talk to her in private tonight. A quiet place where he can pull down her panties and put himself up inside her.

Wait. That's not what he wants. He broke up with her because he wasn't receiving enough back for the energy he was putting into the relationship. Grace he endures. He was young and stupid when he married her. Yet, he did and that's that. Lee was all take and no give.

Flush it away and rejoin the party. Les and Art and Mark, the three painters, are discussing what little they know about minimalism. Les is trying to lead them astray on the subject of abstract expressionism's supplantation by minimalism. Art claims the former mutated into the latter. Mark tells them both that this argument is completely irrelevant in today's society.

"It was vital for artists to geometrically distill the essence of the form. Look at Noland," argues Les.

"But the artist's identity was removed from his work. There's no sense of personality," counters Art. "Unlike abstract expressionism. The inner worlds of, say, Clyfford Still or Pollock are vibrant and full. I don't get that from Noland or Stella. All I get is this germanic sense of systemization, more like Mondrian than anyone else preceding them."

"I think you are misreading both Mondrian and minimalism, Art."

"Fuck both of you," Mark explains, "with your private nepotistic suck up to the galleries' whorish points of view. What's it matter who's what on this weird fashion level? The only art that matters is real art done by real people, not for money but for the guy on the street."

"Right, Mark. That's why the galleries have taken the graffitists indoors, taken away their walls and given them canvas, and are making a hundred grand per piece for this art done 'not for money.' I don't see the guy on the street carrying a hundred thousand dollars around. Do you?" asked Art.

"At that point I'd argue that those artists sold out. You won't see my work in a gallery."

"You're going to tell me if Castelli offered you prices of a hundred thousand per piece, you'd turn him down in order to paint the name of a rock band on a real rock?"

"Yes, that's exactly what I mean, Les."

Art choked on his drink, coughing it out through his nose onto his shirt and the carpeting. The big man then let out a big laugh which engulfed the apartment and everyone turned to see.
Rich took the opportunity to see if Lee was looking over at them. He didn't see her, so he left the group of arguing painters, hoping to locate her elsewhere in the apartment.

*   *   *

Fred's father died. Liv is pregnant, probably with Fred's child. She devotes her energy to manipulating Fred into marrying her.

I've backed off as far as off can be. My love is a candle on its last flame. Only Liv could bring it back.

Just in case, though, I've brought along a few candles in my back pocket. I could light one for someone else but I'd rather not.

Liv and I are friendly but not close. Her mind's in Fredland and baby Fredland and I don't blame her, but I have no business there.

I wonder whether our missed cue was from her mistrust of my love for her or her inability to identify hers for me.

In an effort to locate the positive for me in all this, I can look back on our love and say it was good while it was there. Unfortunately it was only there for a heartbeat or two while we made love staring into each other's eyes.

That had been a genuine connection, which she'd been the first to pull away from even then. She'd averted her eyes self-consciously and told me not to look at her like that—that it reminded her of Fred.

*   *   *

What's that odor? Oh, just old John.

"Hello, John. Good to see you."

"Hello, Rich. You know Mary?"

"Good to meet you."

"Likewise. Congratulations to the new couple. Know what my

father told me when I married Grace?"

"No."

"'Well, son, why should you be luckier than me?'" So saying, Rich turns and walks away. He hasn't meant to be rude. It's this damned mood, that woman Lee, his stagnation speaking for him. He lights his calabash. He pours himself a glass of champagne at the bar. Better be polite—pour two more for John and Mary. Return.

"Sorry. Thought you might like some of my best."

"Thanks, Rich."

"Mary?"

"Well, maybe a little. Thank you, Mr. Moore."

"Rich."

"Rich."

"No problem. How's married life?"

"No problem," answers John as Rich looks Mary in the eyes. One's red and a little larger than the other. Maybe she has an infection or a sty. Better not wallow in it. Mary doesn't flinch. John's been telling the truth. They're a happy couple. Disgusting, isn't it? Actually, it's good. The best thing on earth. Where's Lee? Talking to Carol. Carol has Pat with her. At least Rich doesn't have kids.

"Dick here, John?"

"Over there."

"Oh, I see. Did Phil make it for the wedding? I didn't see him."

"No. Last I heard he was out with Les' kid Mark touring the country in a Woody Wagon."

"You're kidding."

"No, I'm not."

"Jesus."

"Quite right. I must say I appreciate how you and Grace have been over all this."

"We love you, Dad. Excuse me. I see my old buddy Duncan over there. I've got to talk to him. Congratulations again. I'll see you."

"See you. By the way, where's the can?"

"Up the stairs, to the left on the side."

"Thanks, Rich."

Duncan's standing next to a palm tree by the window. Rich wonders which is thinner. Duncan looks like he weighs a hundred pounds. His bones are trying to break through his flesh. He's almost gone. Half a ghost. Should hint he see a doctor.

"Duncan, almost didn't see you."

"Hello, Rich." Even the voice was thin.

"How've you been? You look a little pale." Subtle as a bat.

"I'm getting better. Have a cold but I'm starting to feel alive."

Wonder what it is? Heroin? Cocaine? Something's doing a number on this boy.

"Where's the washroom, Rich?"

"Up the stair, to the left on the side. But John's in there now. Could be a while."

"Oh. Thanks. I'll take my chances." Nothing but addicts and drunks and incontinents. What a party. There's Carol and Lee. That'll do wonders.

As he makes his way towards them, Lee leaves towards the kitchen. Why'd she do that? Is she afraid? Is she avoiding something? So talk to Carol instead. Just a coincidence probably.

What's it matter? Go lie down on my bed and rest a while.

Are you an actress? Are you a liar? Are you a poet capable of honest affection? I'm getting much too old for little girl games. Let's talk adulthood.

No, I don't want you to love my ass. As a matter of fact I'm not sure I want you around at all. There's just a little part of me that has to be with someone. More and more is pretending to die. There it is. Allow me my few peccadilloes. I can dance my death.

*   *   *

I visited Chad and Fran two days after her birthday. I'd had a busy day. I'd checked around the stores to see if my chapbook had sold any copies. From there I met Mary, and we spent some time together comparing dreams. That's my friend Mary the Dionysian, not Mary Moore, though the former wrote the latter's meditation. It's true. Look, this is confusing to me too. Don't sweat the small stuff. All of my life I'd been looking and from nowhere you blind-sided me, broke my glasses, lenses flying back into different cars. Frames probably pocketed by an urchin with a penchant for fool's gold.

Which reminds me of what happened to Chad and Paul from Rockford and me.

"Give me a beer," said a black skinhead to Chad outside the beer store.

"No," came the honest reply. The skinhead took issue with this and began pushing and jabbing, then a quick couple of punches with his best buddy jumping in and twenty other buddies looking on, including one white punk yelling to take it off the street and drag it into the alley. They threw Chad against the wall of a fake church and one kicked him in the balls. Meanwhile I was pulling the other one back by the arm, telling him to relax, so then his buddy went nutzo on me. I remember receiving a punch, then another, then ducking to find my glasses. When I raised my head, the first hit me. I never did find my glasses, but I found Chad's and we walked away. Paul had successfully escaped into the safety of traffic with the beer (hell, it probably would have better to have been hit by a car at 10 MPH than to have gone through this). We met up and made it back without further incident.

Fran, who'd fortunately missed all this, consoled us with humor and whiskey back at the apartment. A strange silence hovered over us all, so we drank our well-earned beers and played Scrabble until it hurt. Fran lent me her glasses so I could drive home. Our prescriptions are similar, and she usually wears her contacts anyway. We all parted just a bit more shell-shocked.

*   *   *

"Guess who?"

"Rich!"

Carol turns around and gives Rich a big kiss and hug.

"How've you been, cutie?"

"Fine. Great. You?"

"Not bad."

Rich bends down to shake Pat's hand.

"How 'bout you, big guy?"

"You're a bonehead!"

"Pat!"

"It's okay, Carol."

"Pat, Rich is not a bonehead. I'm not sure where he gets this language."

"TV maybe."

"Probably. Now behave, Pat. Or I'll feed you to the shark in the swimming pool."

"Carp."

"Shhh. I'm telling him shark to keep him away from it."

"Yeah, Pat. That's a mean shark. Better listen to your mom."

"You're both boneheads!"

"Pat!"

Where's Lee? His one-eyed wanderlust resurfaces.

"Excuse me, Carol. I'll see you in a bit. I promised to go talk to someone and they're waiting for me."

"Sure, Rich. See you."

"Bye, Pat."

"Say 'bye,' Pat."

"Bye."

*   *   *

Sometimes Liv can be very thoughtful. She remembers holidays and even knows how to reassure an unspoken friendship with a touch. Sometimes her defenses are low against a love she feels but doesn't know how to address.

God, hit me in the head with a baseball bat fast. I'm starting to talk about love again. Put me out of my misdirected misery, even though I must be a masochist to keep going at it. Perhaps it's an instinct I can't yet break through will-power.

I've got to move beyond this love trap death.

Slip out the back door, get in the car and head out for good. Before things have the chance to turn ugly again.

*   *   *

The first thing Rich noticed as he approached Chuck and Ralph was that they were wrong. They didn't do it right.

Chuck was saying to Ralph, "Why buy a slice when you can pinch a loaf?"

Ralph farted loudly in response.

"Yeah, I tried, but there's nothing there."

"Sounded like you'd better go wipe it off before it attracts flies."

"Your fly maybe."

"I wouldn't do you with your aunt's dick."

"You couldn't do anyone because yours is the size of an ant."

"That's poor."

"Oh, well. I was under pressure."

"Pressure the name of one of your fat broads?"

"You're repeating yourself and being redundant."

"Rank."

"Private."

"I'll kick you in your privates."

"Corporal punishment?"

"We've been through this."

"Not in specifics. Only in general."

"Fuck you."

"I already said no."

"Who cares?"

"Sicko."

"Just leave me alone, man. Before I puke all over you."

"Chew on it and swallow it."

"I warned you."

Chuck threw up on Ralph.

Rich walked away quickly. He felt better once he thought he saw Lee. He tried to catch up with her. This pursuit reminded him of Newton's first law of motion. He was an object in motion which tended to stay in motion until acted upon by an external force.

Other people's lives didn't affect him much other than he found he could slip through them easily. Slide past. Noticed then gone. Out with a flash of entry.

Keeping moving towards a light at the end. Which reminded Rich of the dream he had last night about a detective on a heroin case. He remembered a junky telling the detective after being busted, "it's the darkness of the calendar—those are the days I want to know."

Flop from your back to your stomach. On your knees. Now get up. Walk up that mountain.

How you get down is up to you. Some stay up there as long as they can. Some get bored quickly and dive off. Some climb down carefully.

It all ends up in the boneyard in the end.

Bowlin' in the boneyard. Teasin' your purple eyes. It can't all be parties and stories. There's the question of what's inside and what to hide and what to lay bare to anyone who cares to look.

What's going on in here? I've been away, I know, keeping busy enough not to have time to think. If that doesn't work I know a few other ways to stop thinking.

I've got to defrost the freezer today. A bottle of RC I'd

forgotten overnight unscrewed its top and flooded the ice-cube trays. It's a mess. It is.

I also have to type letters to a couple of people who wrote me about my chapbook. I do.

Relax. Listen to music.

I will.

I have to. New music juices me up enough to write again.

Fiction.

And a letter to Art.

Keeping rolling towards a light at the end.

Someone reached around from behind and grabbed Rich by the balls. He felt breath in his ear. A whisper, "I want you inside me now."

"Fanny!" Rich exclaimed as he turned around. "You startled me."

"Off in dreamland?"

"Yeah, sort of."

"Let's go to the bedroom. Grace is out on the veranda engrossed in a heavy conversation."

"I'd love to. I'll meet you there in a minute. I'll just get us drinks."

"Okay, but hurry."

"I will."

I have to, he thought. Where was Lee? He didn't have much time to decide.

Fanny left him and entered the bedroom unnoticed.

Rich looked over at the piano and saw Lee there again. He really liked the way her hair looked, the amusing way one corner of her mouth rose higher than the other, her two-color eyeshadow, her rich eyes. She had been good in bed, even better in the shower or on the table or against the wall.

He walked over to her before she could get away.

"Hello, Lee. How are you?"

"Fine. You?" Her reply seemed distant, detached.

"Trying to catch up with you reminded me of Newton's law."

"Which one? The one about two bodies not being able to occupy the same space at the same time?"

"I don't think that's Newton. Anyway, they can get pretty close."

"Not without an accident. Mechanics will tell you that."

"I meant the law about objects remaining in their state of motion unless acted upon."

"Fascinating. What makes you think I care?"

"You should."

"Well, I don't."

"I haven't heard from you. How about getting together again? Let's blow off this party."

"Rich, you're the host."

"So?"

"Look, I told you we can't do that again. It was a mistake." She was serious.

"No it wasn't."

"Yes, it was. Drop it. You know I can't be with you again."

"At least as friends."

"Don't push your friendship on me."

"I'm not."

"You are. You're going to make it impossible for me to even talk to you."

"Look, I don't mean to upset you. I'll see you later."

"See you."

Rich turned to leave. Grace had been standing behind him the whole time with her head turned, assuredly overhearing his conversation with Lee.

He walked into the bedroom and locked the door behind him.

Grace knocked on the door.

"Rich?"

"Go away," he shouted and he looked at Fanny who was in bed, waiting, and smiled. He quickly undressed and slid in between the sheets. He reached over to Fanny, put his hand over her breast and squeezed it. He leaned over and kissed her, putting his tongue in between her teeth and alongside the inside of her cheek, fluttering it over her tongue, against her other cheek, under her tongue, and against the back of her teeth. He pulled it out and let her tongue into his mouth. He sucked on it gently. He let his fore-fingertip and thumb slide to Fanny's nipple and rolled it back and forth gently. She reached down and pulled his hard penis into her and let out a deep growling moan which turned him on so much he shot up into her almost immediately.

"I'm sorry," he said. "Didn't mean to do that."

"No problem," she whispered and she put her middle-finger up his asshole, which kept him hard. She then climbed on top of him and rocked on him until she came in a scream.

They held each other, shuddering.

"Rich! Rich! I hear you in there! Let me in!" Grace was hysterical.

"Shit, Fanny. How're we going to get out of this?"

"The window?"

"I'll suppose we'll have to."

They dressed as quickly as possible, climbed out the bedroom window, ran to Fanny's car, and escaped to a new reality.

Epilogue

I wish you were shaky and old and had to try to read without being able to see this that I'm writing shaky and old and without clear vision. Not that there's much left to see, mind you. The peculiar rot that infects the minds of the elderly has infected mine, but I make do, perhaps clearer about life than I've ever been. Maybe that's only because I'm closer to death, though. Closer to my mortality.

I just found this manuscript in my sister's house. In her attic. My mother's old house. The manuscript I'd lost years earlier and never thought I'd find. How very strange to read one's own words, especially after thirty years.

I'm dying. Just that. A month or two. I don't suppose I'll ever see "Lee" again. Or "Liv." Or "Mary," even. But I lived a strong life. I know they did too.

Oh, excuse me. Did I...?

Oh.

A little brain disease scurrying through my electro-particles, doctor.

Zip zip zip zip zip zip zip zip.

Check corridor seventeen for signs of an intruder, colonel.

A general check?

By martial law!

Oh no, not again.

Well at least it's admirable.

Admiral?

What, are you gun-shy?

Hell, yes. Some folks change, some don't. I don't. Or didn't. Something like that.

It's in my body now. The coughing's more severe. The blood comes up with the phlegm. It sprays out with the sneeze. I've been hiding it all right. There's nothing left to go for. Collapse is not only inevitable, it is necessary.

I was twenty-something when I wrote this book. It seems young and unfocused, but then I spent most of my life unable to focus on anything. Not on work, not on my wife. What's a book? A destroyed tree manipulated about as subtly as humans can manage. Beavers have a better approach. Build something. People spend lifetimes helping other people. All I did was scratch strange marks onto reconstituted sheets of tree mulch. A noble ambition, eh? If I weren't dying I'd say they should shoot me for that. Here was a man afraid to contribute. He hid in his room and scratched strange marks on reconstituted sheets of tree mulch. The penalty? Death is too good for him. Make him clean the shithouses. There's got to be something useful he can do.

Believe in you? Be leavin' you.

What there was was there, what? I mean, it was for me.

A few bows before I go, before I tie one on. The big one. The last one. Before I slip that final knot. Or no? The UFO's will be here soon, looking for the cool and hip. I'll be long gone by then. Treat them well or they'll waste the planet.

Yeah, I know. They'll waste the planet anyway. But who can blame them? Look at this mess. How else are you going to clean it up? Level it and start over. Seems the only logical thing to do.

God, I sound like an old crank. The kind of man who sits by his window so he can throw rocks at teenagers and yell "get off my lawn!" at them.

I don't know quite what to make of my novel. I'm amazed at how well I remember it even though I haven't seen it since I was very young.

It's kind of sloppy, I think. The story gets lost in the telling. And if it weren't for the characters' stupid punny names you'd need a scorecard to tell who was who. They're not well-defined enough. I'm not even sure what they look like. You only see them through their words, their actions, or their thoughts. Or how other characters react to them.

Hugh's awakening at the beginning is a bit confusing. Does anyone dream so silly? I like the cat though, even if I gave him a ridiculous name. And Rain? What kind of name is that for a woman? Especially a red-haired bitch with a nose-ring?

I remember back then this black guy named Jonesy whom I worked with at a liquor store exclaimed, when he met Rain the day she came and visited me in the store, "Hell, man, your woman has a nose ring!"

"How else you gonna keep her on a leash, Jonesy?"

Too bad she drifted out of my life. I'd always liked her. I must have missed giving her what she needed. I suppose I never knew what it was.

That was a long time ago. No use worrying about it now.

Sometimes, like now, I look back on my life and have to laugh at how ludicrous much of it was.

Thirty years. I thought this one was lost for good. Thrown out. Or stolen. All this time all I had to do was go through my mother's attic. I mean my sister's attic. I like the way the text comes in and out of focus, but when it's out it can be very fuzzy blurry abstruse. Starts out of it with the waking sequence. If I hadn't already written a Wakelin waking section in another book I could have given it to the elusive dead musician.

The real St. Charles was my first cat. A sweet-tempered if somewhat jealous black mongrel named for a Howard Wales jazz album. She had a few birth defects—missing front teeth, an extended hind claw—but I remember her as the greatest cat in the world. She did tricks, like sitting up or rolling over, when asked. She knew how to hug me when I said "come on."

Fat Bill's burned down some ten years ago. It was under different ownership, the seventh or so since Bill died, and had a different name. A grease-fire started in the kitchen, and no one who worked there cared enough to put it out.

The inserts, "Hoy Tomb Mutilate the English Lingo," "In the Land of the Estimos," *Salmon Song (for Rain)* and the other poems, the letters, and especially the Duncan Rivers piece, seem out of place, tenuously attached to the body of the book. Consider them the body's extremities. They balance the creature out in the odd symmetry of their extrusion.

The political rot is dated. Politics dates faster than anything and never comes back around.

The sex stuff's embarrassing. I think I meant it to be. It's crude.

There's a considerable amount of vulgarity in my work at this time—foul language, serious alcoholism, decadence from which I never fully recovered.

A lot of bits are, if they stand alone, extreme. I do hope they seem to average out to something normal enough to successfully approach the human heart.

I had come to a standstill in order to write that book. It is a Chicago book—urban, paranoid, uncouth. My acceptance of a position in Dubuque and my move there seem inevitable in retrospect. It was the only option I had which allowed me the opportunity to grow, to learn, and above all to breathe clean air deeply with no one standing nearby telling me not to. It afforded me the chance to relax and be able to concentrate on the first of my pastoral novels and peace. I was finally able to complete my education, which opened the door to greater personal autonomy. Yet, I regret none of my Chicago experience, not even my emotional retardation and inability to sustain an adult love relationship. Good thing, or I'd never have been free to accept what happened to me after that. I would not have met the woman who became my wife and taught me how to be in the state where love comes through play not work. I miss her. I'm glad it was me who had to learn to live without her. I'm certain, whatever happens to me in a month or two, I'll find that woman again, and we'll be able to dance together and play until the end of time.